Copyright: Mediterranean Me 2024

******

SULTRY SPAIN

"Happily Ever Now" Part IV: Floundering

******

To all the dreamers relentlessly making their dreams their reality...

To all the lovers of life...

******

"One is loved because one is loved. No reason is needed for loving."

Paulo Coelho

******

With Appreciation for My Greatest Loves & Blessings,

"Olivia, Leo, Rachel, Liam & GiGi"

*****

Inspired by a Life. Lived…

******

BOOKS BY SOPHIA ELAN

The "KISS" Collection: Holistic Wellness for Health, Happiness, & Harmony

Keep it Simple, Sweetheart

"Brainiac. Mindful Living. Holistic Wellness Habits for a Healthy, Happy Brain"

"Fed Up: Why Can't I Lose Weight? Part I," a "*KISS*" Guide for Weight Loss

"Eat the Cupcake, Savor the Champagne: A "KISS" Guide to Healthy Weight. Look Great. Feel Great. Be Great"

"Mastering the Art of Stress: Finding Calm in the Chaos," a "KISS" 52 Guide

"Release Yourself: PART I," a "KISS" Primer. Stress Less. Live More. Free Your Mind, Body, & Spirit"

"Release Yourself: PART II, a "KISS 25" Guide. Stress Less. Live More. Free Your Mind, Body, & Spirit"

"Release Yourself: PART III, a "KISS 25" Guide. Stress Less. Live More. Free Your Mind, Body, & Spirit"

The "Mediterranean Me" Collection

Holistic Wellness & Simple Pleasures

"Sicilian Seductions, a Mediterranean Love Affair," the debut novel in the "Happily Ever Now" series, a soul journey of an open heart & mind

"Turkish Temptations, a Mediterranean Love Affair," Part II

"Turkish Delights, a Mediterranean Love Affair," Part III

"Sultry Spain, a Mediterranean Love Affair," Part V

"French Rendezvous, a Mediterranean Love Affair," Part V

Coming soon...

"Greek Reveries, a Mediterranean Love Affair," Part VI

"Magical Montenegro, a Mediterranean Love Affair," Part VII

"Idyllic Italy, a Mediterranean Love Affair," Part VIII

"My Mediterranean Musings: Lifestyle Measures for Holistic Wellness Inspiration"

"My Magical Mediterranean: Travel Treasures for Wanderlust Inspiration"

"My Mediterranean Table: Gastronomic Pleasures for Culinary Inspiration"

An Uplifting Memoir of Triumphing Over Trauma

"Roar: Primed for Peace. Self-Heal Trauma for Health, Happiness, & Harmony"

*Please sign up to my website for upcoming releases and events, sneak peeks & perks, blog posts, social media and to connect…

www.mediterraneanme.org

******

FOREWORD

I'm blessed to have lived in the Mediterranean for over two decades, but I'm even more blessed to enjoy the simple pleasures of life, wherever I am. This *"Happily Ever Now"* series is my love letter - not only to the Mediterranean - but to life in general.

I hope to help you *escape* a little and inspire the wanderlust that has kept me curious, energized, spirited, and engaged throughout my life. Travel opens your heart, your eyes, and your mind.

I also hope to *inspire* you to live your fullest, most authentic life, *unapologetically* - my "secret" to happiness and inner peace. I've *lived* life; that comes with its share of heartaches, but its *"heart-ups"* as well.

I forever believe in *fairytales,* but the one where the *"princess"* is her own *"heroine."* After a life of chasing *"Happily Ever After"* with others, I found *"Happily Ever Now,"* within myself. My fervent wish is for you to as well…

✯✯✯✯✯✯

PART I

MALLORCAN DREAMS - REVELATIONS

Chapter 1

Spanish Vibes

Chapter 2

Embracing Simple Pleasures

Chapter 3

Happy Hour

Chapter 4

A Surreal Evening

Chapter 5

Ménage-a-Maybe…

Chapter 6

Reveling in Freedom: That's What Friends are For

Chapter 7

Painted Joy: Dreams Do Come to Life

Chapter 8

A Trio of Pleasures of a Different Kind

Chapter 9

The Best of All Worlds in Sóller

Chapter 10

Dreamy Deià

Chapter 11

Well-behaved Women Seldom Make History

Chapter 12

Medieval Magic in Alcúdia

Chapter 13

The Simple Pleasures of Being, not Doing

Chapter 14

Until We Meet Again, Mallorca

******

"Well-behaved women seldom make history."

- *Laurel Thatcher Ulrich*

******

Chapter 1: Spanish Vibes

Spain had always held a certain allure to me - an enticing magnetic rhythm, like a pulsating heartbeat. I felt its presence, immediately electrified as I disembarked from my flight from Istanbul to Mallorca. What was most distinctive for me - about Spain in general, but particularly the Balearic Islands - was its youthful, vibrant energy. Mallorca was a microcosm of all the elements that made Spain so alluring to me - stunning coastlines and equally beguiling interior landscapes, charming villages, the intriguing multilayered Spanish culture, and my favorite style of eating - tapas-style - not to mention, my favorite wines.

Spain's essence for me is indulgently embracing the simple pleasures of life. No one lives in the moment better than Spaniards while exuding positivity and it's the exact vibe I was hoping to internalize. I definitely wanted to forget the past and didn't want to be consumed with thoughts of my future. I was determined to revel in the unbridled pleasure of living in the present - like never before - with the beautiful locals as my exemplary guides. Indulgence. Decadence. Satiation. These would be my guiding unprincipled principles, I mused in anticipatory delight bordering on giddiness. I had always enjoyed my time in Spain, but this visit held a unique potential. I had lived for others for so long; I had time to make up for and Spain was my intended playground to revel in all my senses. I intuitively knew that Spain would be leaving her indelible mark on my spirit and I couldn't wait to embrace her soul.

I had visited Mallorca a number of times before; this was my first trip to the Mediterranean island solo. I had been previously with a boyfriend after my first divorce and had most recently come with my second husband to search for a restaurant. Starting any business had been a foolish idea from the get go. Neither one of us had any business experience - to contemplate a business in a foreign country in a foreign language we didn't know had objectively been a particularly foolhardy idea. None of that mattered though - I had cast aside all rational contemplation. It was my ex's dream - which I had inexplicably adopted as my own - purely out of my infatuation with him and desire to please him.

My ex had envisioned a restaurant and late night lounge. Just the kind of financial risk, party atmosphere, and into-the-morning hours I was looking for at that point in my life. I scoffed at myself with the benefit of hindsight. Despite the endless rational compelling reasons against starting a business in Spain, I had supported him, blindly diving in, negotiating my heart out to secure a place I had no interest in. Fortunately for me, that's when we had found a space in Napa, something I was at least more familiar with and better equipped to tackle. That endeavor was disastrous as well for me. I sighed, fighting back tears of self-recrimination and abject low sense of self-worth. Stop it, I commanded myself.

This is exactly the type of thinking and past memories I was trying to escape with my current travel plans. I hadn't appreciated how my visit would stir up the past, but I was determined to repress it. Indeed, I consoled myself, coming to Mallorca was a particularly shining example of how differently I intended to live the rest of my life now. Any potentially foolish or impetuous decisions from now on would be purely in pursuit of my own pleasure I vowed with a forced change of heart and a wicked smile. You can't take the impulsiveness out of the girl, but spontaneity would now exclusively be for my desires and dreams.

I grabbed a brochure as I waited for my luggage for The Fundació Pilar i Joan Miró a Mallorca in Palma, dedicated to the works of the artist Joan Miró. I wasn't very familiar with his work, but was intrigued about learning more about the Surrealist movement, of which he had been a luminary. I was focused on myself for the first time in my life - expanding my horizons seemed like as good a place as any to start - and a trip to the museum to explore Surrealism would be my introductory start.

I glanced up as the whir of the baggage claim conveyor belt grabbed my attention before immediately being diverted to a surreally stunning couple entwined together in a hug that bordered on foreplay, their beautiful bodies seemingly designed for each other. Spaniards are exquisite; the women are effortlessly, elegantly alluring, while the men exude a palpable sexual magnetism. Antonio Banderas was my celebrity crush to the extent I had one and this gentleman bore a close resemblance to him. I stared a little too long, comfortable in the safety of his obvious unavailability. He exuded the typical traits that characterized Spanish men for me - he had dark features and a mysterious intrigue - he seemed suave, assertive, yet sensitive, all wrapped up in a delectable gorgeous package.

I interrupted my own daydreaming, laughing at my summation of this stranger's personality based solely on superficial and fleeting appearances. I forgave myself for my stereotyping. I knew no one should judge a book by its cover, but I gave myself a pass since my stereotyping tendencies were always positive. As I watched the gentleman deftly secure the couple's luggage with one hand while maintaining eye contact and still holding his lady's hand, I realized that I was projecting what I longed for on the couple.

I thought briefly of Ali before my thoughts immediately jumped to Leo - was it really what I wanted - to be coupled at this point? Hadn't I just been anticipating reveling in my freedom? I knew deep down that I fundamentally did want to be monogamous. I was just trying to distract myself from the painful reality that a serious relationship seemed so elusive at the moment. I looked up again at the lovely, affectionate couple still hand-in-hand as I struggled procuring my hefty luggage off the conveyor belt. "My goodness their kids will be adorable," I thought as I silently wished them a life of blessings together. The grass is always greener on the other side, I reminded myself. I shook my head to stop my unproductive reverie and focus on my unwieldy luggage.

My luggage procured and the happy couple out of sight, I focused on my reunion with Mallorca. I knew how fortunate I was to be back and promised myself to focus on the positive. Mallorca, immersed in the azure waters of the Mediterranean Sea, was the jewel of the Balearic archipelago with its breathtaking landscapes, rich history, and vibrant culture. While its more raucous sister island, Ibiza, was primarily associated with music and all-night clubbing, Mallorca was considered a more varied and sophisticated destination. Known as "Majorca" in Spanish, the largest of the Balearic Islands, offered a diverse range of experiences catering to every taste from sun-soaked coastlines, bustling beaches and port cities to inland landscapes dripping with wild beauty, dramatic cliffs, and charming villages. It was the diversity and inland wonders that attracted me time and time again to the enchanting island.

Mallorca's history is fascinatingly as rich and varied as its landscapes. Inhabited since ancient times, its cultural heritage is an alluring blend of Roman, Moorish, and

Spanish influences. I particularly liked the impact this fusion of cultures had on Mallorca's architecture and culinary scene. I had stayed in Palma de Mallorca, the capital city, before - it was a cosmopolitan melting pot of these historical layers, evident in its architecture, narrow streets with restaurants and shops, and vibrant markets. I enjoyed seeing its main sites again as we made our way from the airport to the more rural town of Santa Maria del Cami where I was staying.

My transfer took me past the captivating capital en route to the countryside manor hotel I had chosen. It was characterized by a bustling harbor with a long seaside promenade and a vibrant arts, nightlife, and restaurant and cafe scene. The Passeig des Born was a long palm-tree-lined boulevard with elegant architecture and endless exclusive shops. My ex and I had repeatedly strolled the boulevard before - the designer shops encapsulated his version of the "finer things in life." For me the finer "things" in life weren't "things" at all. I was drawn to enjoying experiences and collecting memories instead of material possessions. I preferred the Paseo Maritime with its extensive seafront promenade and hubbub of activity and social vibe with countless walkers, bikers, and rollerbladers enjoying nature and the stunning coastal views.

I also enjoyed meandering around the Cathedral District with its cobblestone paths, lofty trees, park benches, and Palma's most emblematic structure - the 14th Century La Seu Cathedral, perched above Parc de la Mar. It was one of Europe's tallest Gothic structures and an architectural masterpiece. The magnificent golden sandstone Cathedral came into my sight - it was one of the largest cathedrals I had ever visited and I remembered particularly enjoying it at night all lit up. It was also famous for its stained glass rose window and the spectacle created when the morning sun flooded the interior with dazzling beams of rainbow-colored lights. I glanced at it admiringly as the traffic afforded me the opportunity to gaze in wonder for a few minutes - its sheer grandeur never ceased to amaze me. The Cathedral - which fronts the Mediterranean Sea and overlooks the harbor - appeared to me as if a protective guardian angel over the city that had witnessed centuries of history.

My driver thoughtfully indulged me as we were leaving Palma, stopping to let me take some photos at my favorite landmark in the capital, Bellver Castle. The castle was an architectural stunner with a uniquely circular terraced enclave. It was one of the oldest castles in Europe and was remarkably well-preserved. It was a gothic marvel with an inviting courtyard surrounded by a dense, expansive forest. Elevated over 100 meters above sea level, the vantage point from the castle offered breathtaking panoramic views over the city. I smiled at my driver appreciatively as he chivalrously opened my door to get back in the car for the rest of our short journey. I sighed in contentment to be reunited with Spain in general and in particular with Mallorca. I took in my last glimpses of the coastline before we headed inland, happy to be reunited with Mallorca, eager to explore her endless charms.

******

Chapter 2: Embracing Simple Pleasures

I was looking forward to my visit with anticipatory vigor. For the first time in my life, my only "plan" was to indulge myself in my favorite simple pleasures - food, wine, nature, and local culture. Spanish cuisine was one of those quintessential conglomerations of flavors based on the influence of its diverse regions, history, and cultural heritage and I was inevitably drawn to its rich diversity. The heritage resulted in a blend of different ingredients, flavors, and cooking techniques. It was similar to Sicilian cuisine in that regard, I thought, my mind immediately wandering to Leo...

I was deeply drawn to Leo's adventurous spirit and palate. I admired his confidence in leaving his native Florence to immerse himself in the relative greater diversity showcased in Sicily. Although I always loved exploring the regional culinary traditions throughout Italy and appreciated the passion that underlay a region's dedication to its local specialties, my palate and spirit gravitated to the more diverse, multi-dimensional, multi-cultural influence of places where the cuisine represented an amalgamation of varied influences.

I loved Leo's free and inquisitive nature and how he was an exemplary role model for the twins. Exposure to different cultures, cuisines, and traditions were poetry to my soul; travel ideally opened one's eyes, one's mind, and one's heart. I was confident that GiGi and Gabriele would be all the more curious and cosmopolitan thanks to their upbringing. I knew it had to be difficult for Leo and Isabella to leave Florence - at least temporarily - over their parents' protestations. I admired and respected their individuality and determination. Leo wanted to be the best chef he could be and saw a need for greater exposure to somewhere more diverse like Sicily for him to develop and perfect his craft. Isabella and Aldo undoubtedly had challenging times frequently being separated, but they were obviously trying to expose the twins to as much as possible during their developmental stages.

I sighed in resignation, taking a deep breath, refocusing my thoughts on the present to dull the ache of loneliness welling up in my heart. Food was a fairly consuming passion for me and I was anxious to have my thoughts consumed by anything other than Leo. Spanish cuisine captivated my senses. I always quipped that I had olive oil and red wine coursing through my veins. Olive oil is the backbone of Spanish cooking and is used generously in almost every dish. I evidently wasn't the only one enamored with Spanish olive oil either. Spain is the world's largest producer of olive oil - its extra virgin varieties are highly sought after for their rich, fruity flavor that spoke to my sensibilities. Spanish wine and olive oil were some of my favorites with a tendency to gravitate to relatively earthy, spicy characteristics - hmmm, kind of how I like my male encounters as well, I realized.

I was whetting my appetite simply contemplating my first meal. I loved the tapas style of eating - an exploration of a variety of small bites was my preferred style of dining. Unfortunately, the tapas experience at restaurants was an incredibly social, and often intimate, dining experience; one that I was intimidated engaging in solo. My thoughts turned back to Leo. That's ok, I consoled myself. I loved Spanish stores for their variety of options - I would enjoy shopping and making my own tapas and wine flights at home, I consoled myself with feigned conviction.

******

Chapter 3: Happy Hour

I emerged from the shower feeling reinvigorated. It had worked its magic at washing away my thoughts of the past, firmly jolting me into the present. I was excitedly looking forward to my first evening back in Spain. The potential of the adventures of a new destination combined with the tranquility of the property I had fortuitously chosen were working their magic.

As I glanced in the mirror, I was happy to see that my recent time immersed in nature in Turkey had left me with sun-kissed skin. I was feeling blissful – the combination of sun and exploration always satiated my soul - and I was eager to continue that duo during my time in Mallorca. I'm obsessed with that glorious feeling the sun imparts – simultaneously energizing and relaxing. Solar-powered mood.

I also noticed in appreciation that my daily hikes and Pilates were reflected in my muscular legs and toned abs. Not bad for a woman in her mid-40s I thought as I quickly towel-dried my hair and applied some champagne-colored eyeshadow and sapphire mascara. I normally wore minimal make-up, opting for an au naturel look to match my lifestyle. The rosy tint from the sun highlighted my cheeks with a healthy bronzed glow. A little almond oil glossed my lips, completing my "primping."

I put on one of my favorite dresses – a simple but elegant royal blue silk crepe dress with spaghetti straps – a souvenir from my trip to Italy. I never had been extravagant – never spending much money on myself. Nor did I spend much time focused on appearance, but sometimes the aftermath of a breakup - or "breakups" in my case, I acknowledged - makes one desirous of feeling a little special – if only in one's reflection in the mirror.

I ran my hands through my almost dry hair, twirling my fingers around the strands, framing my face to give it a simple beach wave vibe. I didn't have far to walk. I was just going to the hotel bar to have a glass - or two - of wine, so I opted for a strappy pair of silver stilettos which always made any occasion feel elevated to me.

As I walked the short distance to the bar, I took my time to appreciatively take in the lovely ambiance of the beautiful countryside estate. Slowing down and soaking in the moment were new experiences to me – formerly tied to a frenetic schedule of a corporate lawyer at a big law firm that prioritized billable hours. I was happy to have left behind a life where one's value was measured in 15-minute billable bites.

I had opted for a simple, single room at an elegant traditional manor house immersed in sprawling well-manicured gardens. I vastly preferred boutique hotels and I had chosen one in a residential area reflective of local life away from the hustle and bustle of the big beachfront resorts catering to package groups and the somewhat frenetic tourist-centric capital of Palma.

I had not been disappointed. The property oozed charm with lush landscaped gardens surrounding an inviting pool, fringed with fragrant orange trees brilliantly contrasting with the shimmering silver greenish-gray of innumerable olive trees. Sensual inky purple fig trees and white-bloomed almond trees dotted the property enhancing its beauty. Sky-high palm trees seemed to pierce the romantic jet blue sky twinkling with endless stars. The paths were illuminated with an array of oversized Moroccan lanterns with different shapes and colors interspersed with cascading rainbows of bougainvillea and prolific rosemary and lavender bushes that perfumed the fresh night air. Such simple elegance and so romantic I thought. It reminded me of Valentinis' B&B and I longed for someone to share it with - Leo, precisely I admitted to myself.

I was brought out of my solitary musings as I approached the hotel entrance. The door was beautiful - sexy somehow - as I find doors in so many countries to be so often. It was an imposing arched wooden door with beautiful pewter handles and door knocker, a small window cut-out lending it an aura of mystery as to what potential lay beyond it. Even the entrance exuded sensuality I thought as I pushed hard against the heavy door to earn my entrance. I was greeted with a heady waft of jasmine-scented air as I traversed the chic candle lit courtyard past the reception to the hotel bar. Comfortable stylish chairs and inviting loveseats adorned the welcoming area with pastel-colored fluffy feathery pillows contrasting beautifully with the dark mahogany walls and reception desk.

The inside was just as stunning – with soaring cathedral ceilings and a Moroccan-inspired interior décor. Countless more Moroccan lanterns of varying shapes, sizes, and colors fringed the perimeter, casting beautiful candlelit reflections through their stained glass – alighting the room in an intimate glow. Several large lemon and olive trees framed the walls, interspersed with floor-to-ceiling pewter mirrors with Moroccan arches. There was a ceramic fountain as the centerpiece of the exquisite room, the soft bubbling of the water imparting tranquility. So dreamy, I could just curl up in one of the plush beckoning chairs surrounding the fountain and sleep happily here, I thought.

I hesitated for a brief moment, unsure where to sit, painfully aware of my relatively novel status of being single, as I anxiously perused the seating options - evidently designed for couples and groups. I quickly and gratefully opted for a velvety-cushioned burgundy high-backed bar stool at the bar as one of the young bartenders who had noted my dilemma smiled, directing me to one of the stools he invitingly pulled out for me.

Oh my, I thought, as I stared at him unintentionally, perhaps a little too long. His jet black tousled hair, dark features, olive skin, and long dark eyelashes reminded me of a young Antonio Banderas. He couldn't have been more than 25. "Bienvenidos," he greeted me, quickly following with "Welcome," in case I didn't understand him. As I shook his extended hand, I replied, "mucho gusto" or "with pleasure," - one of the rudimentary Spanish phrases I had mastered that seemed particularly reflective of my feelings at that moment. "Ah, que bonito, how beautiful, you know Spanish," he generously complimented, smiling again with a grin, revealing dimples that instantly made me melt.

"Hardly," I replied. "I manage to eat and drink my way around the world though," I nervously smiled. "…and perhaps get into a little bit of trouble," he flirtatiously said as he glanced at my legs and form-fitting dress in appreciation. I was silently grateful that I had worn my heels instead of sandals as I smiled in gratitude.

"I'm Sergio," he said as he took my hand to help me onto the high bar stool and hung my purse on a pretty ceramic hook under the bar. "It will be my pleasure to take care of you this evening," he said as he winked and lightly grazed my bare shoulder as he returned behind the bar. I blushed and momentarily averted his gaze though my heart was warmed and I was grateful for his attention and kindness.

"May I have a tempranillo please?" I asked abruptly, feeling self-conscious under his steady gaze. "Of course, you may, but all good things in time, no senorita?" he playfully called me as it was obvious I was of "senora" age. "You are on holiday, no?" he asked. Without awaiting my answer, he procured a bottle of sparkling wine, saying, "This deserves a celebratory toast. Do you like cava?" he asked as he began unwrapping the cork, anticipating my answer. "Love," I replied sincerely.

I watched intently as Sergio effortlessly - yet somehow with a flourish - uncorked the bubbly. "My colleague, Diego," Sergio introduced me to another equally young and divinely sensual bartender who came into the bar. I greeted Diego warmly, matching his proffered smile. "From us, senorita," Sergio said as he poured the sparkling beauty into a delicate crystal flute, as we all appreciatively watched the effervescent bubbles work their celebratory magic as only sparkling wine can do. Sergio slowly filled my champagne flute to the top as Diego put two additional flutes on the bar for Sergio to fill halfway. "One must never toast alone," he expressed by way of explanation. "Salute," they said in unison as they each toasted me separately making sure to make eye contact as is uniformly politely done in other cultures. One of the things that exuded sexiness to me in foreign lands was the directness and attentiveness of the encounters and these two appeared to have mastered it I thought as I felt stirrings for intimacy deep within me.

I sipped my refreshing effervescent wine, while Sergio and Diego politely exchanged pleasantries with me while they prepared a variety of colorful cocktails in exquisite glasses with expertly-prepared artistic fruit garnishes. They wanted to know where I was from, how long I was staying, and how I was enjoying their magical island. They were surprised that I had a one-way ticket and was planning my travel spontaneously.

I briefly averted to the fact that I had recently divorced by way of summary explanation, was starting a writing career, and was planning to just explore and enjoy my summer. They applauded my adventurous spirit and commented that it struck them as atypical for Americans. I chuckled, fully agreeing. One of the things that drew me to the European culture was their attitude of "work to live" instead of "live to work" as so many other Americans seemed to embody, even if unconsciously. I loved how Europeans embraced the simple pleasures of life and seemed to focus on more day-to-day enjoyment than fixating on how much money they had and how many possessions they could acquire.

I briefly shared some of the things I wanted to do while on the island - a combination of revisiting favorites and exploring new places. I was pleasantly surprised how comfortable I was feeling, thanks to their warm hospitality, charm, and youthful energy. Each time Diego finished making a drink, he poured me a taste from the cocktail shaker inviting me to try it, saying, "For your approval." I don't normally drink cocktails but was happily rewarded with each sip with a tasty new concoction. I loved trying new things and was getting a little taste of a variety of drinks I would not normally have the opportunity to try. The biting acidity and the fresh tang of the just-squeezed citrus and the array of herbs they were using tantalized my taste buds and made the cocktails visually arresting.

"Mmmmm, minty," I noted with my most recent sip. "So refreshing," I complimented with obvious delight, the alcohol and the sincere warmth of my new acquaintances melting my normal shyness and inhibitions. Diego playfully asked me which fruits and herbs he should use to garnish each of the cocktails. I don't know if the patrons approved of my taking a stab at being a newbie mixologist but it was all harmless fun and I was grateful Diego was keeping me engaged despite how busy the bar was.

I had only intended to briefly go to the bar and return to my room early, but I was really enjoying the company. I was dreading going back alone, my restless spirit punctually and annoyingly rearing its head with the approach of nightfall. As Diego left to deliver some drinks, I turned slightly in my bar stool to scan the room, my gaze having been completely consumed by Sergio and Diego until then. I slowly took in the lovely ambiance while noting somewhat self-consciously that all the patrons seemed to be coupled. As I turned back to the bar, my strap slid down my shoulder. Sergio came from behind me and quickly but gently pulled it back up, his slight touch snapping me out of the beginning of my melancholy and grounding me in the moment.

As I turned to him, exchanging smiles, he reached around me and placed in front of me a colorful Dalí-inspired tiny oval ceramic platter decorated with a beautiful assortment of classic Spanish tapas that I knew and loved so well. "From us, for you to nibble on. ¡Buen provecho! Enjoy your meal," he winked as he returned behind the bar and, without questioning, refilled my flute while I was fixated on my adorable little repast.

I was touched and tantalized as I inventoried the generous offering. Food is an expression of love and a sensual experience to me, as was clearly represented by this adorable diminutive combination. There were jamon-wrapped dates, providing that perfect combination of salty and sweet, a fresh cut fig revealing its juicy sensual deep purplish interior, some rosemary-coated marcona almonds, some cubes of sharp manchego cheese, drizzled with invitingly sticky sienna-colored thyme-flavored honey and some little crisps. I was in gastronomic heaven with this hospitable and culinarily artistic offering. It also was not lost on me that a lot of these - the dates, the figs, the honey - were aphrodisiacs.

"Oh my, thank you," I practically gasped in delight and deep gratitude. I loved the intimate tapas-style of eating and the sensuality of eating little bites with one's fingers. "Delicious," I murmured in obvious satisfaction as I slowly started savoring my tapas and sipping my newly-filled glass of cava. I noted in great admiration the lovely attention to detail that had gone into the preparation of my complimentary tapas platter. Little white flowers from the garden's almond trees adorned one side of the oval platter while sprigs of rosemary in a little shot glass decorated the center. There was another little matching platter with a warmed towel to clean my hands.

It's funny how relatively little things can be so comforting to someone's heart and soul when their heart is emotionally bruised. My eyes actually teared up a little from the warmth and hospitality – it felt like a much-needed virtual hug. I hadn't realized how deeply I longed for intimacy - a little tender loving care - and I was grateful for the thoughtfulness.

"I'm so fortunate and glad that I chose this property and met you both," I offered Sergio and Diego a glimpse into my reverie. "We're glad to see you happy," Sergio said with a smile, revealing those make-me-melt dimples again. Diego chimed in, " Yes, you deserve to be happy." I smiled in deep appreciation, noting again how such simple compassion even from strangers can soothe one's aching heart. They didn't have to know me to know I deserved happiness. After all, we all deserve happiness. Yet, my exes had never articulated such a thing - indeed always clearly subjugating my happiness to their desires. It was eye opening to feel greater warmth and sincerity from new acquaintances than years-long relationships…

Just then "Una Noche Mas," by Jasmine Levy – an alluring hauntingly seductive favorite of mine began playing. Translated to "one more night" sounded perfect to me. All my senses were being engaged – indeed satisfied – as I watched Sergio and Diego effortlessly man the bar and take care of their patrons with infectious energy.

I was pleasantly surprised how relaxed I felt - I was unusually in the moment and determined to adhere to my pleasure for the sake of pleasure mood. I had always been drawn to the exotic and these two were checking all the boxes for my sexual appetite. I could feel my cheeks flush as the cava warmed me, the effervescent bubbles working their magic on my head while I could feel mounting desire throughout my body. A little harmless daydreaming never got anyone in trouble after all, I mused. I was relieved to see that I was open-minded and open to letting things play out spontaneously.

"Now, I think it's time for that tempranillo, no?" Sergio brought me out of my contemplation as he put a beautiful crystal glass with delicate etchings in front of me as he opened a new bottle of Faustino – a favorite with which I was very familiar.

"What are your plans for tomorrow?" Diego asked me as Sergio slowly poured a generous sip of the ruby-red beauty into my glass for me to taste. "Spectacular," I murmured in approval, as I gently swirled my glass, taking in its dark inky color, my senses engaged by the deep berry fragrance and the tannic tongue-coating sensation. I told them I was thinking of visiting the Miró foundation which they assured me was well worth a visit before suggesting other places and things around the island to explore.

******

Chapter 4. A Surreal Evening

I savored my wine in relative silence as Sergio and Diego tended to the full bar. I enviously noticed patrons were leaving - couple by couple. I was getting unusually sleepy, but my restlessness and solitude were making me feel uncomfortable. I listened to the sultry guitar sounds of Ottmar Liebert playing in the background, my melancholy and the sting of bitter regrets returning at the thought of returning to my room alone.

I distracted myself by looking up Surrealism to learn more about it in anticipation of visiting the Miró foundation. Surrealism was a fascinating movement that intrigued me for several reasons. Surrealist artists depicted dreamlike imagery taking inspiration from dreams and the subconscious. Their works feature bizarre, "illogical" scenes that feel like they're straight from a vivid dream. Surrealism thrives on combining "unrelated" objects in surprising ways. I recalled the famous work of a man's face in a birdcage by the artist I most associated with Surrealism - Salvador Dalí.

Whereas I had formerly been dismissive of such work because it didn't appeal to me visually, I realized now that I had been viewing art quite superficially. The movement intrigued me as it intentionally defied logic and conventional reality. I laughed as I realized that was a description that a number of my friends and family would use to capture my life of late. I immediately felt an affinity for the movement, surprised that I had never bothered to learn about Surrealism before despite frequently describing a lot of my experiences as surreal.

Dreams had always fascinated me as well and I found it interesting that the psychiatrist Sigmund Freud had significantly influenced the Surrealist movement with his theories on the unconscious mind and his dedication to exploring the depths of the "hidden" psyche. A lot of Surrealist artists explored themes like repressed desires, fears, and fantasies. Just as one can learn a lot about oneself from interpreting the seemingly nonsensical fragments of one's dreams, one could learn a lot about an artist by understanding his or her inspiration.

Presumably to Dalí and the other Surrealist artists, their depictions weren't illogical. For Dalí, obviously the man's face and the bird cage were "related" in some way. I thought of my stream of consciousness persona and how the connection between my thoughts was crystal clear to me while undoubtedly being elusive to others. Surrealism was a movement that aimed to unleash the creative potential of the unconscious mind - a topic of increasing interest to me.

I thought of my recent time in Turkey, fascinated by the fact that apparently a lot of the prophetic messages by the Prophet Muhammad had come to him in his dreams. Giving life to one's dreams synced with me - be it in a simply expressive manner as in art or in reality as Muhammad had done and I aspired to.

Surrealist artists often used techniques like automatic writing and drawing to bypass rational thought and tap into their unconscious creativity. I loved the underlying free-style spirit and refusal to be confined by logic and rational expression. I was drawn to spontaneity and those who "colored outside the lines." The fact that the Surrealists created without planning - letting the hand move freely and seeing what emerged - spoke to my sensibilities and the way I liked to live. Overthinking truly is a primary source of suffering, I reminded myself, vowing to vigilantly embrace my willingness to seize the moment without forethought.

Some people considered my spontaneity thoughtless and my actions flighty in a judgmental way. My impulsiveness and unconventional way of doing things were intentional though. I find predictability and routine mundane and ordinary. I found living life the way I chose to much more rewarding and fulfilling. I was also grateful for the resiliency and adaptability that my outlook had bestowed on me. So many abhor change, yet novelty is how we expand and elevate our life.

I knew deep down that I didn't owe anyone an explanation as to how I chose to live my life. Feeling like I almost had a philosophical movement behind the way I intended to live the rest of my life buoyed and emboldened me though. Living with inspiration from the multilayered depths and intrigue of the subconscious was a much fuller, more extraordinary, exciting way of living as far as I was concerned. I was inspired by the kindred spirit of the Surrealist artists who cast off expectations and so-called realities. To me this style of art was the most elevated expression of what it meant to be an artist; it was inspirational and I considered myself fortunate for my affinity with such good company.

I found it enthralling that Surrealism was a style reflective of what lay beneath the surface - with the potential to provide insights reflective of one's soul. The movement hadn't been limited to the visual arts either - it also influenced the literary world as well as film and theater. Another thing that I found compelling was that the movement appeared to have been born from a reaction to the horrors of the realities of World War I. It's bizarre to think of conflict as rational and I had never thought about the influence that contemporary society had on various art movements.

I was gaining a newfound appreciation for art; it was no longer a mere observation of whether or not I found a particular piece aesthetically appealing. It was becoming a much more contemplative, engaging, educational experience - above and beyond my initial aesthetic impression of a piece of artwork.

I was becoming enthralled learning about what inspired the artist, regardless of the visual appeal of the artist's creation to me. I had thought I had an open mind but realized it had been fairly closed off with regard to the field of art before. I fondly remembered Dr. Seuss' cautionary tale in "Green Eggs & Ham" - basically to not judge something until you experience it. A whole new world of exploration seemed open to me now as I vowed to try not to engage in the proverbial judging a book by its cover.

The movement seemed to be a challenge, I reflected - one I happily accepted - to let go of the logical mind and engage with art on a more intuitive, emotional level. In essence, Surrealism invites us to see the world through a lens where the impossible becomes possible, and the ordinary transforms into something extraordinary and magical. It resonated with me as a life philosophy and a guiding principle I hoped would govern the rest of my life. It was a welcome invitation to suspend the so-called "rules of reality" - a prerequisite to exploring the limitless potential of one's imagination - one's life - I concluded as I finished my introduction to Surrealism, eager for my Foundation visit. I sighed in contentment, feeling dreamy and hopeful for this next chapter in my life.

Chapter 5. Ménage-a-Maybe…

"Have you finalized your plans for tomorrow?" Diego asked me with an inviting smile as I finished perusing the brochure. Before I could answer, Sergio commented, "Tomorrow is our day off. If you would like, we would be happy to escort you, showing you the highlights of Palma and some secret gems around the island. Princesses should not be without an entourage." I appreciated his playful compliments as much as his dreamy dimples as he smiled and winked again.

Be still my heart, I silently thought in anticipation of what sounded like a perfectly glorious day to me despite my normally introverted nature. "That would be lovely," I responded, trying not to expose my enthusiasm. "If it wouldn't be too much trouble," I demurely added. "No, por favor," Diego responded with the uber polite "no please" expression that enamored me. "It would be our pleasure," Sergio chimed in, sealing the deal. I blushed in appreciation and hopeful anticipation. Sometimes a distraction is just what an aching heart needs and these two seemed to be precisely the beautiful distraction I needed. One gets such a different perspective being escorted around a foreign place by locals and I was genuinely thrilled by their offer, emboldened by my Surrealist reflections.

"I finish work soon if you would like to enjoy another glass together on my patio with me. I live on the property," Sergio interrupted my thoughts to my continued delight. "That would be fabulous," I said without hesitation, not wanting the evening to end and embracing my "why not?" life philosophy. I wasn't being presumptuous that the much younger Sergio had any interest. I simply wanted some company to help me feel less lonely before going to bed and was happy to have one more glass of lubricating wine to lull me to sleep.

"La cuenta, por favor," I asked for the check with a little smile, using more of my oh-so-basic and limited Spanish. "No, por favor. No, please. My treat," Sergio said as he smiled deeply in response to my protestations. I was impressed as I saw him print out my bill and put money for it into the cash register out of his pocket.

Sergio offered me his arm as I dismounted from the bar stool before taking my purse off the hook and carrying it for me, a chivalrous gesture that had been bestowed on me in other countries before. Civility and chivalry are gratefully alive and well I mused as we walked the short distance to a small but charming coach house adjacent to the bar.

Sergio led me to the patio and opened another bottle of tempranillo. He put on some more sultry guitar music, poured me a glass, and said, "Please enjoy your wine and ambiance while I take a quick shower." I could feel my cheeks blush as I silently visualized him showering. Maybe I wasn't being presumptuous after all, I mused.

The air was cool and refreshing in contrast to my warm cheeks and the general warmth of desire that was permeating my entire body. The moon was almost full, bathing the patio in a romantic glow. I appreciated the seemingly innumerable stars penetrating the dark canvas of the jet-black inky sky. Stars always mesmerized me – somewhat of a rarity in city living in the US – a starlit sky always made a night feel magical.

I was wondering with positive nervous anticipation what to expect for the remainder of the night. My desire had been mounting throughout the evening and I longed for intimacy. I wanted to be warmly embraced, passionately kissed, and deeply desired. As I was eagerly awaiting Sergio's return, to my surprise, I heard the front door open and Diego appeared to my unexpected pleasure. "We not only work together but we live together too. We're best friends," Diego answered the puzzled look on my face.

"Happy to keep you company while you wait for Serg," he said, pulling up a chair, topping off my glass and pouring one for himself. He lit the several candles adorning the table, further adding to the impossibly romantic ambiance. We briefly chatted about Barcelona, where Diego was from, and his inevitable love for the Barcelona futbol team and their superstar, Lionel Messi. He was impressed with my familiarity with the sport and with Messi in particular – the Argentinean wunderkind I had come to know when I frequented Argentina.

Within a few minutes, Sergio appeared at the patio door, wearing a pair of royal blue silk lounge pants. He was topless, revealing the taut physique of someone who obviously takes care of himself. His obliques were clearly defined and my eyes followed them down to that incredibly sexy part of a man's pelvis just below his chiseled abs and above his waistline that drives me nuts. I gasped slightly in appreciation and slightly in anticipation as there was no doubt in my mind now that my desire would indeed be quenched.

Diego excused himself saying he was going to take a shower also. I interjected asking if I could use the washroom first. Visualizing him showering as well put me over the top and I needed to collect myself, almost overcome with desire. He chivalrously took me by the hand and showed me the way while Sergio took a sip of wine.

His hand was strong but soft and his scent was musky and alluring. My mind wandered, innocently fantasizing about a ménage-a-trois. Their attentiveness was like a salve to my still bruised ego from my ex discarding me and to my lonely heart from the disappointing ending of what I had hoped would be a relationship with Leo.

When I emerged from the washroom, Sergio was waiting in the hallway for me with our wine glasses. He handed me mine and asked if I wanted to finish our wine inside given the slight night chill. I nodded in agreement, took his extended hand and followed him down the hallway to a bedroom with a cozy sitting area. I was impressed with the simple but comfortable elegant décor. There was a velvety white chaise lounge and matching loveseat with fluffy ruby-colored pillows. There was a large round ottoman in front of the seating with more candles.

The lighting was dim, casting a flattering, sensual glow. There were French doors leading to another outside patio, slightly ajar, causing the sheer white curtains to billow in the refreshing night breeze. The king-size bed frame was a deep cherry wood, contrasting nicely with the white seating. A white leather headboard completed the inviting space.

Sergio led me to the loveseat, inviting me to make myself comfortable. He lit the ubiquitous Moroccan-style lanterns, while I took a big sip of my wine to quell my fledgling inhibitions. The candles cast intricate mosaic shadows along the wall. My desire, aided by the wine, soon overshadowed my mounting slight shyness and I began tingling all over.

"You look like a princess," Sergio complimented, his eyes locked with mine. "It's the lighting," I meekly responded, as I blushed and looked down slightly. He raised my hand to his lips and gently but firmly kissed it. My aching heart appreciated the attention and compliments and I instantly melted with gratitude and desire.

We simultaneously took a sip of wine and put our glasses on the ottoman in unison, signaling our readiness to move on. "May I kiss you, beautiful?" he asked, fully aware of my obvious answer. "Yes, please," I slightly moaned as I leaned in towards him, my body tingling. It was a gentle, yet increasingly deep all-consuming kiss. Kissing was sensual heaven for me; I eagerly devoured his welcoming mouth. His lips were full and soft in sharp contrast to the firmness of his kisses. He gently massaged my neck, pulling me closer to him as he began lightly teasing and nibbling my ear, an extreme erogenous zone for me. I tilted my head back fully, ready and excited for whatever was to transpire. "Mmmmm, you're delicious," he whispered. "…and you smell incredible." Ahhh yes, my French perfume, my signature scent, never failed to tantalize.

I put my hand on his firm thigh and slowly started stroking up and down it with my long fingernails. He arched his back slightly in appreciation. His pelvic region was beautifully highlighted in his silk lounging pants. I couldn't wait to taste him, to feel him inside of me.

I grabbed the back of his head, his thick hair still slightly wet, and pulled him to me for a deeper kiss as my strokes became more intense and longer, leaving no doubt as to my desire. The back of my palm brushed up against his lap and I was rewarded with an enticing feeling of his hardness I would inevitably soon enjoy. I lingered there as our eyes locked, his penetrating gaze heightening the intensity of my intensifying arousal. Without averting my gaze, he started stroking my thigh in long, firm strokes, mimicking my lead.

"Where's Diego?" I heard myself ask to my surprise as my longing continued mounting uncontrollably. "Would you like him to join us?" Sergio immediately replied without hesitation. "As you desire," he winked, thereby emboldening me. "Sure, why not?" I replied with my apparent new trademark outlook on life. "I'll go get him," he said as he exited. I took another deep sip of the wine, enjoying its taste and its aid in loosening my already loosening inhibitions. I was surprised by my forwardness and interest in a ménage-a-trois. I hadn't been aware that I desperately longed for raw unleashed desire and passion. An intense sexual encounter with no commitment is exactly what I was looking for. My recent experiences and feelings of rejection and unrequited love had apparently left me longing for a night of unbridled intimacy. I wanted to be taken like never before and my desire was so intense it seemed it could only be satiated - if at all - by multiple encounters.

Sergio quickly returned with Diego, also clad in silk lounging pants and a form-fitting v-neck t-shirt that accentuated his young, fit physique. They each sat down on either side of me – it was a generous loveseat but we were in close proximity. Diego said, "Thank you for inviting me." I coyly replied, "My pleasure." "I certainly intend it to be," he murmured, leaning in to gently kiss me. His eyes were a deep hazel green with a touch of golden sparkle. He was clean shaven and had an intoxicating spicy musky scent. He kissed me lightly and more gently than Sergio had, making me tingle slightly and wanting more – so much more. Sergio poured Diego wine and handed us our glasses as he toasted us, "To new memories," he winked, once more revealing those inviting dimples, as we all clinked glasses and enjoyed a deep sip.

Diego began kissing me softly again, slowly teasing me with his tongue. My back was slightly turned to Sergio. My strap slipped off my shoulder but no one replaced it this time. Sergio began massaging my shoulders as Diego's kisses intensified in response to the firmness and depth of my kiss. I was ravenous and leaving no doubt about it.

Sergio began kissing my neck and whispering, "princess" in my ear, a term of endearment that seemed common in foreign countries. I always found it flattering and sweet and wonderfully novel - not being familiar with it in the US. Mediterranean men had an unwavering gaze and erotic expressiveness about them - they worshiped women and unhesitatingly showed their affections, compliments, and desires. It was easy to feel comfortable in my own skin with such attentiveness.

Diego took a sip of his wine, stood up and took his shirt off, revealing well-defined abs and pecs. To me, they both represented the epitome of the perfect physique – one obtained from an overall healthy lifestyle and physical fitness. They weren't bulky or showing off. Their casual nature about their beauty added to their appeal. They were simultaneously gorgeous and confident but humble. I moaned slightly and closed my eyes momentarily, feeling slightly dizzy with delight and overwhelming desire.

Diego watched patiently, standing in front of me, sipping his wine, purposefully, slowly licking his pronounced sensual lips. Sergio grabbed my hair gently, turning me towards him and started kissing me intently and deeply again. Everything about these two had me in overdrive – including the teasing contrast of their styles. While he was kissing me with ever-increasing intensity, Sergio pulled my dress up slightly and slipped his hand under, slowly stroking my already engorged lips through my thong, my wetness seeping through my panties to welcome his touch.

I was incredibly aroused - the night had played out like a glorious, languid tease, beautifully fraught with heightening sexual tension. It was the foreplay of my dreams and I knew I would release momentarily if Sergio continued. He assertively pulled my panties to the side, assertively stroking my evident desire. Just as I thought I was going to explode, Sergio abruptly stopped, intentionally leaving me wanting more. He kissed my forehead - an endearing gesture that always made me melt - before getting up and moving to the adjacent chaise lounge.

He and Diego simultaneously started removing their pants. I helped Diego with his as I eagerly watched Sergio undress as well. Watching a man pleasure himself was titillating for me and Sergio was not about to disappoint me. He took his hand still wet with my juicy lust and started slowly stroking the glistening tip of his head with it with a feather-light touch - he was teasing himself and it had me in a fixated frenzy. He closed his eyes and leaned his neck back in evident anticipation while starting to firmly encircle his hardness, his grip and his facial expression intensifying as he ran his hand along the length of his shaft. Seeing him deeply enjoying pleasuring himself with my wetness sent me over the edge. He was generously endowed and I envisioned every inch of him penetrating me deeply. He opened his eyes, silently imploring me to follow his lead as he stared intently, purposefully into my eyes.

Sergio's show was making me very hungry and eager to please. I turned my attention to Diego's obvious desire. I could appreciatively gaze at Sergio's performance while I slowly began teasing Diego's erection, encircling my tongue around his head, mimicking Sergio's hand action. Diego moaned and put his hands behind my head, gently imploring me to explore the rest of his beautiful hardness. Sergio started running his fingers up and down himself, sending obvious chills throughout his body. His eyes remained locked on mine, clearly turned on by the fact I was appreciating his display, ready to mimic his every move. I took his cue, running my nails gently up and down Diego's firmness, slowly then with increasing pressure, following Sergio's lead.

I looked up into Diego's eyes – his deep penetrating look mirroring his obvious pleasure. I grabbed his well-defined ass, pulling him deeper into my mouth as Sergio started firmly gripping his rigidness, stroking up and down with a tightly clenched fist. As I stood up from the loveseat to kneel in front of Diego, my strappy dress slipped off, revealing my black lace bralet and matching thong. Sergio and Diego moaned in unison and I slipped a finger under my thong, inserting it to feel my wetness. I took my finger and playfully massaged my wetness on his full testicles as I sucked with greater intensity. I massaged his fullness, knowing he would be exploding soon. I started stroking myself, moaning louder with yearning. Still taking my cue from Sergio, I firmly but slowly sucked up and down the length of Diego's shaft.

I was so turned on between tasting Diego and watching Sergio put on a show for me, I knew I could erupt any time I chose simply by fingering myself. As much as I wanted to feel each of these gorgeous young Spanish stallions inside of me, I enjoyed the thought of prolonging the tease for all of us. I had no doubt this would not be my last sexual encounter with these two.

I was, however, eager to satisfy both Diego and Sergio. I knew they both were on the verge of orgasming and I wanted to prolong and intensify our inevitable releases. I took a long, drawn out purposeful taste of Diego while motioning Sergio to join us. "Please," I begged with my words and eyes, as I began firmly stroking Diego with my left hand while continuing to stroke my sopping engorged arousal with my right fingers.

Sergio obediently obliged, coming to stand before me. "Please. Feed me," I implored, matching Sergio's penetrating gaze. He didn't hesitate, firmly grabbing my head, my hands still pleasuring Diego and myself, and forcefully guided my mouth onto him. As I began to taste him, I moaned in appreciation, knowing it would be challenging to fully absorb him.

I began gripping Diego tighter, my clenched fist running up and down the entirety of his shaft while I started fingering myself, first with one finger then two, my pressure increasing with my passion. With my hands busy, I knew I was at Sergio's mercy or lack thereof. Knowing he was fully in control, Sergio kept his hands on the back of my head, continuing to guide me slowly but ever so deeply inch by inch.

As I was slowly devouring Sergio and firmly stroking Diego, I realized I desperately wanted to feel one of them inside me. I moaned in hunger, slightly gagging on Sergio as he penetrated further in response to my moans. He grabbed my hair and raised my head so our eyes met. I knew we were all about to explode in glorious unison. Diego moaned, quietly imploring me to stroke harder and faster. I obliged as I thrust my fingers deeper inside of me while enveloping more of Sergio inside of me, my eyes welling with tears as I struggled to devour him in his entirety.

As I convulsed from my own orgasm, I caused Diego to release, his warm essence drenching my hand as Sergio extricated from my mouth, firmly gripped himself and let me watch him explode all over my awaiting mouth. As I eagerly licked up what I could, Diego went to clean himself off, returning with a cloth for Sergio who first gently wiped off my mouth before wiping himself off. He collapsed on the couch, pulling me close while Diego laid on the chaise lounge. He looked at me intently with smiling eyes and kissed my forehead softly saying, "Let's get some sleep, princess, shall we? I think we'll need energy for tomorrow." I nodded in silent agreement and heard Diego gently sigh in contentment as he already started drifting off to sleep. I nuzzled my head into Sergio's warm embrace, fully satisfied with my first day in Mallorca and eagerly anticipating the rest of my holiday.

******

Chapter 6: Reveling in Freedom: That's What Friends are For

I awoke with a startle to an incessant ringing. Must be one of the guy's phones I hazily thought as I bolted upright in bed, a feeling of self-loathing beginning to encircle me as I glanced around to survey the remnants of the night before. I shook my head to shake off my sleepy stupor, gratefully realizing I was all alone. Olivia was the one awakening me from my deep slumber and erotic dream.

"Sofia!" I could hear the concern in Olivia's voice. "Ugh," I replied, exacerbating the situation, unable to muster anything more from the depths of my self-recrimination for my fantasies despite my relief that was all I was guilty of. "Where are you? I've been trying to call you," she persisted. "In the land of self-loathing," I answered imprecisely before adding, "In Mallorca." "Oh, ok, I don't even know where that is," she chuckled. "Just as long as you're good, love."

Olivia could hear in my voice that I was troubled and gently prodded, leading me to divulge the gist of the prior night's events before segueing into my dream; my truest friend always assured me there was no such thing as TMI. "Sounds fabulous," Olivia practically cooed, giving me a new perspective on the evening. "Sounds like an ad for Mallorca, in my opinion, wherever the heck it is," she added, lightening my mood. "Did you enjoy yourself? Were you comfortable? In reality and in your dreams?" she clarified. Olivia had immediately and seamlessly shifted the perspective to my viewpoint instead of being judgmental - brilliant and insightful. I silently lauded my kind and sage friend.

"Well, yes, of course," I slowly stammered, letting her opinion that all that mattered about the evening's events was how I felt, slowly color my assessment. "It was quite an experience and it definitely helped assuage my bruised ego." "Perfect," my non-judgmental friend concluded. "Sounds like you had incredible passionate life-affirming sex for the pure sake of your pleasure - if only in your head," she giggled. "Oh, boy do I wish I were blessed with your imagination," she murmured wistfully. "Yessss," I slowly replied, appreciative of her efforts to not make me feel uneasy about my explicit description.

I shared that I felt guilty that I had even entertained the notion of a menage-a-trois especially with two much younger men. I also bizarrely felt that I had cheated on my ex in some twisted sense of loyalty. "Guilty?" Olivia gently, questioningly, asked in response to my feelings of shame. One of my greatest comforts in life was that Olivia knew me so well and listened with her heart to my mood and my tone. Words were blissfully often gratuitous between us.

Of course, feeling disloyal to my ex was wildly irrational. That's the thing about feelings though - they are what they are - frequently not rational or warranted. I loved though that Olivia was helping me work through my feelings instead of being dismissive given their ludicrous nature. It wasn't lost on me that both my fantastical dream and my misplaced feelings of guilt were trying to tell me something.

Hmmm, "fantasy," "fantastic," I silently contemplated the two words, never having thought about their connection before. It slowly dawned on me as I fully awoke from my slumber that my contemplations about Surrealism very likely had something to do with the content of my dreams. It was insightful - I hadn't truly appreciated how discarded

I had been feeling from my husband leaving me. I hadn't consciously realized how desperately I longed to be desired, to be wanted - to feel worthy, to be validated. I hadn't realized how I had been internalizing the actions of all my exe's - I was interpreting them as reflecting some sort of defect in me - not them… Hmmm, I thought as Olivia continued her impromptu "therapy," lovingly helping me wrap my head around what I was feeling.

"Guilty of what, love? Wanting to enjoy yourself for the sheer sake of enjoying yourself? You are not married, remember?" she pointedly went on, knowing I was feeling some bizarre sense of fidelity still to my ex. "You are the most loyal person I know, especially when it comes to him," she referred to my last ex with obvious disdain." "He abandoned you. I abhor how he made you question yourself, your worth, your desirability. You owe him less than nothing. I'm glad you felt wanted - in reality and your dream. You deserve so much - and way beyond sex - of course. I'm thrilled you had some sort of a release - even if only in your dreams," she chuckled. "Besides," she transitioned to a broader commentary, "You don't owe anything to anyone, other than yourself. You are not competing for a community service award. You are not applying to a convent. You do you, sister." Olivia consoled me with an evident smile in her voice.

I hadn't been the one who wanted to be "unmarried" though. I wasn't the one who had nonchalantly cast aside my marriage commitment. I hadn't appreciated that I was unwisely holding myself to a code of conduct that clearly no longer applied because I still bizarrely felt beholden to my commitment. I shared my real-time epiphanies with Olivia, hoping to gain some clarity.

"I know you're struggling, love. I know you want closure. It's totally to be expected that you want to feel desired. Your dream makes perfect sense to me and I'm thrilled you let loose subconsciously, if not consciously yet. You. Do. Not. Owe. Anyone. Anything," my dear friend slowly punctuated her thoughts, making sure they sunk in before proceeding. "You played out your obvious longing to be wanted in the most innocent way possible - in an intense fantasy. Now that's what I call "safe sex," she wittingly quipped. Olivia's words worked their magic as always. I joined in her amusement as I recalled her parting gift economy box size of condoms - obviously she hadn't expected me to refrain from sex. Why would I possibly care what anyone else might think in the abstract? Hmmmm, chaste, chastise, chastisement, I continued analyzing the import of different words I had never given thought to before.

"But they're so much younger…," I fixated again before she quickly interjected, "So what? Good for you! They are full-grown men, Sofi. You take excellent care of yourself; you look much younger than you are. You deserve men to be attracted to you, to desire you. Anyone who thinks otherwise is judgmental and jealous. Screw them," we burst out laughing simultaneously, appreciating the double entendre of "screw them." "…and as far as age difference goes," Olivia was on a roll, "if you add their ages together, they more or less are the same age as we are." My clever, loving friend contagiously broke out in uncontrollable laughter.

She lovingly turned my words "against" me in an effort to finish making her point by citing my oft-quoted Dr. Seuss wisdom to the effect that those who matter, don't mind and that those who mind, don't matter. I had used the advice so frequently when trying to convince Olivia not to worry about what others thought.

"Doing anything for yourself - including sex - instead of in service to another is unfamiliar territory for you." Bingo - Olivia had struck the nail on the head of my feelings. "Get familiar. You're healing from effed up relationships, babe. This is the new you. You're an intensely passionate, go big or go home persona. You're a bad ass beautiful butterfly. Revel in your freedom, pursue your passions, and get some for me too," Olivia finished her somewhat unusual but effective sermon of sorts in a tantalizing manner that served to completely elevate my mood.

Olivia had a wonderful special knack of approaching everything with a we/"team" mentality. Olivia's reaction to my embarrassed, somewhat reluctant, divulgences was a much-needed reminder that I really wasn't alone. She immediately made me feel completely unabashed about my prior night's brush with a tete-a-tete. I craved intimacy more than anyone. Olivia knew I mistook sex for intimacy and love all too often and she had lovingly made me feel that whatever I did was fine with her - her only caveat that it was for me - not someone else...

I thanked my best friend profusely for her wisdom and love before promising I would do a better job of keeping her apprised of my whereabouts. "Don't make me call the US Embassy and beg them to find out what two gorgeous bartenders did with my best friend. I need your itinerary - so you can follow you and I can live vicariously through you until I can join you."

I was so grateful for Olivia and so happy to have started my day with her. She had completely changed my earlier perspective while helping me process my feelings.

Historically, I had felt obliged to demonstrate my worth and have myself externally validated. Ironic that my feeling of self-worth could be premised on acts showing absolute disrespect for myself; things were slowly but surely dawning on me. The idiocy of having self-worth come from actions that fundamentally disrespected myself hit me like a lightning bolt. My realizations were incredibly liberating and made me feel extraordinarily empowered.

Viewing sex from this perspective was extremely titillating to me. It wasn't about pleasing someone else as the be all and end all. My pleasure and my release had been my priority - not subserviently satisfying someone else. The goal was a mutual, though casual, physical connection…. "Well done, Sofia," I silently applauded myself, grateful that I truly was progressing on my healing path.

Olvia's perspective helped me realize how far I was coming in my healing journey. The unconventional sex - albeit in my head - had been so freeing and enjoyable to me because I hadn't confused it with anything other than what it was - it was pure physical passion with the only goal of pleasure. There hadn't been any pretense, any expectations, any ulterior motives. It had been a reciprocal sexual encounter and had been glorious because there wasn't anything more intertwined with it. I hadn't felt compelled to engage in anything I didn't want to for the sheer sake of pleasing someone else. I was a comprehensive serial people pleaser and that persona had permeated all aspects of my life previously - indeed my very existence. I had defined my worth thusly. I had played out in my fantasy what I wanted in life conceptually - if not the details per se.

I thought again about Surrealism and how it reflected one's subconscious. Even if I were still struggling pursuing whatever I wanted purely for me, my subconscious had given me clarity with respect to the direction I wanted to go. I didn't need a threesome - it was just a glorified fantasy to get my attention - to highlight how wonderful and empowering it was to focus on my own pleasure. Obviously, I had pleased the duo in my dream as well - but because I had wanted to - not because I felt compelled to. The fantasy sex had been one of the few times I hadn't subjugated myself - I hadn't been motivated by my people pleasing. I jumped out of bed and into the shower, eager to get on with my day and out of my head and into the whimsical "fantasy" world of Miró.

******

Chapter 7: Painted Joy - Dreams Do Come to Life

The Miró Foundation was an extraordinary collection as well as an unexpected learning lesson and source of great inspiration. I picked up a detailed pamphlet at the entryway to learn more about the artist and the museum. The foundation provided a comprehensive look at Miró's evolving artistic journey, housing over 6,000 pieces - including not only paintings, but also drawings, sculptures, and prints. The gallery was set up to provide insights into the evolution of the artist's distinctive style, characterized by bold colors, organic forms, and playful abstractions, which continually pushed the boundaries of artistic expression.

Miró was born in Barcelona in 1893, but spent his later years on Mallorca, which had apparently imbued new inspiration to his visionary spirit. The museum had been established in 1981 by Miró and his wife, which gave it an interesting twist since most museums dedicated to a single artist are built after the artist's death. It made the foundation feel like far more than just a collection of works; it was a more intimate reflection of Miró, showcasing his sanctuary of innovation and creativity.

The architecture of the gallery itself was a marvelous spectacle, seamlessly blending with the stunning Mediterranean landscape. It was surrounded by lush gardens with an enviable position overlooking the entrancing deep blue of the Mediterranean. For the first time, I started thinking about how an area inspired an artist's creations as I admired the dreamy set up.

The main building masterfully used light and space to create an inviting atmosphere that was contemplative and inspiring. Miró's personal workspaces were adjacent to the main building - they offered a unique glimpse into the environment where he created some of his most famous works of art.

As I browsed the art, I had a newfound appreciation of the imagery of somewhat bizarre and illogical depictions as if a reflection of a vivid dream. Not anything I personally would want to own, but I respected the creativity and refusal to be confined to more rational depictions. Surrealism seemed like the best expression of what it truly means to be an "artist." My favorite types of people were people " who colored outside the lines" - an attitude that defined Surrealism to me. If I had the slightest bit of visual artistic talent, I would enjoy trying to come up with my own creations, I thought.

I had a much more profound appreciation for the artist's work once I understood the source of inspiration. What to me had appeared so simple at superficial glance - almost like a child's rudimentary sketches - actually had an alluring complexity that drew me in. Despite not being a particular fan of the actual artwork, Miró's works seemed to be a challenge to the observer to let go of his or her logical mind and engage with art on a more intuitive, emotional level that resonated with me. I laughed at myself, having frequently using the word, "surreal" to describe my experiences while never having bothered to learn about Surrealism. My novel education and visit gave me a whole new outlook on art in general and on visiting art galleries. I prided myself on having an open mind, but had been missing a fundamental aspect of art appreciation my entire life.

I did enjoy the whimsical nature and vibrant colors of the collection. I had heard of the artist's work being described as "painted joy," a description that encapsulated the visual essence of the art for me. I appreciated the fact that Miró seemed to have mastered the concept of letting his imagination almost dance across the palette in a way I had never seen before. The extensive collection also gave a new dimension to the word, "dreamy" to me, now that I understood the subconscious as a source of Surrealist inspiration. I read a quote by the poet Jacques Prevert - "A simple brushstroke can give freedom and happiness." Although he had said it in relation to Miró, it synced with my novel, profound appreciation for art in general.

I left the museum full of wonder and inspiration. It seemed to me that Surrealism - at its essence - was a welcomed invitation to see the world from a perspective where the impossible becomes possible, and the ordinary transforms into something extraordinary and magical. It amused me that an art movement - that had previously held zero interest to me - had quickly become a favored life philosophy. I was reminded again of Dr. Seuss' message in "Green Eggs & Ham" - to not judge something ignorantly. I loved living life with an open mind and my visit was a stark reminder to apply that to all aspects of my life. Life is so much richer this way, I concluded, thoroughly content with my visit.

The museum was unexpectedly one of the most memorable ones I had ever visited. The architecture and setting of the museum itself were exquisite, while the Miró collection was like a beacon of artistic freedom, which, to my surprise, had ignited a creative spark in me. Although I lack one iota of visual artistic talent, I got an "aha" moment as I was leaving, deciding I would employ artificial intelligence to let my wildest imaginations come to life and create my own Surrealist work.

Chapter 8: A Trio of Pleasures of a Different Kind

I was drawn to Mallorca because it had several diverse villages with their own distinctive charms, unique vistas, and varied attractions. I looked forward to visiting a trio of them in close proximity to each other, as well as to Palma. There were a number of areas along the Southwest coast known for all-inclusive packages catering to tourist groups, particularly Cala d'Or - a region my ex and I had explored that was not my style at all. Most people tend to gravitate towards the beaches on islands and, as a result, they tend to be the most touristy and crowded. They reeked of commercialism to me, whereas I was more drawn to the lush inland landscapes and architecture and romanticism of the smaller villages.

My favorite part of traveling was delving deeper into a place and exploring more authentic areas that retained their own distinctive character - in large part because they weren't so catered to tourists. I was reminded of my trip to Ibiza several years prior - Mallorca's sister island is most well known for its music scene and late night partying into the early morning hours. Although I loved house music and had briefly tipped my toe into the experience at the world-famous Pacha, the club scene was not my thing and I had moved on quickly. My explorations had rewarded me with some of the most breathtaking scenery and beguiling accommodations I had ever been blessed to experience. Going off the beaten path always promised the most memorable experiences from my perspective and I was looking forward to my day of exploration.

Similar to the Greek islands known for their extensive mesmerizing coastlines, I was always surprised at how many tourists concentrated exclusively on the seaside towns when the interiors often had so much to offer;

indeed, they were my favorites. Back to the present, I determinedly chided myself. In any event, it's nice to have such a variety of options with the relative ease of navigating an island.

******

Chapter 9: The Best of All Worlds in Sóller

Thanks to Sergio and Diego's tips, I planned to visit Sóller in the northwest first. There was a tram with wooden carriages - the traditional Ferrocarril de Sóller - that made the journey from Palma, traversing through the mountains, offering a stress-free way to indulge in the scenic vistas. Sergio had told me that "Sóller" was from the Arab "suliar," meaning "golden bowl," an apt description for the fertile valley of orange groves which defined the village, known as the "valley of gold" or "valley of oranges." It had become wealthy in the 19th Century because at the time it was isolated from the rest of Mallorca given the mountainous terrain, leading the locals to export fruit from the valley's abundant citrus groves - and, interestingly, wine - to France from the nearby Port de Sóller. A number of the beautiful properties gracing the village's landscape had been constructed thanks to the thriving businesses.

The unique trip in the wooden carriages of the vintage train had a romantic ambiance. I was grateful that my companions in my carriage were a mother with a young son and daughter - they reminded me of Isabella and the twins. They were adorable and polite and I loved how enthralled they were with the passing scenery - focused on the present and the vistas instead of being distracted on devices. I smiled warmly at the mother in silent appreciation of how she was raising her children.

We all "oohed" and "ahh-ed" in amazement as the train's hour or so journey rewarded us with stunning views of both the coastline and the countryside. I was impressed that the vistas still managed to instill wonder in the family despite not being novel. We often take things for granted when we are familiar with them and I appreciated the trio's evident awe. Gratitude for nature and finding beauty in one's surroundings ensures happiness in my book.

We caught glimpses of almond and carob trees before segueing into pine and olive trees. I had never seen a carob tree before and was grateful that the mother - Sophia - spoke English and helped orient me. We exchanged pleasantries, grinning at our names as we introduced ourselves. It was a lovely way to make the little sojourn - I appreciated the company and how the family's presence was keeping me firmly rooted in the present. I loved the contrasting scenes between the delicate white almond blossoms, the hardy, rigid deep green pine trees, and the appealing glistening silvery gray of the olive trees that forever alluringly captivated me. The air was fresh and the fragrance of pine and citrus wafted into the carriage through the tram's windows. I breathed in deeply in gratitude, the refreshing breeze of the countryside always energized me.

I caught my first glimpses of Sóller as we approached the green valley with terraced olive tree vineyards and bright orange tree orchards - it looked like an impressionist painting. Sophia graciously gave me her number in case I needed anything while I was in Mallorca. We hugged warmly as we departed as if we were long-time acquaintances. I gave the children extra tight squeezes, a bit sad that the train ride was over so quickly. I was always struck by the sincerity and helpfulness of people in other countries - a wonderful sort of civility and feeling of common humanity characterized a lot of chance encounters that left lasting impressions and made one feel less foreign, less alone.

I strolled through the town, stopping to absorb the lively yet peaceful Plaza de la Constitución with its pretty decorative fringe of palm and orange trees. The plaza was clearly the village's beating heart with numerous bars and cafes. I was instantly struck by the aesthetic appeal of Sóller - it had an interesting combination of Mallorcan style houses and French-inspired palaces. I stopped to admire the village's diştinctive landmark - the graceful neo-Gothic church, San Bartomeu. Sophia had shared with me that the architect, Joan Rubid, had been a pupil of the most famous architect I knew - Gaudí.

I had seen representative works of Gaudí in Barcelona where he spent most of his time and had been struck by their grandeur and whimsical nature. I thought about my novel learning about Surrealism, remembering that the famous Surrealist artist, Dalí, had been a contemporary and fan of Gaudí. Gaudí's most notable works always struck me as having a dreamlike fairytale imagination behind them as well but with a more appealing aesthetic for my taste. I knew his work was characterized by vibrant colors and voluptuous forms and a unique freedom of form - he and Dalí apparently abhorred straight lines. I deeply respected individuals who "free styled" and were non-conformists. I admired the shapes of his works - the refusal to adhere to convention in his elaborate works particularly appealed to me. If I designed my own house, I would opt for curves and unconventional shapes. His work was quite distinctive with colorful mosaics and fanciful shapes that made his work easy to identify. Being one with many passions, I found it particularly interesting that Gaudí's passions - architecture, nature, and religion - informed his creations.

I was grateful that it was serendipitously market day. I perused the various citrus offerings at many stalls from afar before stopping at the kiosk of a vivacious, joyfully plump, maternal older woman who reminded me of Nonna in Sicily. I had an impromptu snack, as she insisted on generously offering me samples of her products, happily reminiscing about my memorable time cooking with Nonna for the Marsala wine dinner. My sampling temptation made it impossible to resist purchasing some of the homemade organic orange marmalade, candied orange peel strips, delectable orange-flecked shortbread cookies, and orange blossom tea.

Sóller had a lot to offer in a relatively small and quaint area - including something I had never come across before - an ethnographic museum dedicated to displaying items relevant to ethnography - the systematic study of people and cultures. I realized that I was a bit like an ethnographic wannabe, although no one would consider me systematic, I self-deprecatingly chuckled at myself. I strolled by the Art Nouveau building, Can Prunera, which housed a permanent collection of art - including works by Picasso, Kandinksy, and Warhol - in addition to local artists and temporary exhibitions.

It was a lovely day and I strolled towards the Port, opting to bask in the natural beauty instead of visiting any of the surprisingly numerous galleries or museums. I passed by the Museu Balear de Ciències Naturals - the museum of natural sciences - and the Jardí Botànic - a botanic garden featuring many Balearic plant varieties. I had no idea that Sóller had such a wealth of varied things to do and I promised myself to come back some day with Olivia or Rachel to explore her charms in greater detail.

I sat at the beach at Port de Sóller - the only beach in the northwest - admiring its colorful port and listening to the boats lapping in the waves. I loved the tranquil pace and genteel nature of the area in sharp contrast to the popular beaches in the south that catered to tourist groups. I couldn't resist the wafting aroma of one of my favorite Spanish foods as I bought one of my favorite and simplest snacks - pan con tomate - bread with tomato to enjoy by the water. I knew that Sóller had world class restaurants with exquisite settings but I couldn't imagine a more perfect setting than one seaside with my toes dipped into the water connecting with the earth.

I could never get over how simple yet delectable I found the crusty hearty bread with juicy tomato and sumptuous olive oil, its characteristic garlicky goodness, and a smattering of coarse sea salt. This one had a generous amount of oregano that made it all that more delicious to me. This was my type of al fresco dining, my type of cuisine, my type of day. My heart warmed, thinking of the children in the tram and GiGi and Gabriele. We should all be more childlike, I mused. When you see the beauty everywhere, you're always surrounded by beauty. When you revel in the simple pleasures of life, you get to experience pleasure regularly. When you celebrate daily life, you always have a cause to celebrate at the ready. Life is good, I reflectively thought. Spain is working her magic on me. Life is good indeed, I sighed in complete contentment, slowly finishing my tasty treat before making my way back to the center of town.

With its stunning architecture and characteristic orange orchards and olive groves, Sóller quickly became a favorite village of mine, particularly given its enviable setting nestled in a valley surrounded by the towering Serra de Tramuntana mountains which enjoyed UNESCO World Heritage Site designation. Mountainous regions always drew me in with their peace and tranquility, but I also enjoyed stunning coastlines with lulling waves. I felt blessed to be back in Mallorca which offers the best of both worlds - particularly, it seemed in Sóller.

Sóller had an enticing blend of natural beauty, modern sophistication, and elegant architecture, giving it a dynamic atmosphere. It was precisely the kind of place I would love to call home one day, I thought, as I stood, taking in one last slow glance at the enchanting village before departing to my next destination. It had stunning mountains, a peaceful seaside coastline, and entrancing fertile valleys overflowing with natural abundance. I associated oranges with Spain and knew I would think of Sóller fondly whenever I enjoyed the citrus fruit. I loved how simple daily reminders could be so evocative of places that captivate our hearts.

******

Chapter 10: Dreamy Deià

I was feeling invigorated and inspired as I made my way by scenic bus ride to my next destination - Deià - a UNESCO World Heritage Site of Cultural Landscape. I had never even heard of such a UNESCO designation before and approached it with eager anticipation to explore it. I was struck by how many UNESCO designations Mallorca enjoyed.

The tiny, terraced town was characterized by well-preserved stone houses cradled amidst the mountains with surrounding towering palm trees that looked like sentinels and carpets of terraced olive trees. The village appeared as a dreamlike sanctuary as we entered the outskirts, rewarded with the first picture perfect panoramic view.

I knew it was a village of inspiration and haven for artistic types - like artists, writers, and musicians - due to its exquisite setting and natural beauty. I immediately fell prey to her charms as well as the quaint village perched on a hillside instantly touched my soul in a magical way. I slowly made my way through the town, stopping to take several photos of the stunning, elevated views of the Mediterranean Sea, my heart hoping for similar inspiration for my writing.

Its narrow streets, stone houses, and stunning sea views created an undeniable inspiring setting. I passed by the former house of the British poet and novelist Robert Graves who had lived in Deià for many years. The house had been turned into a museum dedicated to his life and work. I had never read any of his writings but my interest was piqued now. I enjoyed seeing how different places I visited inspired creative endeavors. I passed by numerous galleries showcasing the works of local and international artists inspired by Deià's enchanting environment and browsed through a few of them. Deià's artistic heritage and serene landscapes spoke to my soul - it offered a unique blend of creativity and natural beauty, perfect for inspiration and tranquility.

I could easily see wiling away hours soaking up the ambiance while writing - the town seemed like a muse to me. I left the center of town briefly to make my way to Cala Deià - a small, rocky cove perfect for simply soaking in the Mediterranean beauty. I loved how laid-back these little, less crowded coves were and how different the ranges of blue were in various areas of the island.

I was glad I had only had a simple snack in Sóller. My tummy started demanding attention as I made my way back up into the town center. I was impulsively planning a mini-indulgence at La Residencia - a lovely hotel that had captivated me with its simple elegance the moment I had seen images of it online. I had instantly been drawn to it when I had seen its description as "The Sanctuary of Art Energy."

The hotel had an exquisite fairytale setting in the midst of lush greenery. It was a sophisticated and elegant stone property with well-manicured gardens and a terrace overlooking the dreamy landscape. I was familiar with its signature fine dining restaurant, El Olivo, renowned chef, and indulgent tasting menus. I was opting for the more casual but equally tasteful Restaurante Miró. The friendly maitre'd asked me if I wanted to stop to take photos at El Olivo en route to its sister restaurant. I paused to breathe in the air and the ambiance as I took photos of the enchanting view. I promised myself I would be back some day for a celebratory dinner. The restaurant was famous for incomparable panoramic sunsets and romantic candlelit dinners.

The maitre'd sat me at a cute table on the Miró terrace overlooking the gardens. My waiter brought me a handwritten menu with the offerings of the day, a basket of toasty baguette slices, accompanied by a bowl of earthy green olive oil with artistically-swirled balsamic glaze, and a "gazpacho shooter." The oil was in a cute decorative little ceramic oil bowl and the gazpacho was in an adorable tall shot glass, each with what looked like Dalí-inspired art. Surrealism seemed everywhere now that I had delved into it, I amusedly beamed. The waiter generously told me to take my time and let him know if I had any questions or needed anything. I was happy with my choice of restaurants, planning to leisurely soak up Deià's enchanting ambiance while enjoying a memorable lunch.

This slow pace of life synced with me, I thought as I explored the enticing menu in appreciative detail. Mallorca's culinary scene was a glorious reflection of its diverse cultural heritage with a heavy emphasis on fresh seafood, olive oil, vegetables, and aromatic herbs and spices. Detailed descriptions always captivated me while whetting my voracious appetite. I noted a lamb empanadilla with grilled lemon and peppermint. I was intrigued by the unusual combination which undoubtedly promised to be simultaneously refreshing and cooling. I applauded the chef's skillful pairing of pungent, puckery grilled citrus and herbaceous, cooling mint - such simple ingredients elevated by the contrast in temperature and texture. I decided to borrow the inspiration while finally settling on a salad of tender greens with marinated salmon, seaweed, and pickled apples. I could only imagine what a memorable experience dining at El Olivo would be like as I silently promised myself again to indulge in dinner there some evening when I could enjoy it the most with a companion.

I caught the eye of the attentive but unobtrusive waiter to place my order. The staff was so warm and welcoming - I appreciated that they were making me feel so comfortable, especially dining alone amidst the other patrons. Unhurried service was a hallmark of Mediterranean countries - one never felt pressured to rush through a meal to enable the establishment to "turn tables" as many times as possible. I was emboldened and decided to take my waiter up on his recommendation to take my time as I requested the wine list. I happily sunk deeper in my comfortable seat, grateful for my vista and my lack of schedule.

It always felt celebratory to me whenever I had a glass of wine with lunch - a habit I frequently noted in Mediterranean countries - and I was feeling celebratory about life in general. I enjoyed expanding my knowledge and my palate and was eager to try something new. I frequently recalled different places evocatively based on my dining experiences and the novelty of the cuisine or wine I had. A Garnacha Blanca caught my eye - I was more familiar with red Garnacha and decided to give it a try as I read the description - refreshing with green herbs, Granny Smith apple, and lemon flavors. Sounded like the perfect accompaniment to my lunch. My waiter echoed my silent thoughts as he complimented me on my selection.

I knew my meal was going to be delectable the moment I saw it. I loved how La Residencia honored artists - a respect that extended to the culinary presentations - I noted with the delivery of other diners' beautifully-presented meals. It wasn't lost on me that I was eating at a restaurant named after Miró. I eagerly accepted my waiter's generous grinding of coarse pink peppercorns - a last minute touch that enhanced the already pretty presentation. The color contrast between the pink of the salmon and peppercorns and the green of the baby lettuces, seaweed, and Granny Smith apple created a pretty pastel culinary palette that appealed not only to my sense of taste but my other senses as well.

The crisp bite of the apple against the delicate flaky salmon and almost velvety greens was an excellent example of how textural contrasts can easily elevate a simple dish. My wine - perfectly chilled and served in a small, but generous-sized carafe - complimented the meal perfectly. The attention to detail was incredible and I smiled my delight as my waiter caught my eye to ensure I was enjoying my lunch. I appreciated that my meals throughout my time in Mallorca were undoubtedly locally-sourced. It never ceased to amaze me how truly different fresh, local, seasonal products tasted vastly better - it was a hallmark of Mediterranean eating. I never felt decadent eating out in Mediterranean countries - the meals I ate were almost universally as homemade as if I had made them myself. They left me feeling completely satiated in a comprehensive sense without feeling overly decadent. I thanked my waiter as he cleared my plate and asked him to give my compliments to the chef.

The gracious hospitality extended beyond my meal as my waiter approached with a little almond cake and another glass of wine. He overrode my momentary look of protestation, telling me that the treats were on the house. He winked at me, saying they loved seeing people truly appreciate their efforts and that the chef had thanked me for my kindness. I blushed at the overly generous response to my sheer pleasure and tiny compliment. My waiter told me the wine was a verdejo - a wine I was familiar with that was sort of like a marriage of my favorite white wine, Sauvignon Blanc, and Pinot Grigio. The cake was light, moist, and airy, interestingly with fennel seeds and slices of pink grapefruit. As I tasted the Verdejo with citrus, fennel, and almond characteristics, I realized what a genius pairing it had been. I was in awe of the kitchen's creative talent as I appreciated that they likely had created the cake to highlight the notes of the wine.

I felt like I almost couldn't be any more satisfied - it had been one of the most enjoyable dining experiences I had ever had. I wished though that I had been able to share the incredible experience with a loved one as I scanned the restaurant filled with friends, couples, and groups.

My eye caught a print of Miró's "The Escape Ladder." It was my understanding that it had been created in response to events surrounding World War I. With my recent novel perspective on art, I studied the print to come up with my own interpretation. It struck me as a sort of challenge to figuratively climb into the unknown - an invitation to explore - with a symbolic reward of liberation for making the journey. I internalized it as inspiration to continue on my path of self-discovery. What a perfect way to end a memorable experience, I thought in utter contentment. I was eager to continue my novel art appreciation now that I viewed art as an engaging and interactive pursuit - one that could not only be enjoyable but transformative as well. I left La Residencia - confident I would be back - with a full tummy, a happy heart, and an optimism that others would have the same interactive experience with my writing as I had started having with the visual arts.

******

Chapter 11: Well-Behaved Women Seldom Make History

My next destination, Valldemossa, was 16 kilometers to the south and where I planned to spend the night. Valldemossa is another of Mallorca's many postcard-perfect villages with a rich cultural heritage and vibrant romantic essence. It too was nestled in the Tramuntana mountains and was known for its stunning scenery as well as a few famous visitors and celebrities.

The town's terraced terrain, pedestrianized cobblestone streets, stone houses with green shutters, and overflowing blooming bougainvilleas created an atmosphere of old-world charm in a fairytale-like setting with the dramatic backdrop of the mountain range. It was less than 30 minutes away from Palma, yet felt worlds apart.

The village was home to Costa Nord, a contemporary culture center founded by the actor Michael Douglas, for whom Valldemossa had been a second home for decades. I was particularly excited about visiting its other claim to fame beyond its exquisite setting - Cartuja de Valldemossa - the historic monastery where the Polish composer and pianist Frédéric Chopin and the writer "George Sand" had spent a winter in the late 1830s. Their stay had inspired Sand's book, "A Winter in Majorca" and Chopin had reputedly described Valldemossa as "the most beautiful place in the world" - a laudatory designation more recently echoed by National Geographic. Despite the couple's initial enthralled impressions, circumstances caused them to leave the island with a much more tarnished perspective, unfortunately.

I had previously been unfamiliar with the writer's work and had not visited the monastery on my prior visit. I had recently read about her in anticipation of my trip and was pleasantly surprised to feel a deep affinity for Amandine Aurore Lucie Dupin - the author's real name - and fascinating intrigue over the couple's relationship. Dupin, a prolific and acclaimed novelist, had been a proto-feminist who had divorced her husband and had been a very vocal proponent for equality and non-violence in relationships. A single mother of two, she had apparently engaged in a number of romantic liaisons often with younger men before partnering with Chopin, six years her junior. She also raised eyebrows by adopting a masculine pen name and wearing pants, which was uncommon and frowned upon at the time. The couple had been at the artistic and social epicenter of the French Romanticism movement. They had courageously bucked the contemporary conventions and prevailing mores of the time.

A confluence of misfortunes apparently transpired throughout the winter of their visit, leaving a bitter impression of Mallorca on the couple - particularly of its inhabitants. The winter they had stayed had apparently been unusually cold and rainy. Mallorca is known for its year-round sunny days with around 300 days of sunshine, but sadly Dupin and Chopin experienced inhospitable weather during their stay. Chopin had tuberculosis and the climate made his condition worse. The weather wasn't the only inhospitality suffered by the two - the locals were afraid that Chopin had a contagious condition akin to the plague and disapproved of the unmarried couple's lifestyle together, exacerbated by the fact that they did not attend church. Dupin's progressiveness and fact that she was a chain-smoking divorcee - combined with her notorious romantic interludes - did not exactly enamor the locals to her either.

I was enthralled to learn that Dupin's primary inspirations for her writings were her lifelong love of the countryside and her sympathies for the impoverished. The main setting for her books was the countryside and her underlying theme was one of love transcending the obstacles of class and convention. I was eager to read some of her novels once I learned about her extraordinary life, including "Indiana" - a passionate protest against social expectations binding a wife to her husband against her will with a protagonist who abandons her unhappy marriage and finds true love.

The storyline was reminiscent for me of a favorite book of mine, "The Awakening," by Kate Chopin, although the protagonist in that novel had a much different ending. I smiled at the coincidence of the author's name with the composer. Liam and I had an "exclusive" - aka, just the two of us - book club years prior when I spent more time reading for pleasure and "The Awakening" was one of the books we had shared. Chopin's novel about a married woman seeking greater personal freedom and a fuller life was not well-received at the time it was published in 1899. The thought-provoking book became more highly acclaimed years later. I appreciated the conflict it highlighted between one's individual conception of happiness and societal expectations. Although I didn't approve of her actions per se, I applauded the great lengths the tragic heroine went to to live life the way she chose. Per Seyersted would later note that the novel felt modern because of the main character's belief that: "the physical component of love can stand apart from the spiritual one, that sensuous attraction is impersonal and can be satisfied by a partner she does not love." As someone who would have stayed forever in unfulfilling relationships, I was inspired by the courage and audacity that both Dupin and Chopin had instilled in their strong leading female characters, reflective of the authors' traits themselves. Both of the authors had "ruffled feathers," tackling controversial issues at the time. I admired them for their progressive nature and unwavering commitment to write what they pleased - despite the contemporary backlash.

I fondly thought of Liam, wondering if he would be interested in reviving our tradition of reading books together. It was an endearing one for me - I was always so interested in his opinions and perspective. I laughed, recalling that we were supposed to take turns selecting the book - his choices always struck me as being more academic and a bit esoteric - and I had always cajoled him into reading whatever I wanted to. I wondered what he would think about "Indiana" as the inaugural choice for a revived book "club."

I approached the monastery, feeling I was already intimately familiar with Dupin, anxious to get a glimpse of what life was like for her and "her" Chopin so many years ago. The monastery was picturesquely positioned on a gently sloping hilltop, rising majestically over the terraced jumble of maze-like streets and honey-hued stone village houses. The sand-colored monastery contrasted beautifully with the ubiquitous surrounding greenery and dramatic jagged rocky outcrops of the imposing mountain range. It exuded peace and warmth from the outside. I felt a full-body chill as I entered the monastery - in small part because I was immediately exposed to the "freshness" of the drop in temperature and the coldness of the austerity of the structure with soaring arched corridors. The temperature was welcome in the summer heat but understandably inhospitable in the winter like the one

Dupin and Chopin had endured. The source of my tingling was primarily from deeply feeling an affinity for the famous writer and an inspirational admiration of the couple's passionate love affair despite social convention.

I certainly understood the couple's initial enchantment with the poetic setting of Valldemossa, amidst the green and ochre-hued landscapes of the Sierra Tramuntana mountains, and with the monastery, located on a densely wooded terrain affording tranquil views of the sea. It's no wonder in these inspired surroundings with her lover by her side that Dupin initially referred to their accommodations at the monastery as "the most romantic abode in the world."

The monastery's long corridor was lined with tiny, vaulted monks 'cells' - the ones occupied by the author and composer housed mementoes from the couple's stay, including some of Dupin's manuscripts and Chopin's notes and his piano. Chopin had created some of his most famous compositions at the monastery. I looked out the window at the stunning landscape, recalling Dupin's original depiction of Mallorca to her friend, Carlotta Marliani:

> "The nature, the trees, the sky, the sea, the monuments surpass all my dreams: this is the promised land!"

A description of Mallorca much more favorable than the author would later capture in her book on Mallorca which apparently was so unfavorable that some Mallorcans had threatened to sue her. Chopin's initial impression of Mallorca when the couple started out in Palma echoed

Dupin's favorable impression, as reflected in his letter to Julio Fontana:

"I'm in Palma, between palm, cedar, aloe, orange, lemon, fig and pomegranate trees; the type of trees that will never grow in The Garden of Plants there in Paris. The sky is turquoise, the sea blue, the mountains emerald, and the air? The air is as blue as the sky. The sun shines all day and people are dressed as in the summer time, because here it is hot."

I thought about the couple's harsh winter and equally harsh reception in sharp contrast to the glorious weather and gracious hospitality I was enjoying. The locals' attitude and weather certainly color one's perspective of a place for good or bad. I felt blessed that my weather and the disposition of the locals in the Mediterranean countries I frequented were always sunny and welcoming.

I wandered the tranquil landscaped gardens surrounding the monastery's perimeter, admiring the entrancing vista of bright orange, silvery olive and verdant sentinel-looking cypress trees against the backdrop of the dramatic mountains. Dupin's enthusiastic description of Valldemossa in a letter to her friend, Alexis Duteil, resonated with me: "We are planted between heaven and earth." How ironic and tragic, I mused, that the village now celebrates the famous couple's passionate love affair while they had been terribly ostracized during their actual time spent here.

It seemed almost fitting that the author had a complicated relationship with Mallorca. The contrast between her being enamored with the island's jaw dropping beauty while being repelled by the lack of warmth from the locals seemed to mirror some of the divide in her own life as a societal aristocrat who openly defied social conventions and expectations. Mallorca itself appears as a land of contrasts, I realized - between coastal seascapes and rugged mountains, idyllic villages and bustling port towns, wild beauty and tranquility.

I chuckled thinking of how one of my favorite quotes, "Well-behaved women seldom make history," aptly applied to the protagonist in "The Awakening," as well as to the strong-willed Dupin. I applauded the author for her independence and passions, her quest for true love, her adoration of nature, and her compassionate soul. I felt a kindred spirit with Dupin; my visit emboldened me to continue embracing life my way.

I was still fully satisfied from my lunch and decided to spend the evening at my boutique hotel. It had a beautiful balcony overlooking the gorgeous natural surroundings. Reading "Indiana" on the balcony while having some of the orange blossom tea and orange cookies I had from Sóller sounded like the ideal way to end what had been a perfect day enjoying some of Mallorca's most quintessential treasured villages.

*****

Early the next morning, I reflected on the advantages of my solitude again as I enjoyed the hotel's sumptuous breakfast, basking in the stunning landscape after a blissfully deep sleep. I had appreciated the village's serene ambiance and cultural heritage vastly more than I had on my prior visit with my boyfriend. I chuckled remembering that my most vivid memory from my prior visit was a tiny faux pas of leaving our rental car in the market square. We had been quite surprised when we came out to get the car to find out it was market day and our little car was laden down with endless baskets of fruit and vegetables. The kind purveyor graciously pointed out the sign in Spanish - that clearly forbade parking in the square on market day - with a smile. Although I knew enough Spanish to realize what the sign said when it was pointed out to me, I held my Spanish-speaking Argentinian driving boyfriend at fault. Even though it had changed the day's itinerary spontaneously, I had enjoyed a lovely day browsing the market and having lunch at one of the cute outdoor cafes while he had sulked at our trivial change of plans.

My visit to the monastery and my new literary inspirational hero had made my brief time in Valldemossa quite memorable this time. My intimate glimpses into Mallorca's artistic past were also making me more and more enthralled with the island as well as with the creative arts in general. Mallorca was truly a treasure trove with so much depth and character beyond its famous coastline, touristy beaches, and cosmopolitan capital. My trip thus far had been a shining example of how travel can open one's eyes, mind, and heart - something I now realized I had not been taking full advantage of when I had been rushing through life and catering to my exes.

My heart warmed as my thoughts went back to the one "ex" who had firmly remained present throughout my life - Liam - recalling his wisdom about embracing my solitude. I chuckled, suspecting he likely wouldn't be as excited as I was to read Dupin's "Indiana" and touched knowing he would join me in the endeavor in any event.

Chapter 12: Medieval Magic in Alcúdia

My next destination to explore before heading back towards Palma was the medieval walled city of Alcúdia nestled on the northeastern coast of Mallorca. My spontaneity in deciding to visit Mallorca was paying off. Despite being the largest of the Balearic Islands, it was a pleasant surprise how easy it was to get around the island with public transportation. The bus system was not only well organized and inexpensive but it was enabling me to see a lot of places without the stress of driving around by myself.

I immediately thought of Olivia as I began exploring the Mediterranean charmer. Alcúdia had a multifaceted appeal - it was at the intersection of dreamy meets adorable. Not only was it steeped in history with well-preserved medieval walls and ancient ruins, but it was also a picturesque blend of sun-drenched beaches with coves of crystal clear water surrounded by pine forests. The old town captivated with charming narrow cobbled streets, stately Renaissance houses with coats of arms, and several pretty churches, including the Baroque chapel, Sant Crist. The scent of freshly baked local pastries wafted through the air, mingling with the aroma of strong, rich coffee from the local cafes.

The Plaza de España was clearly the heart of the old town - a vibrant square pulsing with the comforting rhythm of daily life with locals and tourists gathering to enjoy tapas, shop for handmade crafts, and immerse themselves in the lively ambiance. There was also a 1,600 hectare nature reserve around the bay, La Albufera, with hundreds of species of birds and a network of trails and viewing platforms to experience the serene beauty of the protected area up close.

I knew I would be back to explore in greater detail with Olivia so I contented myself simply strolling around and soaking up the ambiance. I languidly walked through the maze of cobblestoned streets, admiring the quaint pastel-colored houses, towering palm trees, and numerous large clay pots boasting a stunning array of flowers. I tried to capture the essence of Alcúdia to share with Olivia but knew mere photos were not doing her justice.

Alcúdia's history stretched back an astounding over two millennia with its origins rooted in Roman times. Walking through the old town, one could almost hear the echoes of centuries past. The medieval walls - a testament to the town's strategic importance through the ages - were some of the most meticulously preserved ones I had ever seen. I stopped by an information kiosk to learn a bit more about the Roman legacy of the town, particularly for Olivia's benefit.

The ruins of the Roman city of Pollentia, founded in 123 BCE, were some of Alcúdia's most significant historical treasures and just a short walk from the medieval center. Pollentia - a thriving hub of activity in ancient times - had remnants providing a fascinating glimpse into the past. There was an ancient theater, with stone tiers carved into the hillside that still hosted performances, bringing Roman culture to life under the Mallorcan sky. Adjacent to Pollentia, there was a Roman museum housing artifacts uncovered during excavations, including pottery, coins, and tools that painted a vivid picture of daily life in this ancient settlement.

Although I enjoyed briefly imagining the hustle and bustle of the Roman marketplace and undoubtedly fervent philosophical discussions in the forum, the ruins and excavations were definitely Olivia's thing and I decided to wait to explore them together. I smiled warmly, thinking of my treasured friend exploring ancient treasures for hours while I awaited her seaside. One of my favorite things about our friendship was that, although we were so close and shared some common interests, we also were very different and had distinct passions. It made our friendship engaging and an interesting learning experience as we exposed each other to different things.

With my heart warmed by thoughts of Olivia, I made my way to one of the nearby beaches - Playa de Alcúdia - to take in the stunning array of blues reflected in the sea from the deepest blue to the lightest transparent turquoise blue. It was reminiscent of the colors that had entranced me in Kaş in Turkey. The beach was stunning with powdery white sand. I sat down on the cushiony slice of heaven, took off my sandals and burrowed my feet in the refreshing coolness of the sand, while taking in the hubbub of activity. The sea waves were gentle - ideal for swimming - while the steady breezes provided excellent conditions for sailing and windsurfing. Oliva enjoyed people-watching and could spend countless hours here too. I fondly thought of her again, anxious to tell her about Alcúdia as I made my way along the scenic coastal promenade, lined with palm trees and dotted with inviting cafes and boutique shops.

I was drawn to a restaurant along the promenade with an enviable view of both the Mediterranean Sea and the medieval walls. The menu was a traditional celebration of Mediterranean cuisine - featuring fresh seafood, locally grown vegetables, and aromatic herbs - but a couple of dishes I was unfamiliar with had piqued my curious spirit. I asked my friendly waiter about them who advised me that they were traditional in the area - tumbet, a vegetable casserole, and frito mallorquín de marisco, a mixture of local seafood and vegetables. As I hesitated between the two, he graciously suggested that I get half-size portions of each to try both. Alcúdia was a particularly blessed agricultural area adjacent to the sea and I quickly accepted his suggestion, eager to not only try local specialties but novel dishes as well.

As I waited for my order, the sun began its descent over the Mediterranean, the sky was painted in a gorgeous mix of pastel baby blue and pink, the sun's rays casting a golden glow over the ancient walls and shimmering waters. The glorious sunset and setting imparted a sense of wonder and awe. I worked on a collage for Olivia with a picture of the medieval walls, the sunset, and the Plaza with the Baroque chapel in the background. I sent it to her with the message: "A trifecta of historical, natural, and spiritual treats await your exploration. Please add Alcúdia - with me! - to your bucket list!"

My meal arrived timely just as I sent my message. I equally enjoyed each of the very different options and was grateful that my kindly waiter had made it possible for me to not have to choose. Both were rather flavorful and wonderfully satiating though relatively light. The tumbet reminded me of the classic French ratatouille and Italian caponata I loved. I felt a heart pang as I thought of Leo before determinedly turning my attention to the frito mallorquín. It was as pretty as it was delicious - the seafood was meltingly fresh - it had a silky texture and was accompanied by a colorful array of peppers and aromatic herbs. It was simply divine.

Although I had asked my waiter for my check and was rather full, I smiled at the gracious hospitality as he brought me a complimentary dessert, insisting I try another local specialty. It was the local pastry I had smelled wafting through the streets earlier - ensaïmada. It was a spiral-shaped doughy treat topped with powdered sugar. My waiter told me this version - cabell d'angel - or "angel's hair" contained a pumpkin filling. My meal had been a culinary adventure of novelties from start to finish. I thanked my waiter profusely for introducing me to the local specialties before I gathered my things to catch the next bus back to my hotel in Santa Maria del Cami.

My phone dinged with a response from Olivia "Oh boy!" with an awe-inspired, gaping open-mouthed emoji. "Added," plus check mark emoji. I loved how trusting Olivia was - never hesitating to follow my lead unquestionably. Next I made a collage of the sea, the sunset, and my meal to send to Rachel. I counted my blessings for having visited the timeless gem of Alcúdia as well as for life in general. I fervently wished Olivia and Rachel were there to share it with me. Alcúdia seemed to have something for everyone. My heart skipped a beat, envisioning returning to Mallorca with my two best friends - it would be our first trip together - and undoubtedly a special and memorable one. I missed my friends terribly and took heart as I left, knowing I would visit Alcúdia again one day, confident together with the two of them.

******

Chapter 13: The Simple Pleasures of Being, not Doing

It was my last day in Mallorca and I decided to spend it exploring nearby Andratx and having lunch al fresco seaside at its adjacent port - it would be a mix of traditional charm in the town and modern elegance along the port.

It was a beautiful bright sunny day with deep blue skies and fluffy white clouds. I took my time leisurely strolling through the town, basking in the warm rays of sun and the characteristic Spanish atmosphere. Like so many of the other Mallorcan towns, Andratx was an inspiration to artists and writers. Life was lived largely outside in Spain and particularly in the islands. Mallorca was especially blessed with natural beauty with its stunning coastline, azure Sea, and the majesty of the dramatic jagged green and gray mountain range. Andratx had an enviable setting cradled by the surrounding Serra de Tramuntana mountain range.

The town center was relatively compact with rambling narrow streets while there were outlying sprawling farmlands providing an abundance of produce. The area was known for its oranges, almonds, olives, and grapes. I enjoyed meandering through town and browsing the quaint shops with local products. An enticing scarf store caught my eye with a seemingly endless selection of gorgeous scarves with beautiful decorative pewter scarf accessories I had never seen before.

The melodious ringing of a church bell from one of the many churches announced the arrival of mid-day, prompting me to finish my town tour and head towards Port d' Andratx for a languorous seaside lunch. My ex and I had spent a day at the port before - the chic port was more his style - it had a beautiful marina, luxury yachts, and upscale boutique shopping. I had indulged him while he had shopped, insisting we visit each and every store along the port. I had never been one for designer brands and luxury shops. I had never really been a shopper and my tastes were much simpler. The luxury part and high end shopping were his lifestyle language - it didn't speak to me as it did him.

I was always more focused on immersing myself in nature and the local culture. I was intent on collecting memories while he had been intent on collecting possessions. I sighed as I acknowledged that both of my exes had similarly been inclined. I felt the sting of regret as I walked past the shops before focusing on my good fortune to be living life now as I chose instead of to foolishly please someone else.

I determinedly put the past and the pretentious shops and exes behind me as I approached the waterfront to select a restaurant for a light lunch. I always enjoyed dining al fresco and Andratx's location on the waterfront was particularly alluring. I chose a cute cafe framed with flower boxes and herb planters located on the water. I approached hesitantly, a bit self-conscious being alone and hoping I would get a good seat, too shy to inquire. I was appreciative when an impeccably-dressed gentleman greeted me with a warm smile and immediately escorted me to a table, perfectly positioned to enjoy the view and the soothing sound of the waves. I quickly left my trip down memory lane behind, eagerly planning to create new memories on my solo sojourn.

My waiter warmly greeted me with a complimentary flute of cava and a platter of roasted marcona almonds with rosemary and coarse sea salt and plump green olives with orange zest. I smiled in contentment and gratitude as I sipped the refreshing sparkler, and enjoyed the sea view, appreciating the fact that the gratuitous nibbles likely had been sourced from the nearby fertile Andratx farmlands.

I slowly perused the specials of the day as the gentle, rhythmic waves lulled me into serenity. I realized how far I had come from my hurried days as a lawyer. The frenetic pace and pressures of life at a big law firm had seeped into my everyday life so that even when I wasn't working, I had approached everything in a hurried, frenetic manner. At that time, days had been a blur - filled with endless deadlines and suffocating pressures, rushing from one non-rewarding thing to another - all in the name of satisfying the materialistic desires of my exes.

My life was vastly richer now, reveling in the simple pleasures of life, focused on pursuits I was passionate about. I was loving not having a schedule whatsoever, soaking up life authentically, and reveling in simply being, rather than doing. My attention turned back to lunch as my appetite demanded attention as I watched my waiter deliver a tempting platter of grilled seafood to an adjoining table. I enjoyed trying different varieties of traditional classics whenever I had a chance. The restaurant had an intriguing variation of the classic gazpacho cold tomato soup - gazpacho blanco - made with grapes, cucumbers, garlic, olive oil, bread, and almonds. I immediately decided to try the refreshing sounding version.

I knew I would also be having one of my favorite Spanish dishes the moment I saw it. I actually had smelled the enticing garlicky aroma the moment I sat down and was hopeful it was what I was expecting. Gambas al ajillo was not only a favorite Spanish dish of mine but a favorite one of all time that I often made at home. I loved recreating meals from my travels to evoke memories of the places I experienced while sharing my culinary favorites with friends and family.

My gazpacho arrived quickly - it was a refreshing combination of cool and acidic flavors. I was so glad that I had come back to Mallorca, I reflected as I contemplated my next destination - another Spanish favorite of mine. I had a tendency to explore new places, but I was comforted revisiting some more familiar places as well - it gave my life a semblance of continuity - something that seemed to be sorely missing these days. I also appreciatively realized that I was experiencing locales in a much more immersive, enjoyable, and rewarding way without my exes and with the benefit of my novel embracing a slower pace and a more authentic life. All too often before I had hurriedly jumped from one place to the next - some places had been distractions from my inauthentic life or attractions merely to please my exes - more than destinations and areas of enchantment to me.

Mmmm, I smiled broadly at my waiter as the smell of garlic emanating from my meal announced its arrival. My garlic shrimp dish was sizzling, but I couldn't resist waiting - the shrimp were cooked to perfection and were practically swimming in the classic terracotta cazuela tapas serving dish with minced garlic, citrusy lemon zest, paprika, and olive oil. It was generously served with chopped parsley and paired with some toasted crusty bread to soak up the addictive sauce. The simple meal highlighted Spanish cuisine at its best for me.

I breathed in the fresh air deeply, grateful for my blessings. I chuckled thinking of my first ex who would have been drooling over the plethora of fancy yachts moored in the port and the second ex who would have indulged in shopping at the high-end boutiques. In contrast, for me, the "riches" of life were reflected in my simple yet richly satisfying meal with gracious service and the natural beauty surrounding me.

Andratx had an alluring combination of the Mediterranean, the mountains, and the marina. The stark contrast between what made me happy and what pleased them highlighted the ludicrous nature of how I had lived my life historically. I felt devastated when my ex abruptly terminated our marriage. Time, distance, and reflection were slowly giving me a new perspective - an optimistic one. Whereas I had viewed the end of our marriage as a destruction - in reality it had turned out to be the beginning of the construction of a more enriched and happier life.

******

Chapter 14: Until We Meet Again, Mallorca…

I loved my time in Mallorca, I summed up my visit in my head as I sat in the lobby bar of the hotel that night - this time in one of the cozy armchairs, watching Sergio and Diego from a safe distance. Mallorca had an intriguing blend of breathtaking coastal and rural landscapes, rich cultural heritage, and distinct picturesque villages. Although it was the largest of the Balearic Islands, it held a small town appeal for me given its quaint villages. The enchanting towns each offered timeless beauty and inspiration - for my writing - as well, I realized, for my life in general.

My visit solo had been vastly different from my prior visits with my exes. My solitude had enabled me to explore Mallorca on my terms and my explorations instilled in me a profound allure for the captivating island. My visit had been fulfilling and memorable - part self-reflection, part relaxation, and part exploration. I had revisited favorites and enjoyed my introduction to novel experiences - villages, art movements, and new foods.

Exploring the island's rural villages provided me with an intimate glimpse into traditional Mallorcan life that I found so much more alluring than had I stayed in bustling Palma or the touristy beach towns in the south of the island. Palma was lovely for a visit and I enjoyed the coastal promenade, but it was in the villages that I felt at ease, at home. I didn't need the glitz of the fine dining restaurants, the so-called glamor of the high-end designer shops, the pulsating vibes of the night clubs, or the indulgence of the all-inclusive party-centric large beach towns that had largely characterized my prior visits based on the preferences of the exes.

Each of the Mallorcan towns I had visited offered its own unique charm and attractions, leaving an indelible mark on my memory. Their combined historical sites, natural beauty, and artistic inspiration, reflected the multilayered richness of experiences that define the diverse and enchanting character of Mallorca - and Spain - for me. Mallorca was always a truly captivating destination for me, and each visit captivated me a little more. I had originally felt self-conscious and shy coming to sociable Spain alone. I smiled as it dawned on me that Mallorca had earned the designation of being my favorite island thus far, a designation made possible by having visited by myself. I took comfort in knowing that I would be back, envisioning sharing her endless enchanting charms with Olivia and Rachel.

My restless soul felt unusually satiated and I was happy to realize I was starting to feel sleepy. I finished my drink, planning to go to bed early. I wanted to be refreshed for my early flight to explore another Spanish city and one of my all-time favorite places in the world. I approached the bar to thank Sergio and Diego for their hospitality. I blushed each time I caught their eyes. We hugged warmly as they each made me promise to keep in touch, and not to hesitate to reach out if I ever needed anything. If only they knew my inner thoughts, I grinned. If only I knew theirs, I thought, as my mind started drifting, curious what my dreams would be like that evening...

******

PART II

SEDUCTIVE SEVILLE - BE STILL MY HEART

Chapter 1: Ravishing Rafael

Chapter 2: Blessings

Chapter 3: Local Pleasures

Chapter 4: Neighborhood Treasures

Chapter 5: Heaven on Earth

Chapter 6: Culinary Foreplay

Chapter 7: Romantic Flirtations

Chapter 8: Plaza Perfection

Chapter 9: Tardeo

Chapter 10: Vineria San Telmo

Chapter 11: Deja Vu

Chapter 12: Sprouting - Tranquillo

Chapter 13: Confessions

Chapter 14: You are Loved

******

Chapter 1

Ravishing Rafael

I felt energized the moment I got off the plane from the short trip from Mallorca. I had spent a few days in Seville before - I was even enthralled with its melodious, beckoning name - the pretty Spanish Sevilla seemed to hint at the glimpses of her sophisticated, seductive charms. My first brief visit had been solo and my last had been with my last ex. We had mostly just aimlessly wandered around and enjoyed a few tapas bars. I had immediately been captivated by Seville's immense charm and knew I would be back. Even from my relatively brief exposure to Seville, I knew it was my favorite city in Spain. Although I gravitate towards smaller cities, sprawling Seville - like Istanbul - seemed to seamlessly maintain its enticing allure.

I had enjoyed visiting the gorgeous parks and world-class museums in Madrid and the market and Gaudi architectural masterpieces in Barcelona. Seville was vastly more my style though. For a big city, it felt quaint to me and the pace of life seemed to sing with a sweet melody. Seville was one of those places I just couldn't get enough of. There was beauty everywhere you looked and that - combined with the ubiquitous Spanish energetic vibe - made Seville a special charmer. I was looking forward to exploring her more, taking endless photos, and simply soaking in her seductive splendor.

Lost in my head with anticipation in my enthusiastic rush to reunite with Seville, my foot accidentally got caught on the luggage ahead of me as we were alighting from the plane and the toehold of my sandal on one foot tore apart. Murphy's Law, I thought as I realized this was one of those disembarkations where we had to go down a flight of stairs to the tarmac instead of directly into the airport via a jetway. I chuckled nervously, trying to figure out how best to manage my somewhat challenging predicament. There weren't a lot of options, so I made my way down the stairs as best as I could in a rather comical manner - trying to grip the toe hold and lift my foot high enough to where the bottom of my sandal would cooperate slightly and not buckle under. I looked like a clown with extra big shoes with elevated steps. I was extremely self-conscious as I was not only looking quite silly but holding up the disembarkation process, commanding a lot of attention at the precise moment I wanted to fade into oblivion. C'est la vie, I thought. What can I do? I kind of shuffled my foot along the ground once we reached the tamarc and made my way very slowly into the airport arrivals.

As I slowly slid my way to the baggage carousel, I caught a glimpse of a stunning young man observing my tiny plight with a bemused smile. I grinned and shrugged my shoulders at him. I'd be able to swap out my shoes when I retrieved my suitcase so my self-conscious shuffle would soon be over.

I sighed in relief as I saw my luggage approaching. I was struggling awkwardly as my large suitcase was jammed between other heavy luggage, as often seems to be my lot in life, and I noted with some concern that the handle was up. I finally stopped trying to wrestle with it and waited for it to come around again. I looked up to catch the eye of the same man I had made eye contact with before; he was watching me and still grinning. Glad I can amuse someone, I wryly thought.

As I was scanning the carousel looking for my bag to come around again, the gentleman approached me. He had a duffel bag over one shoulder and was carrying my heavy bag in one hand. I sighed, seeing that my luggage handle had broken, an apparent casualty of the carousel melee. "Ugh," involuntarily, ineloquently escaped my lips as the statuesque man approached me, still grinning. Not the best introduction I realized but I was preoccupied with thoughts of struggling with my bag. So much for my blissful reunion with Seville I sighed, as I politely smiled in gratitude, taking in his sheer beauty up close.

He was dressed simply, classically but in form-fitting clothes that left no doubt as to his evident physical prowess. He had on a light gray V-neck cashmere sweater that made the twinkle in his dreamy blue gray eyes even more apparent and body-hugging trousers, evidencing his firm derriere and muscular legs, finished with stylish understated classic boots. He had a 5 o'clock shadow - my seductive kryptonite - and well-groomed black silky hair. He caught me inadvertently staring and smiled at my tacit compliment saying, "May I help you?", as he extended his hand in greeting and introduced himself, "Rafael. Mucho gusto. Pleased to meet you." His handshake was firm and his gaze unwavering as he lingered holding my hand. "Sofia, mucho gusto," I replied, shaking his hand and slowly pulling mine away, steadying myself from the electrifying charge from our brief touch. I could feel the immediate sexual chemistry despite my shyness and embarrasment. "Gracias, pero... Thank you but - you've already done enough."

"You are going to the historical center - no? I'm going that way. If you are too, let me help you," Rafael softly persisted in a sultry commanding voice. "Por favor. Please, allow me," he continued. I loved the endearing habit in Latin countries of making it sound like you were doing someone an honor by letting them help you - it was swoon-worthy charm to me and I was having difficulty concentrating in his presence. I bit my lip from a combination of being self-conscious, touched by his offer, and unsure what I should do. "Are you nuts?" I was already playing the monologue in my head of what some of my family and friends would say if I accepted this stranger's assistance. "I insist," Rafael continued over the unexpressed objections in my head. "It's not easy to navigate the center - there are a lot of pedestrian-only small streets and often several steep flights of stairs. If you take a taxi, it may not be easy finding your accommodations because they will have to drop you off at the outskirts," he persuasively concluded.

"Ugh," I unattractively monosyllabically groaned again in response to his polite offer of assistance. I hadn't thought of those logistical considerations and was not looking forward to the inevitable challenges that lay ahead. I looked down at my feet, feeling a little forlorn, my enthusiasm for Seville unfairly waning. Rafael apparently mistook my downward glance, "Wait," he said. "Por favor. Please," he briefly took my hand, squeezing it for emphasis before disappearing.

"Ugh," I said to myself for the third time since my arrival. I'm not the risk-averse type. People always think I'm reckless. I wasn't concerned about my safety; I just hated accepting help. I'm tired of always struggling alone though, I was silently debating myself. I couldn't suppress a smile as Rafael returned and I realized what he had done. Without question, he knelt in front of me and started wrapping yellow duct tape around my sandal to secure the broken strap. I didn't have the heart to tell him I was just going to change my shoes. How dangerous could this sweet guy be, I thought, as my decision decisively shifted towards accepting his help.

Rafael continued his negotiation with me not appreciating he had already sealed the deal with me. "You need help. Your luggage is heavy. I do heavy for a living," he winked as he handed me a business card. He was a personal trainer. "Ah," I winked back in acceptance, relieved to have help. To ensure I didn't change my mind, Rafael confidently took me by the hand with his free hand while effortlessly dealing with my monstrosity of a suitcase, escorting me to his car.

As Rafael arranged the bags in the trunk of his car, I unobtrusively snapped a photo of him and his business card. I sent the photos to Olivia - at least someone would know with whom I was last seen offchance something went awry. This was as responsible as I got. Of course, I didn't want to alarm her so I simply said "Arrived in Seville. This is my ride," ending with a winking emoji.

Rafael asked me for my address. "Lovely," he responded as I showed him the address of the apartment I was staying at and we started driving. "You're staying in Triana - a wonderful residential area just across the river from the historic center. It's a lively area with great markets and cafes. It's the birthplace of flamenco and very romantic," Rafael complimented my choice, while flirtatiously winking as he slowly drawled "romantic" - or so it seemed to me in my heightened aroused state. I didn't want to be presumptuous, but I was happy to have met someone so unexpectedly, so soon even if it were just a brief flirtation. "Perfect. I love living like a local to really experience the culture."

We chatted amicably, exchanging pleasantries. The time flew by. I realized I wasn't even paying attention to the views as we drove from the airport to the center; Rafael was commanding my attention. He inquired about my trip

- whether it was my first time, what my plans were, etc. I noted with great interest that he asked me if I were alone or meeting anyone. I quietly nodded my head no, trying to contain my budding enthusiasm that perhaps I was not being presumptuous that he was interested. He was so gorgeous and much younger that I didn't have anything in mind other than a potential fling, but I was surprised to realize how much I was interested in one. I always felt self-conscious about being by myself in big cities in Spain given its extraordinarily sociable culture.

Perhaps my adorable escort would entertain allowing me to take him for dinner one night as an expression of my gratitude, I thought, trying to get up the courage to ask him. Baby steps, I thought as I couldn't find the bravado to ask him as I started worrying again that I was being presumptuous. How could this stunning younger creature possibly be interested - he was just being a chivalrous gentleman, I concluded, deciding I would just enjoy the ride and the assistance and quit while I was ahead.

Rafael was an attentive and wonderful conversationalist and made me feel uncharacteristically at ease. Our conversation felt natural and effortless once I decided against asking him to dinner. I began to relax and take in the scenery as we approached the center. I was no longer pettily blaming Seville for my minor mishaps and was looking forward to my visit and simply seeing the sites with renewed anticipation . I grinned as my thoughts went back to the "We'll see" parable when something seemingly bad happens. But for my tiny troubles, I wouldn't have met ravishing Rafael nor had the benefit of his assistance.

I tried to focus on the scenery and my solo itinerary, but kept getting distracted by Rafael's presence. There's something about the mastery of driving a manual car, the roar of the engine, and surge of power shifting gears. I looked down at his hand as he expertly shifted back and forth. It was large and powerful and I was mesmerized.

I tried diverting my attention, willing myself not to stare at him. It was hot and I was appreciative of the fresh breeze as the wind whipped through my hair, tousling it. I started my nervous habit of talking too much. I told Rafael how much I loved cooking, Spanish markets and the tapa style of eating and how Spanish wine and olive oil were my favorites. "… and the men?" he boldly inquired. I blushed and looked down. "Yes, definitely," I said to myself, and it was true. I was at a loss as to how to answer; I knew he was just innocently flirting at best and I didn't want to expose my feelings. I had always thought that Spanish men and women were some of the most naturally beautiful people in the world in general. I had always had a crush on the Spanish goalie, Iker Casillas. Ah, futbol - a new topic I was comfortable chatting about to try to dilute the obvious sexual tension - at least on my end. Spaniards - like so many Europeans - are passionate about the game. My random stream-of-consciousness thought "process" came to my rescue as we talked about our favorite players and Rafael's favorite team as we approached the historic center.

When we got to my apartment building, I was so grateful that Rafael had persisted in persuading me to accept his generous help. He had been right about everything. He had to ask several people for directions even though he was using maps on his phone. We had to park quite a distance from my building and then I was up six flights of stairs - no elevator - as was par for the course. A gorgeous helper, however, was not par for the course and I was deeply grateful for Rafael's intervention above and beyond my undeniable attraction to him.

He merely smiled in a sweet, tacit "I told you so" manner before directing me to lead the way up the stairs. I was self-conscious having him so close behind me and kept trying to help with my luggage. He insisted my luggage was no trouble as I tried to foolishly help over his protestations - it did enable me to be in close contact with him though so maybe not so foolish afterall. I blushed from sheer desire as I continued making my way up the several flights of stairs self-consciously, quite grateful I wasn't hauling my luggage. I racked my brain as to the appropriate way to repay his kindness. I would certainly give him money but I also reconsidered inviting him for a thank you dinner. I unquestionably wanted to see him again but equally unquestionably didn't want to look too forward. I was trying to muster the courage to invite him. I was surprised at how quickly I was drawn to him - not just his physical beauty but his personality as well. I loved that he was a personal trainer too.

Just then, as if on cue, he whistled appreciatively, complimenting me on my legs - apparent from my dress and him following closely behind me up the several flight of stairs. "I love a woman who takes care of herself," he said looking at me in the eyes as we arrived at my door. I blushed and quietly murmured "mucho gracias," mixing Italian and Spanish, as I also fumbled ineffectually with the keys and the door, unable to hide the evident impact Rafael was having on me. His voice was delicious - simultaneously soft, sweet, and assertive. "Let me." I was mesmerized as he insisted on taking my keys to help me. …and his lips - equally soft and sweet plus voluptuous - I stared a little too obviously as he opened the door effortlessly.

My apartment was small but cute with an adorable little balcony and a fully-equipped kitchen. Rafael generously refused when I tried to pay him, taking me by the hand - again - and pushing the money away as he reiterated it was his pleasure. "Pleasure," I fixated, entranced by him - by his….. everything, I concluded, as I looked him up and down, trying to memorialize every detail. He seemed like a dream about to dissipate as I still couldn't find the confidence to ask him out.

His voice was a sensual melody and his cologne was driving me into a frenzy I was desperately trying to suppress. My combined determination not to live with regrets and to seize the moment was uncharacteristically overriding my normal inhibitions and fueling my confidence to do something - anything - to ensure I would see Rafael again.

 Despite being turned on by his politeness and chivalrous manners, little introverted me was fantasizing that he would just take me then and there. I couldn't believe how instantly amorous I felt - it was so unlike me - at least consciously, I thought as my face flushed from memories of my Mallorcan menage-a-trois fantasy dream. Seville was already working her seductive charms on me and I was overwhelmed with desire. "Please," I looked around at the kitchen, willing myself to do something to make sure I would spend more time with Rafael. "You must come to dinner one night," I was surprised to hear the words escape my lips, emboldened by my desperate desire for Rafael not to escape from my life forever. "As a thank you, of course," I immediately added, unconvincingly trying to make my invite appear as a simple expression of gratitude - rather than a reflection of the burning desire that was my real impetus.

Rafael looked at me bemused as I nervously started shuffling from foot to foot in my duct-taped sandals. I put my hands together in an exaggerated pleading way as he seemed to be toying with me, enjoying watching me squirm. "It would be my pleasure," he grinned, responding affirmatively - after what seemed like an interminably long pause - to my great relief and excitement. Pleasure, pleasure, pleasure, was on repeat in my head, as he took my suitcase to the bedroom.

"It's your first day here; get settled today." I followed him to the bedroom with my eyes, worried I may shockingly take initiative if I joined him. His combined assertiveness and thoughtfulness was sending me into a sexual tizzy. … and his voice - I was so seduced by it, I had to focus to pay attention to what he was actually saying. As your host," he began. Be still, my heart - my host! - I waited for him to finish with baited breath, thinking - hoping - perhaps I wasn't being presumptuous after all. "I insist on taking you out for dinner tomorrow and helping you get oriented."

I loved how he casually referred to himself as my "host" - what a simultaneously polite designation and sensually-appealing characterization. I may be obsessed with the civility of other countries, but it was obvious that I was more obsessed with the prospect of seeing Rafael again. I wasn't used to being helped and I was touched by his insistence. I was immediately charmed by him. As he exited the bedroom, he took my hands in his, lingering - again - while looking deeply into my eyes. We both knew no response was required to his invitation as I meekly smiled and looked down trying to avert his penetrating gaze and my penetrating thoughts.

I was tingling everywhere and practically jumping up and down inside. I purposely tried not smelling his intoxicating fragrance. I shuffled nervously from foot to foot, turning my gaze downward before laughing about his impromptu sandal rescue, grateful after all that my broken strap had led me to this gloriously unexpected chain of events. "I'll take you shoe shopping if you would like. We have fabulous shopping here. And luggage too," he winked, kissing me slowly on each cheek as we said goodbye, agreeing to see each other the next day. He politely asked if he could give me his phone number. I handed him my phone in response. He made me promise that I would call or message if there was anything at all I needed, seemingly emphasizing anything again with his dreamy intent eyes.

I shut the door behind him, leaning my back against it, steadying myself from my flood of emotions and rush of blood. How adorable is he, I reflected. I wasn't a big shopper, but no man had ever offered to take me shopping before. I was more used to following my ex around on his shopping sprees. I realized that one of the reasons I was so attracted to so many men recently was because their personalities were so refreshingly different from my exes' self-absorbed personas. I looked down at my broken sandal and thought of my broken luggage handle. My reunion with Seville hadn't gone quite as planned and I couldn't be more thrilled. Yes, "we'll see," I recalled the parable. We will see…

******

Chapter 2

Blessings

I was anxious to get out and about to reunite with Seville so I decided I would wait to unpack until later in the evening. I was pleased to see a street flamenco performance as I exited my building on my way to the historical center. My thoughts immediately went to Rafael as I paused to watch the entrancing performance. Seville pulses with the fiery rhythms of the passionate dance. I had known that flamenco had originated in Andalusia but was surprised by Rafael's tidbit that the Triana neighborhood where I was staying was considered the birthplace of flamenco.

I was drawn to the raw emotion and fluid artistry of the dance. I was sure I would be enjoying a number of impromptu dances in the area - flamenco seemed to be part of what infused a sense of romanticism to the neighborhood. I was happy I had chosen the more local, less touristy area as my base to soak up authentic Spanish culture. I was excited about my evening with Rafael, but I was grateful that he had proposed it for the next day. I was anxious to revisit the highlights of Seville and determined to tamp down my enthusiasm for my new encounter. I knew we would have a mere, casual fling - if. My vulnerable heart had a tendency of falling too fast, too furiously and I was intent not to make that mistake with Rafael.

I crossed the Guadalquivir River that bordered my neighborhood, weaving through the city with picturesque promenades and stunning views - it separated the old town and main shopping district from my neighborhood. I had chosen the riverside district - famous for its artisan workshops, traditional ceramics, and lively atmosphere - because it had a more local vibe while still being conveniently located to the more touristy historic center.

I surveyed my surroundings in appreciative awe as I approached the center and meandered my way around, reacquainting myself with Seville's impressive array of architectural wonders. Seville was a city that seamlessly segued between contrasts that spoke to my sensibilities - the energy of the iconic tapas scene spilling out of cafes adjacent to the serene grandeur of the Cathedral of Saint Mary, known simply as the Seville Cathedral - the largest Gothic cathedral in the world. Its grandeur was matched only by its intriguing history - it had been constructed atop the ruins of a mosque during the Christian Reconquista, reminiscent of the storied Hagia Sofia in Istanbul. I gazed up at the imposing Giralda Tower - it had once been the minaret of the mosque and was now possibly the most iconic symbol of Seville. Visitors who summit it are rewarded with the most breathtaking panoramic views of this enchanting Spanish gem. It seemed to bridge the past with the present. I respectfully paused by one of the many horse-drawn carriages under the shade of one of the ubiquitous trees of oranges to listen to the timely call to prayer that was melodiously emanating from the tower - it was serendipitous timing that beautifully completed the atmospheric scene.

It seemed fitting that I silently gave thanks for my blessing to be back in Seville as the call to prayer finished. Seville oozed seduction set against a backdrop of jaw-dropping architectural splendor in the midst of the tranquil embrace of Mother Nature. It effortlessly blended old world charm and romanticism with an undeniable, underlying electrifying sensuality appealing to all senses. With its ancient history and magnetic modern energy,

Seville created a captivating ambiance that was both timeless and dynamic - similar to Istanbul, my other favorite large city, I mused. The two cities were vastly different, but their shared characteristic of multicultural layers and blend of antiquity and modernity made them forever intriguing to me and endlessly exploratory.

Seville was a shining testament to the rich history, vibrant culture, and architectural splendor that Spain is renowned for and had quickly earned my designation as not only my favorite Spanish city but my favorite overall city the first time I had visited it many years before. It was the kind of special place where everywhere you look unveils beauty and a place where my restless soul could uniquely simply bask for hours in her endless glories.

Seville was simply elegant and felt intimate despite her sprawling size since the main attractions were fairly concentrated and easily navigated on foot. One of the characteristics that defined and drew me to her was that - notwithstanding a significant number of tourists - Seville had somehow been able to maintain her charms, lacking the type of in-your-face capitalism and behemoth buildings that often marred large touristic cities. Accommodations and shops in the center were largely independent and boutique-like. Although the center also had more than its fair share of shopping to suit any taste, it was more refined and alluring than a lot of other big cities. Everything felt refreshingly local, charming, and authentic.

I was hungry and anxious to explore the food markets and get something to tide me over until dinner so I made my way back across the river to Triana. Olive oil, fresh seafood, and Moorish influences feature prominently in Andalusian cuisine. I was on the lookout for some of my favorite seafood given the region's extensive coastline - prawns, calamari, and octopus. The country's bountiful farmland also yields an array of fresh vegetables - including tomatoes, peppers, and onions - frequent colorful components of Spanish dishes. The cuisine was the best array of "surf and turf" given the region's proximity to the sea and its agricultural traditions. Local markets, known as "mercados," offered an authentic glimpse into the vibrancy of Spanish food culture and I was anxious to explore my neighborhood. I was all culinary excitement and anticipation as I ventured back across the river and was immediately greeted with an intoxicating waft of an array of aromas emanating invitingly from the several unassuming tapas restaurants.

******

Chapter 3

Local Pleasures

I wanted an even more immersive experience, however, so I continued passing by the beckoning eateries as I made my way to the Mercado de Triana, located on the west bank of the Guadalquivir River, fairly close to where my apartment was. The façade of the market had distinctive red, ochre, and white ceramic tiles, a testament to Seville's rich Moorish heritage. I paused to read a plaque to find out the market had an interesting history dating back to the 19th century; it originally was a castle, later a pottery factory, and even a prison, before becoming a culinary and cultural hotspot - the pretty structure wore her history well.

I strolled through the market, surveying all the wonderful colors, aromas, and offerings before settling on my destination. There were purveyors of fresh seafood sourced from the nearby waters; specialty jamon and cheese kiosks with a dizzying array of pork and cheese offerings; fruit and vegetable stalls with a kaleidoscope of produce; artisanal bakeries with several types of bread, adorable cupcakes and other homemade baked goods; and tapas and wine bars. The Mercado was bustling; it was an experience way beyond mere shopping for groceries. The market was a microcosm of the traditions and heritage of the people of Seville. There was an undeniable sense of community with locals and tourists strolling through the market aisles. I enjoyed observing friendly vendors passionate about their local products sharing cooking tips with tourists and groups of locals engaged in lively conversations and laughter sharing a wide variety of tapas and drinks.

Although food is undoubtedly the star, the Mercado de Triana also had a variety of boutiques selling specialty items like handmade ceramics, jewelry, flamenco attire, and leather goods. It was an alluring embodiment of the spirit of Seville; a sensory journey through the heart and soul of Andalusia with its tantalizing culinary fragrances and flavors as well as artisanal shops highlighting the region's traditions and local products.

I finished my aimless stroll around the market, my senses whetting my appetite. I couldn't resist sampling a few of the local delicacies any longer as I selected a cute little tapas bar. There were several long high-top counters with bar stools, many of which were already filled with patrons chattering away as they indulged in delicious-looking bites.

I made my way to the counter in front of the open and simple kitchen. The waitress welcomed me with a warm smile, handed me the menu in Spanish, and told me in English that it would be her pleasure to help me. I nodded and smiled in appreciation. I asked her what the orange wine was that I saw several patrons sipping. She told me it was aptly-named "vino de naranja," orange wine, a dark-colored fortified wine that has bitter orange peels added during the fermentation process. Without asking, she graciously poured me a taste. I nodded in approval and she filled my glass while graciously giving me a little bowl of Marcona almonds with dried rosemary and coarse sea salt. My drink was not only pretty but refreshing and I was happy to try something new. It reminded me of Italian Aperol spritz but I vastly preferred the vino de naranja. I thought of Leo, wondering how he was, before turning my attention to the menu as my grumbling tummy commanded my contemplation.

I started with a little platter of local chorizo and three varieties of cheese, accompanied by a generous bowl of orange blossom honey. I began snapping photos for memories as well as to share with Rachel before enthusiastically starting my tapas selection. I love the flavors of Spanish chorizo; it's made with garlic and pimentón, Spanish smoked paprika - either sweet or hot - which gives it its deep brick-red color and smoky flavor I enjoy. I noted happily that I had a mix of sweet and hot. I enjoyed a trio of different variations of my favorite cheese - Manchego - never appreciating before that there were different options based on aging.

The sampling enabled the perfect point of comparison. I took my time happily trying each and noting the differences that my waitress kindly explained. Manchego fresco, as the name implies, is in the first stage of aging, aged for about two weeks. It was pure white in color with fresh, mild, and milky aromas and flavors; the texture of the sheep's milk cheese was similar to goat's cheese, but the flavors were much richer and more buttery. The Manchego curado - in the third stage of aging from 3 to 6 months - had a smooth texture and was creamy with mildly sweet, nutty, caramel-like notes and a pleasant slightly piquant finish. Manchego viejo, in the fourth and final stage of aging, was aged from a year to two years in natural caves. The texture was firm and crumbly with a deep, rich yellow color.

I had never experienced a guided cheese sampling before and appreciated learning about the different varieties - it was a memorable experience going to the source of the product. I was thoroughly enjoying my first tapas experience in Spain and made a mental note to pick up Manchego curado, which was my favorite. I used the honey wand to drizzle the addictive honey on the chorizo and the cheeses and kept it as my waitress cleared my platter, knowing it would pair well with all of my tapas.

I wistfully thought of Rachel, wishing she were with me. We both obsessed in the best way about food and she particularly loved cheese. I immediately thought how wonderful a tasting trip through the Emilia Romagna region of Italy would be together, sampling Parmesan cheese and Parma ham and Modena balsamic vinegar while enjoying the sights. A cooking class there would be a bucket list experience for me.

I softly chuckled at myself as my waitress brought my next tapa - Rachel and I had a tendency to be daydreaming about our next meal while already immersed in one. I couldn't resist the grilled skewers of meat I had seen a lot of the patrons enjoying so I had ordered a chicken and lamb "pinchitos" next - an Andalusian dish with Moorish influences, consisting of marinated chicken, lamb, or pork cubes seasoned with warm aromatic spices like cumin, coriander, cinnamon, saffron, and paprika. I had watched attentively as my two skewers were grilled over the open charcoal fire, the wafting seasonings making my mouth water. The pinchitos were served on a cute little cutting board adorned with lemon wedges and a few slices of grilled bread on the side. "Culinary heaven," I simply noted in a message to Rachel with photos of my sumptuous tapas with my vino de naranja in the background before adding "Next stop - Emilia Romagna together…"

When I complimented the waitress on the divine spice blend on the skewers, she kindly shared that I could easily emulate it with a spice blend known as "ras el hanout." I made a note to pick it up for myself as well as Rachel. My phone dinged with the anticipated - though surprisingly quick - affirmative response from Rachel - "absolutely" with her trademark happy dance emoji of a woman who coincidentally looked like she was wearing a red flamenco dress.

For my final tapa, I had ordered something I had never had before, "Zanahorias aliñadas," carrots parboiled to al dente perfection and then marinated in another Moorish-inspired spice blend and vinegar. They were the most flavorful carrots I ever had and I was glad to end with vegetables. I knew I loved Moorish architecture and now realized I loved Moorish-inspired cuisine as well as I made my way to one of the little shops to buy the distinctive ras el hanout spice I had delighted in.

I was so happy, I couldn't stop smiling. I was fully satiated I thought until at that precise moment I got a message from Rafael asking me if I were happy and if I needed anything. I replied that I was indeed happy and sent him a few of the photos. He instantly replied back, inquiring if I could be even happier. I smiled, acknowledging that although my tummy was full, I was definitely craving affection. I was glad that we weren't getting together until the next day, the anticipation heightening my desire. I demurely replied that I would be happier when we got together.

I stopped by a few more of the boutique shops on my way out to get a bottle of wine, the Manchego and chorizo varieties I liked best, some Jamon Serrano, some artisanal crackers, and some thyme honey. I bought the crackers and honey from a lovely older gentleman that had insisted I sample a few different crackers and honeys. Although I was full, I loved the experience of my second sampling of the day and gratefully acquiesced. He also kindly gave me a couple of complimentary pears that I knew would be delicious with my other purchases.

I felt a deep sense of contentment as I languidly strolled back to my apartment, soaking up Seville's atmospheric charms. My first afternoon reunited with Seville had been an intoxicating experience of soul-stirring melodies of flamenco, delectable tapas, the grandeur of historical sites - and the undeniable mounting anticipation for my rendezvous with Rafael the next evening.

******

Chapter 4

Neighborhood Treasures

That evening I unpacked what I thought I would need for the next few days before opening my wine and arranging a small tapas platter from the items I had gotten at the Mercado. I took my little meal to the balcony to enjoy while I planned my itinerary for the next day and watched the daily evening events taking place. I was glad I was staying in a residential area and that I had a perfect view over the neighborhood with the river in the background. The sounds of simple evening life were music to my ears as I enjoyed my market purchases and sipped my wine. I had purchased one of my favorite Spanish varietals, a slightly spicy ruby red Tempranillo.

In Spain, life is lived out in the streets. I watched as cafe terraces filled up with chattering patrons spilling out of bars onto the cobblestone roads beneath me. I enjoyed watching the children playing in the pedestrian street in front of my balcony. Several boys were passionately engaged in a friendly futbol match with makeshift goals. I loved how eagerly they were playing, simply for fun. The passion for futbol is so palpable in other countries, uniting young, old, men, and women. I loved how enthusiasts rallied around their favorite teams - watching matches was a regular pastime that I enjoyed immensely as well, the locals' excitement was always infectious - every game was as intently watched as if it were the World Cup Finals.

My heart warmed as I observed young girls watching over younger siblings, creating simple games, reminiscent of my childhood. Most were based on some sort of physical competition, but I also saw one with a group of aspiring musicians taking turns singing into a pretend microphone.

Other children were affectionately petting and feeding the handful of docile cats and dogs that were participating in the evening's street interactions. I loved how interactive, engaged, and present the children were playing outside in the fresh air, getting some exercise while enjoying some camaraderie. They weren't inside or glued to phones or tablets and I loved how inclusive the physical interactions were - sport was spontaneous - not reserved for school clubs. There were women and couples strolling hand in hand and older gentlemen sitting on park benches conversing or at little fold up tables playing dominoes. Al fresco and sociability are the dominant ways of life in Spain for all ages - life collectively unfolds in the streets, plazas, and parks - it's one of the things that gives Spanish culture its contagious, energetic vibe.

I planned to get up early the next morning to spend more time in the historic center. I was only planning to spend a few days in Seville - at least that was before I had met Rafael... I started daydreaming, my thoughts getting more fluid and uninhibited, thanks to the full-bodied wine. I shook my head to escape my reverie - surely Rafael's interest in me was fleeting at most. That's fine, I consoled myself. I was only looking for a little affection and pleasurable company to dine out anyway, wasn't I? I asked myself unsure of the answer. In any event, I was anxious to make the most of my time here however long I ultimately decided to stay. I preemptively concluded my curt analysis, not in the mood to bring it to a conclusive answer.

I hadn't remembered how much of a hold Seville had on me before coming back. My first day was already the best time I had ever had in Seville and I was looking forward to immersing myself and exploring more of her wonders. I noted with satisfaction that I was enjoying my time more than I had during my prior visit with my ex and with even greater satisfaction that thoughts of him hadn't really entered my mind. I was afraid my visit might start triggering regrets and heartache. I thought of Rafael, suspecting he had something to do with my temperament. My heart particularly ached when I felt the full brunt of being alone - thanks to Rafael, I wasn't feeling isolated.

I finished savoring my glass of wine and thoughts before getting ready for bed. I surveyed my welcoming bedroom with approval. The room had an understated sexiness about it, I thought as my thoughts segued to Rafael. The bed was an oversized king with a wrought iron headboard and footboard and plush white linens starkly contrasting with the blackness of the iron. There was a cozy-looking, velvety-plush burgundy chaise lounge positioned opposite the bed. My mind drifted, contemplating Rafael's company. The room was alluringly decorated with alternating full-length mirrors and gorgeous black and white photos of the city's landmarks.

I crawled into the cozy bed, burrowing into its cushion welcome, embraced by my happy thoughts of how thoroughly I had enjoyed my first and simple day in Seville, eager to drift off to sleep. Who am I kidding, I silently queried myself - my anticipatory excitement delaying sleep. Yes, I was happy to be back in Seville but my chance encounter with Rafael was undeniably responsible for my simultaneous feelings of contentment and excitement. I glanced at Rafael's business card that I had put on the nightstand earlier.

I saw he had Instagram and couldn't help but check out his page. It wasn't surprising as a personal trainer that Rafael had an incredibly toned physique - textbook chiseled abs and beautifully-sculpted chest and arms, highlighted in a couple of beach photos of him and others playing volleyball. I worked hard at staying in shape and I had mad respect for his body, reflecting commitment and passion. It was particularly noteworthy to me that he didn't flaunt his incredible body on social media, choosing to highlight the progress of his clients instead. There were only a few isolated pictures of him - always with friends or a setting - never narcisstic-type ones of him alone - show for show. Nonetheless, his incredible looks and fit physique were undeniable - a sort of understated testimonial for what his services could help potential clients achieve. He was beautiful and he undoubtedly knew it but he was understated about himself and that humility and class made me all that more attracted and eager to see more.

My interest was clearly piqued by my respect for the discipline, hard work, and commitment it took to attain such a taut, well-defined body. I also couldn't help but note that he appeared extremely well-endowed in his beach shorts. I fixated on the few photos of him for a few minutes, whiplashing between staring at his abs acquired through dedication and his God-given beauty. I drifted off to sleep thoroughly excited for what my second day in Seville would hold…

Chapter 5

Heaven on Earth

The next morning, I awoke early, feeling refreshed and energized with anticipation for the day. I could barely contain my excitement as I thought about visiting one of my favorite places in the world and a Sevillean iconic landmark. Not to mention - I reluctantly admitted to myself - that I was looking forward to seeing Rafael again - my part trepidation blended with my budding interest in him making me feel tingly all over. Some places - not just Rafael, I chuckled - were absolutely mesmerizing and for me that most definitely included two of Spain's most famous sites - the Alhambra Palace - the exquisite structure in Granada that was uniquely designed to represent "Heaven on Earth" - and Seville's stately palace, the Royal Alcázar.

I read about the palace complex briefly to refresh my recollection about its history while I enjoyed my tea on my cute little balcony watching local life slowly play out underneath me on the streets below. In contrast to the pulsating Sevillean evenings, mornings had a pace all their own - it was as if energy were being conserved to make the most of the evenings' inevitable sociability. The air was still and quiet, punctuated melodiously by the soft cooing of birds. I watched two doves interacting before turning my attention back to my reading. I adored how they mate for life and my heart always warmed as I admired their inseparable - aspirational - love.

The history of Seville itself was an intriguing tapestry woven with threads of diverse cultures, each leaving an indelible mark on the city's character. The Phoenicians, Romans, Moors, and Christians had all contributed to its fascinating multilayered heritage. The Royal Alcázar, a UNESCO World Heritage Site, reflected centuries of history, culture, and architectural brilliance, blending some of that history - reflected in Moorish, Gothic, Renaissance, and Baroque styles. The history of the Royal Alcázar is a story of evolution and adaptation, spanning over a millennium, I read. Kind of like me I chortled - though quite shy of the millennium mark.

Originally designed as a Moorish palace, it was built on the site of a former Muslim fortress and has been in continuous use by Spanish monarchs since the 10th century. Wow - it's the oldest royal palace still in use in Europe. It served as a residence, a fortress, and a symbol of power for various dynasties, including the Moors, the Catholic Monarchs, and the Bourbon monarchs. The palace was apparently a filming location for the "Game of Thrones." I had never seen the popular series but had visited a number of stunning locations where it had been filmed and could at least appreciate that it must have great visual appeal.

It was a beautiful day and I took my time strolling to the Alcázar in the heart of the historic center. One of my favorite things to do in touristy cities was to explore early in the morning to fully absorb the "spirit" and "purity" of the place before throngs of people descended en masse. I felt as if I paused endlessly, unable to pass up the indescribable beauty that permeated Seville without taking countless pictures to try to capture the memory, the essence of the special city. I loved how even the bottoms of the many residential balconies were decorated in pretty-colored mosaic tiles. Everywhere I turned, I was struck by an eye-attention grabber. Seville felt like an outdoor gallery - as if someone had decreed that no spot could be left un-" beautified" in this captivating city.

I arrived early at the Alcázar notwithstanding my appreciative dawdle. I saw with relief that fortunately the line to enter wasn't that long. I had seen lengthy queues the day before and was glad I had gotten an early start to my morning. I enjoyed visiting before it was too crowded or filled with tourist groups, which always detracted from the serenity of a place and made picture taking challenging. I vastly preferred focusing on architectural and natural beauty without the distracting presence of people.

As I entered the intricate gates to the Royal Alcázar, I was immediately struck by the enchanting Moorish architecture adorning its interiors as if I were seeing it for the first time. It was mesmerizing with intricate geometric patterns, horseshoe arches, and beautifully-carved stucco work. The "Patio de las Doncellas" had a central courtyard surrounded by stunning galleries, apparently a testament to the Moorish mastery of symmetry and aesthetics. It is no wonder that this palace was chosen as a "Gardens of Paradise."

The transition from Moorish to Gothic and Renaissance influences was evident in the "Hall of the Tapestries" and the "Hall of the Admirals." The intricate detailing, vaulted ceilings, and grandeur of these spaces reflected the evolving tastes of Spanish monarchs. The "Hall of Ambassadors" was a masterpiece, with an astonishing domed ceiling adorned with celestial motifs.

One of my absolute favorite parts of the Alcázar was the intricate ceramic tilework that adorns its walls. The Azulejo tiles are a resplendent hallmark of Andalusian artistry. I wandered through the "Hall of the Dolls" and the "Hall of the Justice," entranced by the complex patterns and narratives masterfully depicted on the blue and white tiles, each telling a unique story of history and culture. It reminded me of the "Blue Mosque" in Istanbul, I realized as I made my way into the interior courtyards to explore the lush and expansive gardens.

I would always be taken aback by the sheer grandeur and beaut of the Royal Alcázar's gardens, which were as impressive as its interior. The Gardens of the Alcázar are a maze of meticulously-maintained greenery and gardens and bubbling fountains. There were reflecting pools, intricate mosaics, and an enchanting "Mercury Pond." The scent of orange blossoms perfumed the air, adding another layer to the incredibly sensory experience. I had never appreciated the art of landscape design and horticulture more than in this lush paradise with stunning, graceful, towering palm trees that seemed to pierce the sky.

I took countless photos inside and out. I knew they wouldn't do justice to the splendor and grandeur but I did my best to capture the essence. The gorgeous arches served as natural frames to the beautiful gardens and ubiquitous palm and orange trees. I took my time admiring the courtyard from every angle, each highlighting a unique vista.

What a treasure trove of history and art, I thought as I reluctantly left, knowing I would be back some day to share it with Olivia and Rachel. It was simply breathtaking and my favorite palace of all time. I had been to other palaces, like Versailles, but was frankly underwhelmed - seemed to me essentially an ostentatious showing off of wealth; I really hadn't found anything remarkable of interest to me. By contrast, the Alcázar - with its multicultural heritage - was an architectural splendor that provided a fascinating journey through history as well as through the evolution of architectural styles and the changing tastes of Spanish monarchs. I'm an architectural enthusiast and loved all the gorgeous tiles. The captivating architecture reflected the influence of each era, offering an ever-evolving design. The result was almost a magical harmonious blend. My visit immersed me in the rich tapestry of Spain's history and cultural heritage.

Seville in general was leaving an indelible mark on my heart and soul and the Alcázar was one of my most memorable tours ever. It slowly dawned on me that I had changed a lot since my last visit and that is what had me wowed more than ever by the stunning palatial gem. I used to hurry from one thing to the next - sites had been more of a distraction than a destination before. By being alone, more present, more open-eyed and contemplative, I was saturating myself in a multidimensional, multi-sensorial way. I felt like a human sponge, soaking up the experience in all its enchantment. I knew the Alhambra had been designed to represent "heaven on earth" but, for me, the Alcázar had earned that distinction…

******

Chapter 6

Culinary Foreplay

"¡Buen provecho!" we said in unison when our array of tapas began their initial culinary descent. Rafael and I started what promised to be a scrumptious feast of a variety of tastes with Chorizo a la Sidra - the richness of the slightly spicy sausage was expertly cut by the tangy cider it had been cooked in, a simple dish which I noted would be easily replicable in my own kitchen. If I had a kitchen, I briefly good-naturedly mused at my homeless status. I loved hosting guests tapas style, I was drawn to the variety and intimacy of the dining style.

Next we had Patatas Bravas. The lightly fried potato cubes were elevated with a duo of spicy tomato sauce and garlic aioli - yum, two of my favorites I thought with delight. I loved making my own aiolis, a healthy take on the store-version of mayonnaise that I always abhorred. I thought of my mom because she loved the store version and always teased me about my aversion. Tortilla Española, a Spanish type of omelet made with eggs and potatoes always made me think of my mom too. She was always suggesting that simple combination when I was hungry as a child and although I liked it, her suggestions were never timely to satisfy whatever I was craving at the time. It was too bland the way she made it - no offense mom, I silently clarified, fondly remembering her. I just always knew she would get a kick whenever I would order a relatively expensive version of her standard fare as a tapa. I was relieved Rafael hadn't ordered it because it was heavier than a lot of the other tapas and generally served cold whereas I always preferred hot tapas.

Rafael could see I was a bit lost in thought and inquired if I were ok as he refilled our wine glasses. "Oh, yes, everything is marvelous," I assured him. I was truly enjoying our dining experience. It was a rare treat for me to be enjoying tapas at a restaurant since my introverted nature frequently preempted me from venturing out alone - especially for such a sociable and intimate experience. I also liked that it was a slow, savored meal. I laughed at myself also realizing I was happy I got to try so many more things sharing with another; I could never order so many tapas alone.

Tapas culture had intrigued me for as long as I could remember - it was a trifecta of perfection for me body, mind, and spirit. My curious spirit and love of novel experiences always enjoyed this style of eating which also synced beautifully with my culinary wellness priorities and my love of intimate experiences. I was beyond excited to share the evening and dining experience with Rafael but was a little shy about being with Rafael and self-conscious about our age difference. Most of the patrons were in groups of Spaniards and I felt like we stuck out a bit as the only couple I observed combined with the fact that I was foreign and older. Rafael was very attentive and I wasn't used to it. I appreciated his presence and the fact that he wasn't distracted by his phone or the throngs of people around us. I was a bit uncomfortable nonetheless, not being accustomed to someone's laser focus on me and the fact that Rafael seemed more thoughtful than talkative as was my tendency as well. It made me more attracted to him but I was getting uncomfortable with our relative silence juxtaposed to the chattering groups. I squirmed a little, smiling at him meekly, before casting my eyes down briefly to avert his intense gaze. I was a bundle of equal parts energy, enthusiasm, and nerves.

As I watched the endless stream of tapas being delivered to the boisterous tables around us, I took it as a prompt to fill the silence that was making me uncomfortable and grabbed it as an opportunity to share my adoration of the Spanish style of eating with Rafael. I told him that Chef José Andrés was not only one of my favorite chefs but one of my favorite people as well given his extensive humanitarian efforts. I had frequented his tapas restaurant, Jaleo, in Washington, D.C. years prior when my legal work often took me there. I loved how humble he was - particularly given his notoriety and richly-deserved accolades for his work feeding people in the aftermath of disasters and crises like hurricanes and wars.

Although José was Spanish by birth, he was also a US citizen and had built an impressive restaurant presence throughout the US during the decades he had been there. Rafael wasn't as familiar with the chef's World Central Kitchen charitable work and listened to me attentively discussing the chef passionately while my eyes lit up in admiration for the talented chef and his humanitarian efforts. Rafael continued thoughtfully listening as I told him that the organization provided chef-made meals immediately to people in the wake of natural disasters and in humanitarian crises. He whistled in amazement as I told him the team had already served over 400 million meals. "Food is love to me and I can't imagine a better expression of that than people coming together in a time of crisis to nourish the bodies and spirit of the individuals affected." Rafael nodded in agreement, as I continued. "It's an aspirational goal of mine to similarly help people one day. Meeting Senor Andres is on my "bucket list" of things I want to experience in my life," I concluded, matching Rafael's warm smile in response to me sharing some of my dreams.

Discussing food had been the perfect way to ignite our conversation as we quickly transitioned into discussing our "bucket list"-type agendas. "Interesting," Rafael commented with that same bemused smile that had caught my attention at the airport. "Please, tell me. What else is on this bucket list of yours, beautiful?" Rafael politely listened as I shared some more of the vastly diverse items on my list - including meeting my spiritual icon, his Holiness, the Dalai Lama; visiting the Buddha Eden Garden in Portugal; following the St. Francis of Assisi path with Olivia and seeing Imagine Dragons and Coldplay together; stand-up paddling with Rachel; making pasta with "nonnas" in Puglia and going on food tours in Parma, Italy with Rachel; grape and olive oil harvesting in Spain; bike riding through the Champagne region in France; making pizza in Naples with my nephews; meditating with monks in Chiang Mai, Thailand; cooking with Jamie Oliver; chatting with Nigella Lawson as I watch her cook; and taking boxing and fencing classes. I looked up at Rafael. I had been focused on a litany of desires, emboldened by the rare query as to what I wanted. I had such a curious spirit and so many passions. No man had ever asked me what I wanted. Rafael's simple question had unleashed an exhaustive monologue I had spontaneously spewed in a geyser-like manner. I bit my lip, momentarily hoping I wasn't too much for him. He smiled deeply in response, motioning me to continue releasing the thoughts in my apparently pent-up head.

Emboldened by his kindness, I was on an unusual conversational roll. I was shocked by how comfortable I was feeling with Rafael. I never erupted authentically with a volcanic-like explosion of extemporaneous speaking with a virtual stranger. I could go on endlessly with nerve-inspired superficial chit chat, but this was blissfully different. I was more or less baring my soul because

Rafael seemed different - sincere. He was making me feel uncharacteristically interesting because he truly seemed interested. I was so used to my male companions reveling in the spotlight. I could truly envision prior relationships sharing their desires without even reciprocating the question.

"Sofia," Rafael finally managed to get a word in. I tilted my head downwards to avert his gaze, chastising myself for babbling on. I was wrong - I was boring him and he probably wanted to leave. My ex had always monopolized the conversation - our interactions hadn't been a dialogue but a monologue where I just listened, feeding his ego while ignoring mine. Once I had finally started finding my own voice, he had just left. Just like Rafael was undoubtedly about to leave me now. I was foolish to think he found me interesting.

"Sofia," Rafael repeated, gently placing his fingers under my chin to lift my head to meet my eyes. He paused for what felt like an eternity while I tried to maintain my composure for the inevitable. "You are amazing. Your zest for life is wonderfully contagious. Please, go on." My heart warmed with relief with Rafael's kindness and attentiveness. I briefly thought of the Buddhist tenet that most suffering is unnecessarily caused by misperceptions. Touche, I silently thought, smiling at Rafael in gratitude. He took my hand and I realized he was still politely, genuinely waiting for me to share more.

I felt like a bubbling bottle of uncorked Champagne that eluded having the cork popped back in. My stream-of-conscious persona effervescently continued, summing up my feelings, "So many people wait so long to pursue what they want. Indeed so many people don't even know what they want." I paused thinking of how I had formerly spent my life in the former camp - subjugating my desires to others - but that I was blessed with many passions and clarity as to what I wanted. "I think it's tragic that so many people delay what they want - putting it off to another day - often until the end of their life when it's usually too late. Life is meant to be lived. Every day deserves a celebration in my mind. Indeed," I laughed as I reflected, "I think that's why I'm a tad obsessed with sparkling wine - it's the symbol of the celebratory nature of life to me." Rafael smiled, still endearingly being attentive, silently absorbing my long-winded desired itinerary of experiences. "Although I have always wanted to visit the Champagne area, cava is actually my favorite sparkler," I clarified before asking Rafael to share his so-called bucket list.

Rafael grinned, noting with pleasure the eclectic mix of my list and my enthusiasm for a celebratory outlook. "Sounds Italian-heavy and that you really enjoy spending time with your friends. "Oh, yes," my eyes started misting, "Italy is so special to me and my friends are my world, they are my greatest blessings." "That's wonderful, although I hope Espana at least gets an honorable mention," he teased. "Oh, yes, I adore Spain as well. I think Mallorca is my favorite island and Sevilla is my favorite big city. Spain resonates with my soul because Spaniards seem to vibrantly live life. I love the youthful energy that permeates every day life here," I sincerely gushed.

"Wow, that definitely qualifies as more than an honorable mention." "Plus, remember my love of cava and tapas-style eating," I winked at him, hoping I hadn't "dissed" my companion's native country. "No worries, I love Italy too," he revealed before chuckling, thanking me on behalf of Spain for the nod to cava. He noted with a slight blush, "Hmmm, you enjoy the youthful energy, good to know," before contemplating his own list. I loved how comfortable Rafael had made me feel divulging my thoughts.

"I never really thought about it; no one has ever asked me." "I feel it's a quick and interesting way to get to know another person. It can provide insights into another's dreams, passions, and perspective," I explained before eagerly awaiting to hear Rafael's desires, while he thoughtfully paused again before considering his answer. "I see what you mean. Not only is it a great conversation starter but it is a unique way to get to know someone. Fairly easily. Quickly. Intimately." His voice and thoughtful nature had me in a distracted tizzy. I was enjoying - and appreciative of - his contemplative demeanor and thoughtful responses. I felt like he was truly listening. Like he truly cared. It reminded me of Ali, I mused. Without the language barrier though - or the rush to enter into a serious relationship.

"It's funny, I think most people would elaborate on more lofty desires - like yachting in the Caribbean or driving a Ferrari in Italy, for instance." I immediately thought of my exes - Rafael's more "exclusive"-type examples, more reflective of their preferred lifestyle dreams. I was happy to realize again that I hadn't been wallowing about my last husband or wasting time on regrets - thanks to Spain and Rafael. I anxiously awaited Rafael to continue, my happiness quickly transitioning to fear that Rafael thought my "bucket list" goals were too mundane. Perhaps, he too preferred the so-called "finer" things in life like my exes instead of the soul-stirring, authentic experiences I craved.

I involuntarily sighed, certain I had misread Rafael, feeling self-conscious for having uncharacteristically shared what I wanted and deeply embarrassed about having monopolized the conversation - "taking up too much space" with my incessant, nonsensical chatter. I looked away, distracting my attention to the groups of happily animated patrons. I felt so ignorant, so out of place. I wished I could just blend into the background.

To my amazement and relief, Rafael gently took my hand and thanked me for sharing. Apparently, he had simply been reflecting on everything I had said. It dawned on me that unlike a lot of self-absorbed individuals, he hadn't been focused on what he wanted to say - he had clearly, deeply listened to me. "In just a couple of minutes, I know you enjoy simple pleasures - like food and wine and music. You're spiritual while being down to earth. You're grateful and appreciate your friends and nature. …and, …" he paused while looking at me for what felt like an extremely long time, "you're active. It shows and I appreciate it." I squirmed, uncomfortable with the extended attention, "… and you?" I prodded, my mood re-elevated, yet still anxious to transfer the spotlight to him.

"Well, as for me," he finally started, "I'd love to visit the US and take you to dinner at one of Senor Andres' restaurants to have you meet him." I smiled, appreciatively brushing his thigh. I knew that it was an impromptu - likely insincere - desire but it was endearing nonetheless that the first experience he chose was to cross off one of my items. "I guess I'd have to think about it more. I have always wanted to visit Canada and go hiking. It sounds like your Italian hike is already spoken for," Rafael charmingly winked before adding to his list. "I'd love to try stand up paddling and explore the Champagne region together with you. If…," Rafael slowly started as I eagerly waited to hear what his condition might be, "…you agree to visit Monet's gardens in Giverny with me after we tour Champagne."

I blushed slightly and bit my lip, hmmm sexy and sensitive - a combination I couldn't resist. I grinned as he looked at me inquisitively, clearly awaiting my obvious answer. "Ooh that's a good one. I would love to, of course," I murmured. I was happy I was feeling more relaxed. I was enjoying getting to know each other more and growing more desirous of Rafael by the minute - sharing passions and food was such a sensual and intimate combination for me.

I focused on culinary desires as our garçon brought us Pulpo a la Gallega next - slices of octopus drizzled with olive oil, paprika, and served on boiled potatoes. Octopus was definitely a take it or leave it type-food, as well as an entreaty not to judge a book by its cover. I thought of "Green Eggs and Ham" and wondered if GiGi had ever had octopus. It was one of my favorites and a treat because I would never attempt to make it at home. It was an involved and somewhat precise process - definitely not my cooking style - so I enjoyed it whenever I had the opportunity.

We segued into Albóndigas - Spanish meatballs. I was pleased to see ours was in an almond sauce instead of the more common tomato sauce which I could easily recreate. I hadn't had it this way before and planned to emulate it; one of my favorite things about traveling was being exposed to new foods and preparations. Recreating my own versions at home was a lovely way to challenge myself, expand my repertoire, and provoke memories of my travels - as well as share with those I loved. It's one of the biggest reasons I enjoy going out. I'm constantly thinking of how I would make dishes my own as I'm enjoying them - almost inevitably more spices, herbs, and citrus.

I'm kind of a kitchen sink type cook which doesn't resonate with everyone. I had always used copious amounts of herbs and spices once I had started traveling frequently and been exposed to so many. Growing up was basically table salt, ground pepper and garlic and dried parsley - never a fresh herb. I loved how eating is such a simple way to boost health, energy, and happiness and I was confident that my copious use of herbs and spices was integral to my wellbeing. I was taking mental notes for my writings. If I could redo my career, I would be an epidemiologist; I am fascinated with how lifestyle factors impact our relative incidence or avoidance of disease. I considered myself an amateur observational epidemiologist. I loved not only reading about the Mediterranean lifestyle but immersing myself in it which instructed the writing I was so passionate about.

Back to eating, I interrupted my silent reverie as our garçon brought us Croquetas, little yummy fried balls typically filled with ingredients like ham, chicken, or seafood - ours were filled with ham and were delectable. He also brought us each a glass of cava - I hadn't realized that Rafael had thoughtfully ordered it after I mentioned it was my favorite. I was touched by Rafael's gesture and its crisp, refreshing effervescence perfectly balanced the richness of the croquettes. I smiled in deep contentment and satisfaction as Rafael and I toasted. "No more I hope. Are we finished?" I melodramatically pleaded with my hands together in prayer-like fashion. "Not quite," Rafael responded with twinkling eyes gazing, as he placed his hand on my thigh. I felt a warmth spreading throughout my body from his touch, his gaze, and the wine.

I was relieved when the garçon brought our last two tapas - they were two of my favorites and relatively lighter vegetable dishes. My eyes lit up when I recognized the tapas. "You really are simple, aren't you?" Rafael admired. I smiled briefly before eagerly turning my attention to our dishes, enthusiastically diving in despite my protestations mere moments before. I started with the "Pimientos de Padrón con Queso," grilled red bell peppers generously stuffed with goat cheese then broiled. The preparation and presentation were simply poetic. The peppers were visually appealing with the colorful vibrant red of the peppers and the golden, bubbling cheese garnished with bright confetti strips of basil and a drizzle of deep green virgin olive oil. The slight smokiness from the char and the natural sweetness of the peppers and basil together with the earthiness of the pungent olive oil and coarse black pepper, beautifully complemented the creamy, slightly tangy cheese. "A culinary masterpiece of contrasts. Seemingly so simple yet so meltingly delectable," I appreciatively declared as I finished my peppers. "As you are too," Rafael cleverly quipped. I blushed - slightly embarrassed I had unintentionally set up an easy lay up like that - before quickly distracting us by focusing on our final tapa.

The last tapa was one of my all-time favorites and featured one of my most beloved foods. "Tapa de alcachofas a la plancha," artichokes grilled until slightly charred, imparting a mildly smoky flavor and a lovely, slightly crispy texture to the artichokes, drizzled generously with gloriously green olive oil, topped with coarse pink salt, and a splash of citrusy lemon. I was in culinary heaven. I slowly savored my last bites. Fresh artichokes were something I rarely prepared given the laborious cleaning preparation and this tapa was the best way to end our memorable experience.

The last tapas were the perfect marriage of flavors, textures, and aromas. "Mmm, mmm, mmm, mmmm, mmmmm," I could think of no better way to sum up the meal than with my trademark sounds of delight. I had never had a more enjoyable tapas experience in my life and my pleasure was evident even without my mild groaning. "So you're glad we weren't finished yet?" Rafael winked. "Oh, my indeed," I responded. "Great," he winked again before continuing, "…because we're still not finished."

******

Chapter 7

Romantic Flirtations

"Let's take a little stroll shall we?" Rafael proposed after insisting on paying for our dinner over my protestations. I wasn't used to be treated by a man - it felt a little uncomfortable to me because it was unfamiliar. It was the type of unfamiliar I wanted to get accustomed to, so I simply thanked him, touched by his generosity and the fact that he nonchalantly took my hand as he led us out of the crowded maze of patrons to the square nestled between the Alcázar and the Cathedral.

There was no area anywhere in the world that was more romantic to me than this plaza at night. It felt exotic and sultry. The sun was serendipitously just beginning to set as Rafael led me by the hand to the Plaza del Triunfo. The plaza was particularly magical at night - made more so by my undeniably intensifying attraction to Rafael. His hand felt so protective, so comforting. I knew we had just met and I had a tendency to fall too fast, but being with Rafael just felt easygoing, it felt right. Opening up during our conversation at dinner had quickly unknotted my introverted tension and I was happy to realize how surprisingly comfortable I was feeling together.

I knew that Volkan had just been a fling and, although I could have fallen for Ali, he had scared me moving too seriously, too fast. I thought of Goldilicks and the Three Bears, smiling, as I stole a glance at Rafael. Mmmmm, I thought to myself, he's so ravishing, and charming, and maybe, just maybe "just right" in the middle of the extremes as in the fairytale. It had been a magical day exploring the Royal Alcázar, capped off by a lovely dinner with Rafael, and my mind was wandering dreamily. I felt positively smitten with Rafael - a description I had never had occasion to use before, I realized, as I squeezed Rafael's hand in appreciation.

I was grateful the historical square was relatively empty without throngs of boisterous tour groups to detract from the amorous ambiance of the evening. The sky was painted with hues of orange and pink, casting a warm golden glow over the iconic landmarks. La Giralda - the imposing tower standing tall next to the Cathedral, statuesquely seeming to pierce the sky - glimmered in the fading light, providing a picturesque backdrop. The tower had been a minaret when the building had been a mosque - it was now the church bell tower and an oft-visited site for elevated views of the city.

We stood in silence - comfortably this time - simply gazing at the awe-inspiring view. We kept holding hands, as the sun continued its glorious show-stopping descent. I felt all warm and tingly from Rafael's close presence, the firm grasp of his strong hand, and anticipation for what the rest of the evening may hold. The Muslim call to prayer - or adhan in Arabic - timely started melodiously - from somewhere nearby, seemingly as if emanating from La Giralda, as it had done so many years before. "Adhan" means "to listen" and I liked to respectfully do so, taking a cue from the eloquent, gently commanding voice of the muezzin. I shut my eyes, focusing on the moment, reveling in my other senses, as I silently gave thanks for my blessings. The Muslim ritual not only served as an alert that prayers were about to begin, but also as a reflection of the shared faith and belief of the Muslims. Whenever I heard it, it gave me pause to be grateful.

There was something so peaceful and beautiful about the symbolic tolerance of the juxtaposition of the Islamic adhan with the catholic Cathedral and the co-existence of the call to prayer in the midst of the bustling rhythm of daily evening life in Seville. The ritual imparted a comforting calm amidst the chaotic energy - a sense of reliable order combined with the exciting possibilities of uncertainty - it was the best of all worlds for me.

As the adhan concluded, I thought of Helen Keller, concurring with her that sight can sometimes be a "distraction." I listened intently to the rhythmic clip-clopping of horse-drawn carriages, as I breathed in deeply, rewarded by an intoxicating whiff of jasmine combined with the citrusy fragrance of the ubiquitous orange trees. Rafael squeezed my hand, bringing me out of my almost trance-like tranquility. I squeezed back, opening my eyes, beaming at my companion with pure happiness. "It really is magical, isn't it?" he winked at me, obviously pleased by my evident bliss-like state. "It truly is," I murmured. "I'm having a lovely evening. Thank you so much, Rafael." "My pleasure, princess."

I blushed as I looked away. With perfect timing, the pretty church bells of La Giralda started chiming as we began leisurely strolling along the cobblestone paths, wandering through the labyrinth of courtyards, fountains, and lush greenery with a palpable feeling of intimacy. We continued languidly walking, soaking up the atmospheric evening, stopping to browse some of the pretty boutique shops. One in particular, dedicated to scarves, caught my eye - there was a large assortment of the decorative pewter "scarf charms" that I had noticed in Mallorca. Rafael looked at me quizzically, having noted my gaze. "They're so pretty. I had never seen them before,"I shrugged as I moved on.

"Would you like to take a carriage ride around town?" Rafael generously offered. "Oh, no, that's not necessary.

Thank you," I replied shyly, feeling out of my element, feeling uncomfortable that I wasn't "holding my end of things up," as I paused and gently stroked one of the horse's heads. "Have you seen the city view from a rooftop at night?" Rafael queried, just when I thought the evening couldn't feel more romantic. "Why, no, I haven't," I smiled, touched that Rafael was determined to make the night particularly memorable. I was having a fabulous time and I didn't want the night to end.

Rafael took me by the hand, escorting me to a chic boutique hotel in close proximity to the Alcazar. He paused en route, getting me a trio of long-stemmed red roses from one of the several boys selling them in the square. I gazed at him appreciatively, as I sniffed the distinctive soft fragrance, trying not to focus on the butterfly feeling fluttering in my tummy as we took the elevator up to the rooftop bar. I could have never imagined the incomparable views and I knew I would have missed out on them had I not been in Rafael's capable hands. The roof afforded 360 degree panoramic vistas with unobstructed views of the illuminated Cathedral, La Giralda, and the Alcázar.

I stood at the ledge of the terrace, transfixed by the majesty while Rafael excused himself, presumably to go to the bar to get us a drink or use the washroom. I gazed at the Gothic mastery of the Cathedral with its intricate façade, happily reminiscing. I recalled that the Cathedral had replaced Hagia Sofia in Istanbul as the largest cathedral in the world at the time of its completion. It was still the largest Gothic cathedral and fourth largest church overall. The elevated view was giving me a uniquely impressive vantage point to appreciate its sheer grandeur. I thought of how Istanbul and Seville - though so different - were similar in appeal to me in many ways. They both somehow maintained a sense of authenticity and charm despite being so sprawling, I mused, before turning my attention to the Alcázar, with its captivating blend of Mudéjar and Renaissance architecture. The jet black backdrop of the sky with its luminous stars and the twinkling lights of serene Seville completed the entrancing fairytale-like scene.

Rafael returned just as I was thinking I couldn't imagine a more romantic setting and was grateful that I wasn't alone. He came up behind me, nonchalantly wrapping one of the scarves I had been admiring loosely around my neck. Before I could say anything, he politely excused himself again as he turned towards the bar. "Oh, no, please, allow me," I started as I headed to get us a drink. He grabbed my hand, lifting it up to his lips, kissing it, replying, "No, por favor." I stood somewhat paralyzed, melting in his unusual thoughtfulness and charm.

I turned away to focus on the view again, tears welling up, my thoughts briefly contrasting how Rafael was treating me versus how most of my historical partners had. He quickly returned with a couple of rebujitos, a drink that was novel to me, and I appreciated that he had catered to my curious nature. I just smiled meekly in response, uncertain how to express how meaningful the way he was treating me was. He stood behind me with one arm wrapped around my waist and his body pressed up against mine as we sipped our cocktails, while admiring the view together. A tantalizing warmth was spreading through my body. I was grateful for the evening rooftop breeze and the slightly cooling effect of the sherry-based drink thanks to the fresh mint, ice and citrusy lemon-lime soda.

Soft flamenco music was playing, adding to the already undeniable intimate atmosphere. Rafael and I started swaying in sync with it as Rafael pulled me closer to him. I shut my eyes as we seductively moved together. I suddenly felt an irresistible desire to kiss him. I was quite aware that my evening would have turned out vastly different had I not had the pleasure of Rafael's company. I was also touched by his generosity and chivalry - something I wasn't used to. He was making me feel special - indeed almost princess-like - in the entrancing setting overlooking the Royal Palace.

Although I usually didn't initiate intimacy with someone I hadn't been with, I struggled to think of a good reason not to. I put my drink down on a table and turned towards him, briefly looking into his eyes before I slowly started kissing him, lightly, teasingly on the lips. He put his drink down too, eagerly accepting my mouth, pulling me closer to his body, while intensifying, deepening our kiss. My body flushed with heat in response to Rafael's hungry mouth and my unusual boldness. Our bodies started to meld together with a passionate intensity.

I pulled back, feeling self-conscious about my forwardness and our public affection. Rafael encircled my waist tighter, "Well, that was an unexpected surprise," he noted in an amused tone. I shrugged, looking sheepish, nervous as to how he felt about it. My slight trepidation was quickly allayed when he softly whispered in my ear, "You're delicious." I grinned in relief and because his words echoed my silent sentiment.

I fanned myself off with my hands in a somewhat exaggerated but sincere manner, Rafael's closeness and warm breath on my ear making me burn with desire. I laughed, wondering if the sizzling interactions of the Spaniards were partly responsible for the ubiquitous fans I had bought earlier. I took off my scarf, admiring the unique accessory, as we both reached for our refreshing drinks in unison.

Rafael asked me if I wanted another drink. I demurely turned my eyes downwards before shaking my head no. He squeezed my hand, "Good," leaving no doubt we were both eager to move on. He wrapped his arm around my waist while taking my other hand as he led me to the elevator. Before the doors even closed, he stood in front of me, leaned in, gently pressing me against the mirrored back of the elevator, lifted his arms, grabbing my hands in one hand, holding them over my head. I gasped with pleasure as he started kissing me hungrily, keeping me firmly in position. His firm grip was intensifying my desire. I couldn't move had I wanted to - I indicated my acquiescence, pushing against him harder, while matching the ferocity of his tongue. Our closeness left no question as to his desire either.

We gasped together, breathless, as the elevator doors opened - far too quickly - ushering us into the refreshing night air. "Thank you for a lovely evening, Rafael, and for my gift," I clutched my scarf appreciatively, "it will make the night memorable." I started getting shy again, presuming he would want to go meet up with his friends as so many Spaniards do later in the evening. He looked at me, pausing, looking into my eyes for what seemed like forever, holding my hands in his. "You're welcome, senorita, but I hope that's not the most memorable part of the evening."

My cheeks flushed - in recognition of the senorita just as I was worrying if I were too old for Rafael - and out of embarrassment that I may have offended him. "Oh, no, of course, Rafael. I'm sorry. I didn't mean it that way. Forgive me. Every minute has been memorable." Rafael put his fingers to my lips, indicating my profuse apology was unnecessary, with his bemused expression. "I guess I can forgive you, if…" he pausingly toyed with me as I shifted from foot to foot, "you give me a kiss." He endearingly pointed to each cheek as I obligingly kissed him. "…and," he made me wait again, pondering his terms in anticipation, "if you let me escort you home." "Oh, no, that isn't necessary," I started protesting before Rafael put his fingers to my lips again, followed by a directive to affectionately peck each cheek again. "You are in Spain, with me, but of course it is necessary." Oh my gosh could he be anymore adorable I thought as I grabbed his hand in agreement and we headed towards the river.

We walked hand in hand in silence along the riverfront, taking in the sweet vista en route, the ubiquitous twinkling lights gently guiding us home. When we got to my apartment building, I tried to encourage Rafael to lead the way up the several flights of stairs, self-conscious as I had been the first day about him following me up in close proximity. As I hesitated, to my surprise, he bent down and picked me up, carrying me in his arms as we started our ascent. I briefly squirmed, thinking of when Leo had carried me at the beach when I had twisted my ankle.

Rafael held me closer, tighter in his strong arms. I was already so self-conscious about him carrying me, worrying I was too much, I stopped my futile resistance to not add to his burden. He felt so safe, so loving, my body quickly surrendered. I stopped thinking and happily nuzzled my head against his chest, rewarded with his soft, irresistible alluring fragrance. I felt myself get lighter as I stopped resisting and my head started feeling ethereal. I realized this was exactly how I wanted to feel - enwrapped in a caring, capable man's protective embrace - I just wasn't used to it.

He paused, still cradling me in his arms when we got to the door. He gazed deeply into my eyes before giving me a slow, long, tantalizing kiss. I shut my eyes to catch my breath, murmuring "you're delicious," as he had commented earlier and as he was. This time, Rafael blushed, as he gingerly set me down. Now it was his turn to shift from foot to foot nervously as I anxiously tried to read his mind. He probably didn't want to come, he was just being a gentleman, insisting on taking me home. I was probably too heavy for him. I had been rude not paying for anything. I bit my lip to not invite him in, I didn't want him to do me any favors by coming in and I didn't want him to think poorly of me for being so forward. I was being presumptuous. I refrained from slapping myself in the forehead, as I willed him to speak.

Rafael finally responded by pressing me up against the door and lifting my arms up over my head, kissing me passionately as he had in the elevator. I moaned involuntarily before moaning again as our lips finally parted, hoping Rafael sensed my tacit desires.

"It's late and you've had a full day," Rafael abruptly announced his departure before kissing my forehead. My knees felt rubbery from the impact of the sweet kiss while my heart felt like it dropped to my stomach. My feelings were a rollercoaster. I knew Rafael was acting gentlemanly, but my past was making me extraordinarily insecure about his feelings. Men and instant gratification were my normal pattern. Rafael seemed different than other men, but I was struggling not to interpret his behavior as indicative of me not being undesirable, unworthy. I resisted the urge to invite him in - my low sense of self-worth was screaming at me that I owed him. He was treating me so differently than I was used to most of the time - it took all my strength not to sully that by acting like he was expecting sexual payback. I thanked him again, heartened by his departing words, "hasta pronto," princess - see you soon.

As I got ready for bed, I briefly started down a path of unproductive thinking. Left alone and feeling my characteristic restlessness borne out of solitude, his "see you soon" now struck my troubled head as too casual, too imprecise. I jumped to conclusions as a troubled heart tends to, expecting never to see him again. It was still early for Spaniards' time - he was undoubtedly going out to meet up with his friends - or even another woman.

I looked at myself in the mirror deep in literal and figurative reflection. Who was I kidding? I was too old for Rafael and didn't have anything to offer him, I ungenerously concluded. My last husband left me after so many years of marriage, why would I expect anything better from Rafael. I bit my lip as I stared in the mirror - hoping for some comforting thought. I knew I wasn't being fair to Rafael, but I simply couldn't talk myself out of my unflattering assessment of myself at the moment. That's what you get when you outsource your self-worth, Sofi, I gently scoffed at myself.

My scarf still had a lingering scent of Rafael's scent. I wrapped it around myself in an attempt at a makeshift feeling like I was being hugged. I crawled into bed with nothing else on, taking comfort in the added weight of the comforter as I drew it tightly around me despite the warm weather. Words fascinated me and I couldn't think of any more apt name for the bed covering as it worked its weighted wonder in comforting me. I was determined to shift my perspective and channel my c'est la vie philosophy. It was whatever it was, no sense fretting over it.

My phone vibrated, alerting me to a message. I hesitated to look, not wanting anything possibly negative harshing my budding sense of peace. I hesitated again when I saw it was Rafael, assuming the worst, and not sure I wanted to deal with confirmation of my insecurities before trying to sleep. "I had a spectacular evening with you, Sofia. You're an amazing, beautiful woman and I can't wait to get to know you more. I must confess - it was difficult for me not to invite myself in (embarrassed emoji) - you are irresistible - but I didn't want you to think badly of me. Sweet dreams, princess, and I hope you will share the pleasure of your company with me tomorrow evening as well - you top my bucket list. (red heart emoji)"

I laughed at myself, touche, Buddha, I thought, realizing that my misperceptions had almost caused me to emotionally spiral out of control. Rafael was simply being a gentleman - I should have invited him in but I had overthought it. Just as well though because I was happy that I had already started shifting my mind even without the aid of Rafael's message. I always attached too quickly, too intently because I struggled being alone. It made me clingy and destroyed me if I were "unclung." It wasn't how I wanted to be and I wanted to work on it.

I was excited I would see Rafael again, but I was actually glad how the evening had turned out and was proud of myself for self-soothing without resorting to more wine or any sleeping pills. I was determined to get "comfortable" with feeling uncomfortable from time to time - letting the discomfort pass instead of numbing or distracting it - it always passed. I wanted to find more adaptive measures to cope with it until it did.

I glanced at the message again, my heart warmed by Rafael's charm and expressiveness, before simply replying,

"Thank you so much. I had a great time too and look forward to being together." I hoped my reference to "being together" intrigued Rafael as to my import as it was intended to. I intuitively, protectively placed my hands over my naked, exposed chest and vulnerable heart, silently reciting my gratitude litany. Happy tears started slowly streaming down my face as I felt the waves of gratitude almost instantly rhythmically flood over my body. I smiled as my heart coherence practice quickly worked its magic, transforming me from the impending meltdown I had previously been to a state of hopeful optimism. Tomorrow is another day I reminded myself, echoing the famous quote from one of my literary heroes, Scarlett O'hara, from Gone with the Wind. Tomorrow is another day indeed…

Chapter 8

Plaza Perfection

I awoke the next morning feeling refreshed and energized. A much better way to start the day than with regrets or self-loathing. I applauded myself for my behavior the night before as I enthusiastically left to greet the day. No plaza, piazza, or main square had ever captivated my attention more than Plaza de España - my destination and a true architectural masterpiece harmoniously blending Spanish Renaissance and Moorish Revival styles. It had been built for the Ibero-American Exposition - a world fair in 1929, and commemorated the 500th anniversary of Columbus' voyage to the Americas. The square was designed to showcase Spain's splendor and its profound historical ties to the American continent. It was a stunningly exquisite example of the Neo-Mudéjar architectural style, which incorporates Moorish and Renaissance elements. The most captivating feature to me was the massive semi-circular curved building adorned with endless colorful tiles representing the provinces of Spain. It was my favorite plaza or piazza thanks to its unique design and extraordinary charm and elegance. The semi-circular building fringing the square had a massive tower at each end. I'm a huge fan of vibrantly colored ceramic tiles - azulejos - and was awestruck by the sheer beauty and number of them adorning the central building and towers. The tiles created a mesmerizing mosaic. Apparently each tile tells a story of Spanish explorations and conquests, adding to the historical relevance and mystical allure of the plaza.

The unique central canal feature was adorned with four remarkable bridges symbolizing the ancient kingdoms of Spain - Castile, Aragon, Navarre, and Leon. Each bridge was adorned with more intricate ceramic tiles depicting historical events. The central building housing the Provincial Government of Seville had galleries and exhibitions providing insights into the history of Seville and Spain.

I was content simply spending time in the central courtyard of the square absorbing its beauty and observing its lively activity. There were artists with pop up galleries showcasing their handiwork of prints and paintings of Seville's exquisite architecture. I stopped and watched one artist with an easel set up as he was painting the Plaza. I bought a couple of postcard prints of the Plaza and the Royal Alcázar. I tried to buy a few prints of each place I went; they were inexpensive and easy to carry and I enjoyed decorating wherever I was with these little mementos. No matter how transient I was, it helped make wherever I was staying feel more personal and homelike to me.

There were also vendors all along the semicircular courtyard with large displays of decorative Flamenco-type fans. I took my time perusing the varied options before selecting a few. I thought they would be pretty as little wall hangings so I picked out a couple for me as well as for Olivia and Rachel.

There were boat rides and paddle boats on the central canal and horse-drawn carriages offering rides around the plaza, a prevalent site throughout Seville. The square was popular with couples, families, and tour groups but maintained a sense of serenity given its size. A vendor blowing huge colorful bubbles was a particular hit with the numerous children who gathered round; I had never seen anything quite like the bubble "show" he made.

I picked a spot in the courtyard with a good vantage point to stop and enjoy my homemade lunch. I was mesmerized by the grandeur of the semicircular façade's intricate details, soaring towers, and the grand central porch. Fortuitously, an impromptu Flamenco performance was just starting on the porch. I listened to the hauntingly beautiful plaintive music while admiring the beauty of the dancer's dress and flowing movements. It was the perfect accompaniment to my lunch.

I had picked up some ingredients at the market to make my simple meal. I had gotten a wheat baguette and cut it slanted in two. My first sandwich was my favorite Spanish sandwich as well as one of my all time favorite meals. I had toasted the bread before rubbing garlic on it, drizzling the soft interior with extra virgin olive oil, generously grating ruby red tomatoes, sprinkling oregano, and adding slices of manchego cheese and Jamon Serrano. I toasted it some more on a panini press so the cheese sealed the sandwich together. I had fallen head over heels with the sandwich the first time I had had it outside the magnificent Alhambra in Granada, Spain years ago. It never ceased to amaze me how delicious the textural and flavor combination was and how transformative the garlic rub is. It always transported me back to that trip as well, the Alhambra being another architectural marvel that was one of my favorite Spanish gems.

I loved how food can evoke memories so easily. My other panini had Jamon Serrano, fresh mozzarella, and fresh fig jam - it was a creamy delight with the mild saltiness of the ham and slight sweetness of the jam. A perfect lunch I thought as I clapped as the flamenco dancer finished; my tastebuds were delighted with some of my favorite flavors and I had enjoyed the unexpected performance with the beautiful setting of the Plaza.

Despite its palpable energy, Seville somehow managed to exude a pervasive sense of tranquility as well. A retreat from the bustling streets was never far away with the expansive parks. None was more exquisite than the inviting Parque de María Luisa, adjacent to Plaza de España, with its lush gardens, fountains, statutes, and tree-lined pathways. I walked through the gorgeous park en route to my next plaza.

*****

I realized my designation of Plaza de España as my favorite plaza of all time was up for debate as I approached Plaza de América. Plaza de América is a magnificent square adjacent to the extensive Parque de María Luisa. I realized as I stood surveying the majestic oasis that Seville was really a place where beauty takes on new dimensions.

This Plaza was also built as part of the Ibero-American Exposition in 1929, and was intended to showcase Spain's close ties with its former colonies. The square was designed by the same renowned architect as Plaza de España, Aníbal González, and exuded the elegance of the Spanish Renaissance and Neomudéjar architectural styles. Seville was dripping with architectural marvels of design and ingenuity and this Plaza was no exception. I was amazed at how effortlessly various influences were blended to create such tranquil and harmonious visual gems.

While the highlight of Plaza de España was essentially the one massive curved building, Plaza de América showcased a few extraordinary buildings, including twin structures, the Pavilion of Peru and the Pavilion of Colombia, representing the exquisite Neo-Mudéjar style. I was awestruck by the buildings' intricate ceramic facades, delicate arches, and meticulously crafted details. I couldn't stop taking photos - every way I turned demanded to be captured.

The Pavilion of Peru was adorned with vibrant tiles and stonework, telling stories of Peruvian history, culture, and traditions. It was almost as if the building itself spoke to visitors, inviting them to discover the mysteries of this faraway land. The equally breathtaking Pavilion of Colombia featured intricate stonework and mosaics, and artistic representations of Colombia's natural beauty, serving as a gateway to the lush landscapes and vibrant culture of the South American nation. I had never spent so much time admiring tiles and mosaics; I couldn't remember ever seeing so much ceramic work as the means of detailed storytelling.

The entire square was graced by the remarkable Royal Pavilion, featuring beautiful sculptures and regal architecture. This central pavilion provided a visual link between the twin pavilions of Peru and Colombia, apparently to symbolize the unity of the Ibero-American nations.

The splendid buildings were surrounded by lush, meticulously-maintained gardens with winding pathways. It was a green oasis offering a tranquil retreat from the hustle and bustle and heat of the city and I took my time strolling throughout and admiring the buildings from different angles. I was serenaded by the sweet songs of birds chirping as I took note of the plentiful vibrant colors of the flowers, the soothing shade of the trees, and the cool flowing breeze, all senses were engaged.

My favorite part of Plaza de América may have been the majestic fountain commanding attention at the heart of the plaza, glistening in the sunlight. The intricate design and gentle flow of water created a calming ambiance that I appreciated as I pondered the beauty of the plaza from a park bench. As with Plaza de España, this Plaza also hosts various activities such as concerts, art shows, and cultural activities. What an incredible venue for festivals and events I mused as I watched a family starting a horse and carriage ride throughout the park between the two plazas. I made a mental note to visit the Plaza at sunset one day because I had read that the fountain becomes illuminated at sunset, undoubtedly adding a touch of magic to the already enchanting atmosphere.

Plaza de América, like so many other sites in Seville, seemed like more than just a "square" or "place"; there were so many fascinating living testaments to Seville's historical and cultural legacy. It's one of those enchanting places where you can lose yourself in the past while savoring the present, making it particularly memorable. Seville's cultural heritage and artistic brilliance came to life in so many spots throughout the city, I thought in awe - she oozed charm in every direction.

There was an air of romance everywhere as well, I reflected as I watched couples and families enjoying the plaza together. Just as I was getting a little wistful and feeling lonely, I received a serendipitously timed message from Rafael. "Are you up for tardeo?" he inquired with a winking emoji. Emojis get me every time. "Not sure what that is, but sure why not?" I replied with my own winking emoji. "Trust me," he responded, asking if I could meet him at the Royal Alcázar. I cheerily agreed, relieved he had picked such an easy place to find as it's easy to get lost in the endless winding paths and mazes that characterize Seville.

My oldest nephew, Jackson, was always asking me what my favorite country was. He was an intelligent and inquisitive soul with a kindred adventurous spirit. Forced to choose, I had always picked Italy with a twinge of disloyalty for all the other countries I dearly loved. I was increasingly challenging myself to articulate the nuances that made me fall madly in love with the different countries I visited and the different cultures I was blessed to be exposed to. As a novice travel writer, it had become more important to me to be able to eloquently distinguish amongst the countless places I visited.

If I had to identify the "essence" of Spain, I would have always said it was "energy." Spain was more vibrant than anywhere else for me and Spaniards lived in the moment like no others. This palpable energy and zest for life made any visit feel like a vibrant immersive experience. It was one of the reasons though that I felt a bit intimidated going out in Spain alone. Just as I was self-conscious about being single in Italy with its evident familial emphasis, I felt my solitude in pained contrast to Spain's undeniable sociability. Although locals of both countries were warm and welcoming, my introverted nature had always made me feel like an outsider. I had no idea what to expect from the evening but I was excited about seeing Rafael and equally excited about exploring something novel, something I was sure I would have missed out on had Rafael not asked me out. I was giddy with anticipation and practically glided as I made my way back to the center.

******

Chapter 9

Tardeo

Rafael was waiting for me as I approached the Alcázar. He greeted me with an enthusiastic grin and equally enthusiastic kisses on my cheeks before taking me by the hand to experience "tardeo." As we walked, he explained the Spanish ritual I was previously unfamiliar with. "It typically occurs after we have had our cherished afternoon siesta. I guess you could say we know how to relax," he observed good-naturedly. Rafael told me that around 17:00 - 18:00, the streets come alive with people, rejuvenated and ready to revel in the leisurely hours ahead.

He's right, I thought admiringly. I had always noticed the relative carefree nature of Spaniards. I knew that by no means did everyone take a midday nap, but the fact that it was a cultural rite was a reflection of the balance that Spaniards seemed to have found. They were energetic, but also prioritized rest and relaxation. It was as if they had mastered stress management - wisely not wasting precious time on things beyond their control. I remembered being struck at how unbelievably crowded cafes and restaurants were years prior on a visit when unemployment in Spain among the youth was exorbitant. I had found it refreshing that they had maintained their exuberant enthusiasm and continued with their way of life. Sociability - connection - was ingrained in them.

"Wow, tardeo, my new favorite ritual. Like happy hour for older adults," I self-deprecatingly quipped. Who else but the Spaniards would make a ritual out of celebrating afternoons - they made an art of leisure, tapas and wine, and camaraderie. I loved everything about it and I realized it encompassed how I would characterize the culture. The palpable pleasure of enjoying simple things and conviviality. Dinner typically starts late in Spain and lasts until the early morning hours. Work days generally started noticeably later in the mornings - understandably, given the typical social calendar. I loved my mornings, preferring to start my day quite early. Tardeo synced way better with my lifestyle and I was grateful for the exposure.

We strolled through Barrio de Santa Cruz - a vibrant neighborhood that oozed history, charm, and an undeniable sense of enchantment. I particularly enjoyed observing the merger of Moorish and Spanish influences which created a mesmerizing tapestry of culture and architecture for me. The Barrio area included the Alcázar and Cathedral, but this Jewish neighborhood, more or less tucked away behind the Alcázar seemed like worlds apart from the massive iconic buildings.

Rafael endearingly acted as my impromptu tour guide sharing glimpses of the history of the neighborhood with me, which, he noted was as rich and diverse as the intricate patterns adorning its buildings. In the past, the neighborhood had been the thriving Jewish quarter of Seville. I loved how seamlessly different religions coexisted in many countries, leaving an imprint on the culture and neighborhoods. Rafael explained that the winding streets and narrow alleys that characterized the area were designed intentionally to provide shade. I tried listening intently to Rafael's words. I was so distracted by his sensual, slightly husky voice, as well as his intoxicating scent, I was struggling to pay attention to what he was actually telling me.

I didn't know if it was Rafael's presence or simply the setting but the neighborhood felt cloaked in a romantic ambiance. We passed by many serene courtyards perfumed with the scent of orange blossoms, or azahar in Spanish, as Rafael advised me as I paused to deeply inhale the intoxicating scent. He also informed me that the patios were reminiscent of the Moorish tradition of designing homes with inner gardens and fountains, offering respite from the Andalusian sun. I was a huge fan of interior courtyards - a magnificent one was the distinctive feature in the hypothetical home of my dreams that I had designed in my head. I loved the idea of having ready access to a pretty serene outdoor space while retaining privacy.

Meandering through the cobblestone streets almost felt like we had stepped into a living museum. It seemed there was another hidden gem to discover every corner we turned as we wandered the labyrinthine streets. There were beautiful plazas, charming boutiques, and cozy cafes already filled with patrons spilling out all over the neighborhood's narrow, winding lanes. Apparently, tardeo had already commenced in full force in the lively quarter.

Barrio de Santa Cruz seemed to be a particularly palpable manifestation of Sevillanos' zest for celebrating life. The neighborhood had a captivating charm; its history was unmistakably evident in the architecture, but it was a living, breathing neighborhood full of passion and energy.

I was truly excited to partake in my first tardeo. I grasped Rafael's arm tightly as we navigated the bustling sun-drenched streets echoing with laughter, the air thick with the tantalizing scent of tapas. Rafael was obviously pleased at my anticipation. As we exited the maze of tiny, twisting streets into a beautiful long park, "Jardines de

Murillo," Rafael remarked he hoped I didn't mind that a couple of his friends from work would be joining us. Tardeo is typical on weekends and holidays and apparently Rafael and his friends regularly enjoyed it on Sundays. I felt a little nervous but decided to embrace the company. Rafael had obviously included me in the plans he usually had with his friends and I appreciated his generous invitation. I squeezed his hand in silent acquiescence as well as in gratitude for having thoughtfully selected a meeting point I could easily find instead of just telling me to meet him where we were going.

We strolled through the Murillo Gardens park as we made our way to the tapas wine bar we were going to which Rafael indicated was at the end of the park. The gardens were named after a famous Sevillian Baroque painter, Bartolomé Esteban Murillo. I made a mental note to look him up online to learn more - the expansive park felt like a lush, tranquil oasis providing a peaceful escape from the nearby bustling activity of the Jewish Quarter.

Rafael casually took my hand, igniting my trademark tingly excitement. I tried to concentrate as he pointed out some of the park's highlights, including a sculpture of the park's namesake, Murillo, and a towering monument dedicated to Christopher Columbus. I particularly enjoyed seeing the soaring palm trees, fragrant orange trees, and flowering bushes. The park was lively with walkers and bicyclists and readers on park benches along the perimeters, and children running around, families picnicking, and couples lying together on blankets soaking up the sun in the expansive interior. The park was so vast that it still felt serene despite the number of locals and tourists enjoying it. The garden was graced with several fountains and statues, adding to its allure.

I loved how Spaniards frequented outdoor spaces, like parks, and Rafael noted that the garden was a popular spot for locals to unwind and escape the somewhat frenetic pace of the center. It really did feel like we were worlds away. I appreciated the juxtaposition of the vibrant quarter with the peaceful park, something to suit everyone and cater to different moods. Rafael noted we were adjacent to the old city walls of Seville, as he pointed out a portion of the ancient wall and its accompanying gate.

It was a rare treat for me to be guided around with a local, it made my experiences so much more informative and multi-layered. As we approached the end of the park, I stopped to admire the orange trees with a profusion of fragrant blossoms, telling Rafael how much I had enjoyed the vino de naranja I had tried for the first time at the Mercado. He told me he enjoyed it as well as he plucked a few of the fragrant oranges for me.

******

Chapter 10

Vineria San Telmo

Rafael's friends had already secured a prime table at Vineria San Telmo on the inviting umbrella-covered terrace, perfectly positioned with a view of the gardens. Adriano and Garcia each politely stood up to greet me. Adriano had an equally classy and exotic look. He was tall with broad shoulders - his toned physique was evident in his sweater and form-fitting trousers. He was dressed in a light silky black short-sleeved sweater that matched his piercing black eyes, and dark, perfectly coiffed silken hair. He had voluptuous lips and I instantly thought what a striking couple he and Olivia would make with the contrast between his darker features and her fairer, angelic like beauty. He kissed each of my cheeks and whispered softly, simply, in my ear, one word fraught with meaning, "pleasure."

I felt my body temperature visibly rise, feeling a bit awkward, trying to ignore the impact his soft greeting had on my erogenous ears. I turned to greet Garcia, hoping my reddening cheeks weren't exposing my embarrassment. Garcia was also very alluring but in a more rugged way - he had wavy, tousled brown hair and deep hazel green lipid eyes that could instantly melt someone with his attentive gaze. He was wearing dark jeans and a fitted v-neck white t-shirt.

They both had "bad boy" written all over them - the type I never seemed able to resist. I silently gave thanks that I was escorted by Rafael - both of his friends seemed like the type that could easily woo a woman only to leave her in a melting puddle of heartbreak. I knew I was making assumptions, but Rafael felt more sincere and polished to me. I knew I would have been putty in either Adriano's or Garcia's hands even though.

They reminded me - appearance-wise - of my two favorite soccer goalies, the Italian GiGi Buffon and the Spanish Iker Casillas. The comparison ended there though. Rightfully or wrongfully, I summed these two up as men who didn't like to be tied down to one woman - who would swoop in and passionately seduce a woman before departing with equal speed - leaving her confused and heartbroken. Garcia took my hand, holding it firmly as he too leaned in, kissing me on each cheek as well, pausing to appreciate the subtle yet intoxicating fragrance of my French perfume. "I wonder if you taste as delicious as you smell," he queried as he continued holding my hand firmly. I knew I would have been easy prey to either of these two overly-expressive flirtatious young men given my vulnerability and discomfort about being alone.

I thought of my menage-a-trois dream in Mallorca, turning nervously to Rafael, worried maybe I was giving off the wrong vibe. "Ok, guys. Give the lady some room for heaven's sake," Rafael chastised as he protectively moved in between us, possessively putting his arm around my waist, as he pulled out a chair for me and sat down closely next to me. I relaxed as he remained steadfast next to me with his arm around my waist in a comforting yet firm manner. His friends - who worked with him as personal trainers - were just being harmlessly flirtatious I decided. I was glad nonetheless that Rafael had interceded; I didn't want anyone getting the wrong impression.

I observed Rafael as he and his friends discussed the menu and good-naturedly debated what we should have. I was growing more and more attracted to Rafael's personality. I loved how he was humbly self-assured and expressive and affectionate without the tinge of cockiness and exaggerated show that seemed to characterize Adriano and Garcia. Although my bruised ego was in need of some flattery and feeling desirable, I found Rafael's approach magnetic, whereas I would have been uncomfortable with his counterparts' over-the-top interactions.

I was self-aware enough that I would quickly go down a people-pleasing spiral with either Adriano and Garcia and grateful that I felt comfortable being myself around Rafael. I softly chuckled, thinking of our initial encounter at the airport - it seemed like so much time had passed although it was so recent. I was grateful I had fortuitously met Rafael upon my arrival - he felt a bit like a sexual guardian angel, having potentially saved me from less gentlemanly encounters.

I loosened up and started enjoying finally experiencing a lively group tapas experience instead of feeling out of place alone amidst throngs of sociable groups. We chatted amiably, particularly about their backgrounds and my impressions of Seville - they were all lovely conversationalists and I was really starting to enjoy myself, relieved I was feeling comfortable despite my normal shyness.

I knew my elevated mood was in large part thanks to Rafael. I was falling for him more and more each moment I spent with him. I realized that I had fallen for Leo rather quickly while I was still in the throes of heartache and that my dalliances in Turkey had largely resulted from a desire to numb the heartache not only from my failed marriage but also from my deep disappointment of not being with Leo.

With the passage of time and distance, aided by my introspection, I felt ready to explore a real relationship with Rafael. I loved Seville and was blessed with no fixed schedule. I looked at Rafael admiringly, thinking I could easily extend my time in Seville indefinitely as we got to know each other more. I was anxious for his friends to like me - especially since I planned to be around - and I was relieved how quickly the initial awkwardness had dissipated and transitioned into a lively conversation.

As we waited for our drinks and tapas, Adriano explained that some Spaniards tended to visit a series of tapas bars, each specializing in a unique culinary creation while others basically stuck to one venue. In some places, he told me it was common to receive a complimentary tapa with every drink ordered, making these places particularly popular for those who were drinking. It reminded me of the hospitable aperitivo time in Italy, my favorite drinking and eating ritual.

I looked around, soaking up the lively ambiance with all my senses. The waitstaff brought out a steady stream of aromatic and adorable little culinary creations that were visually whetting my appetite. Even the sounds were festive, elevating my mood and heightening my anticipation - the frequent popping of a cork, the fluid sound of wine slowly being poured into a decanter from an elevated position, the obligatory clinking of glasses and incessant toasts of salute, the animated laughter and conversations of friends, a guitar performance from across the street in the park...

Rafael gently caressed my thigh, rounding out my sensory delight. The hum of activity blended into a symphony of celebration it was impossible not to get caught up in. I was reminded why I was uncomfortable the rare times I had tried to pierce through the social veil of the tapas experience alone. I looked gratefully at my companions for having included me, enabling me to fully enjoy the experience like a local.

Garcia informed me that tardeo is particularly prominent in Spanish cities where the sun's rays are most intense - after escaping the sun's intensity with an almost obligatory siesta, tardeo was apparently an honored awakening rite. He told me that Seville, Malaga, and Valencia are especially renowned for their afternoon celebrations.

As the sun began its descent, casting a warm and golden hue upon the city, the tardeo took on a particularly magical quality. Rafael advised me that the tardeo isn't just a prelude to the evening; it's an event in itself. He shared that for a lot of people, the tardeo morphs seamlessly into the night, with people continuing the festivities at dinner. For others, it's a precursor to a night out, with the lively streets and clubs of Seville pulsating with the rhythms of Spanish nightlife, confirming my observation about Spaniards' high energy levels. Oh, my, I silently thought to myself as I thought I was high energy.

I excused myself to use the washroom. Rafael immediately got up to chivalrously escort me. I was tingly all inside and a little light-headed from my growing amorous feelings. He put his arm around my waist, gently guiding me inside. The interior was gorgeous with beautiful colorful intricate Spanish tiles covering the floor, warm terra cotta walls, a cozy, rustic inviting bar with candles and soft lighting, and an engaging array of plaques with quotes adorning the walls, and, surprisingly, the ceiling.

Rafael introduced me to the proprietor who had immediately approached us with a warm smile and the ubiquitous, welcoming kisses on the cheeks. Juan was a very distinguished-looking man with well-groomed salt and pepper hair and sparkling blue eyes. He seemed a gentle soul with an intriguing combination of a soft, soothing voice and a palpable inviting energetic presence. I was instantly drawn to his easygoing charm and welcoming nature. He immediately made me feel at home - he was a living embodiment of hospitality - a reflection of his genuineness and passion for his life's work.

I anticipated frequenting his establishment as I had now more or less decided to extend my stay in Seville. He excused himself to graciously tend to his patrons as I perused the plaques, curious to know what they said. I was able to appreciate the gist of most of them, but asked Rafael to translate a couple that I was finding particularly intriguing.

The first was, "Life isn't about finding yourself. It's about creating yourself." "Ooh, I love that," I cooed, making a mental note to write it in my journal. "Philosophy of life," Rafael began translating the second one - "I do not understand how nobody has come up with proclaiming "la tapa" the alimentary expression of a lifestyle in which everything is tested, talks a lot, drinks intelligently, and comes to the not easy conclusion of that, in small doses, the world is beautiful."

Dear heavens, I thought, what a perfect encapsulation of Spanish culture and its appeal to me. Although I had always been drawn to the tapa style of dining, I had never thought of it as an expression of the traits of life that I had always admired - the energy, the camaraderie, the variety. "Brilliant," I murmured as I briefly left to wash my hands. I was touched that Rafael was waiting for me when I returned to escort me back to our table. I was giddy with excitement to spend time with Rafael and to immerse myself in my first tardeo.

I was having the best time, basking in the company and the atmospheric terrace before actually eating or drinking anything. I could only imagine how fabulous the experience would be. I realized I was missing my regular weekly call with Olivia as I grabbed my phone to message her so she didn't worry. The task of keeping tabs on me for my family and friends had fallen on her. I lovingly thought of her, knowing I wasn't so easy to keep up with.

I tried to succinctly but poetically grasp the essence of the tardeo in a message to her. Juan's quote about "la tapa" inspired me as I wrote: "It's a ritual that will not only tantalize your taste buds but also leave you with cherished memories of the Spanish art of living life to its fullest." I went on to tell her how early it started and how late it went sometimes. "Oh, boy," Olivia replied immediately. "With your energy levels, maybe Rachel and I need to tag team you. You two start with the tapas and I'll relieve her for the late night festivities," she teased. I smiled as she had quickly summed up the situation. Rachel was definitely more the foodie of the two while Olivia would be more interested in the socializing and people-watching aspects. "It's a plan. I wish you were here now," I conjectured, desperately wishing she were. "Not as much as I do, sister! Enjoy for me too…" she signed off with a kissy emoji.

I flipped through the food menu, forever obsessed with all things food. I appreciated the mix of local and international offerings as well as the combination of traditional and innovative items. Next I turned to the extensive wine list - it was well-detailed and user-friendly, but I was glad to have expert guidance. The staff at the Vineria were not only professional and friendly, but they were also international and multilingual, further adding to my ease and helping to educate me about the various wines and foods they brought.

Juan brought us a chillingly refreshing bottle of bubbly cava - I loved how respectful he was of his staff and how hands on he was. Our waiter, Damario, snapped a photo of our happy group while Juan deftly opened the bottle. The sound of a cork popping never lost its celebratory novelty for me and I smiled approvingly in delight. He endearingly poured me a taste to confirm I was happy with it. I felt shy being the center of attention, feeling everyone's eyes on me. I quickly nodded my head in approval even before taking a rushed gulp to indicate it was fine.

Juan poured the bubbly into my glass, patiently waiting for the effervescence to sufficiently subside to fill it to the top before serving it to the rest of the group. I watched, enamored with the bubbles - never taking their happy brilliance for granted - fondly thinking of the declaration by the monk Dom Perignon that it was like drinking stars. We toasted to new friends and health - I loved how each person in foreign countries clinked glasses with each other and always made eye contact - civility always elevated experiences for me.

Rafael toasted me again, saying "To bucket list experiences." I smiled in return as he kissed me, whispering in my ear, "together." "Together" was one of my favorite words in any language. I squeezed his firm thigh in happy acknowledgment as he gently caressed my exposed back. I had worn a simple but feminine dress with a plunging back - I was able to dispense with a bra, one of the perks of small breasts given the intense Sevillean sun - and I was enjoying Rafael's skin on my skin.

I felt completely blissful, further energized by the vibrant crowd spilling out onto the terrace. The Vineria was full and I realized this tardeo was going to be a lovely and languid affair - precisely as intended. For once, I didn't feel like the outsider, I contentedly realized before sampling the generous bowls of plump green olives and cassava chips that Juan had brought us to accompany our cava. The chips were expertly crunchy on the outside while light and airy on the inside with a side of delectable cilantro lime aioli. I bit my tongue to prevent my customary delight of "mmmmm mmmmm mmmmm mmmm" from escaping my lips, not eager to garner any more unwanted attention from Rafael's friends.

I was in foodie heaven as our tapas started their anxiously- anticipated arrival. Rafael had ordered three of everything so Adriano and Garcia each had their own tapas while Rafael and I shared. The portions were generous and I loved the intimacy of Rafael deciding to share with me. Rafael started feeding me - to my pleasant surprise, my self-consciousness quickly gave way to appreciative desire - Rafael's public affection was adding to my mounting arousal.

We shared an arugula and burrata salad with refreshing cubes of watermelon; a scrumptious flaky Moroccan pastry filled with chicken and almonds; grilled pork tenderloin with pumpkin in curry oil with flash-fried arugula; and grilled Argentinean beef with an addictive mustard sauce. I was soon satiated, but the flavors were so phenomenal I was struggling to resist Rafael's persistent profferings. I pleaded with my eyes for smaller bites, but I was admittedly finding his insistence on feeding me as addictive as the food. Food for me is an act of love and sharing was intensifying my amorous feelings. Although the conversation amongst the four of us was engaging and animated, there were moments I practically zoned out on the friends' presence, singularly fixated on Rafael despite the surrounding boisterous tables. Rafael seemed equally focused on our interactions and amused at my zesty appetite despite my mild efforts at protestation.

I snapped a picture of the splendid array of food for Rachel and of my three companions for Olivia. Olivia responded immediately when she received it. "Oh, my like a Spanish version of "The Three Musketeers," she commented. "More like the three sex-eteers," I teasingly retorted. "Lol. Think of them like gelato flavors and choose your favorite - or sample all," she wink faced emojied me. It was my turn for an "Lol." "Unfortunately, they are all my type. Sigh…" I jokingly joined her teasing, dramatically acting as if I were in a real quandary. "I was thinking of playing musical chairs until there is only one left. Seriously - and fortunately - though, there's a clear winner - no sampling required." I knew my choice with conviction and sent her a photo of Rafael he indulgently let me take.

The knowledgeable waitstaff had expertly paired our tapas with a bottle of white wine - a delicious blend of Garnacha blanca and chardonnay - and a full-bodied zesty red blend of tempranillo, cabernet franc, and syrah. Rafael asked if I had enjoyed my first tardeo and I unhesitatingly declared it had been perfection. Juan beamed at me as he heard my compliment as he approached our table with a small platter of complimentary croquetas del dia - the croquettes of the day. I savored one of the croquetas de pisto - encased in light, crispy panko and filled with a savory combination of mushrooms and herbs.

Just when I thought I couldn't possibly eat another bite, Juan brought two slices of pecan pie for the table. I was practically groaning inside, but couldn't turn it down when

Juan proudly advised that his wife made all of their desserts. I had actually never tried pecan pie and figured I would just take a small taste to try it and be polite. I wasn't a big dessert person but was so grateful I had followed my "why not?" philosophy - it was heaven on a plate and one of the absolute best desserts I ever had. Fortunately, my sincerity was evident as Juan had waited and we exchanged knowing smiles.

I put my head contentedly on Rafael's shoulder. The meal had been one of the most delectable ones I had ever had and the tardeo had been one of the most memorable dining experiences I had ever had. The evening was even more fabulous than my first tapas dinner with Rafael because of the warmth of Juan and his staff. I was confident I would be a repeat customer, but it was the type of place - thanks to the genuine hospitality, caring service, and generous commitment to detail - that would last in my memory forever - even with just a single visit.

I recalled the description of the essence of Spain I had been writing in my head earlier. I realized that the tardeo ritual was a shining example of my description of what distinguished Spanish culture for me. One of the things I had profoundly and immediately felt when I had started visiting Mediterranean countries years prior was how different cultures distinctively prioritized relaxation and social connection. They were gloriously non-negotiable parts of everyday life - they weren't afterthoughts, they weren't enjoyed off chance busy schedules permitted, and they weren't reserved for vacations.

I remembered how shocked I had been when I had found out that some of my law firm colleagues regularly, intentionally skipped taking some of their vacation days - thinking they could "get ahead" that way. Certainly not a way to "get ahead" in life or happiness, I mused. I had always aligned more with cultures that "worked to live" rather than "lived to work" as so many of my American counterparts seemed to. I admired the focus on relaxation and connection all the much more with time as I appreciated how these things were integral to holistic wellness.

To me, Spanish culture was a living, breathing example of the fundamentals of the "essentialism" philosophy I had recently become aware of. Whereas I was used to "essentialism" as a school of thought in contrast to existentialism - the philosophical movement that viewed us as "blank slates" and the masters of our destinies vs. an essentialism belief that our essence is more or less determined - this version that was novel to me was a philosophy akin to minimalism. The philosophy of this essentialism of "less but better," as succinctly summed up by Greg McKeown, resonated with my soul - at least aspirationally.

I, too, had fallen prey throughout most of my life to the stressors and consequences of living life stretched too thin, constantly overextending myself thanks to my people-pleasing persona, and taking on too much in hopes of validating my worth. A pattern not only destined to result in chronic stress and sleep deprivation, but also in psychological and physiological consequences. Like all too many others, I had been dismissive of endless stress and woefully inadequate sleep in quest of pacifying my exes and satiating their desires by working tirelessly. Incessant stress and little sleep were more or less badges of courage in America. I had no interest in losing any more time to regrets, but I was grateful that I now fully appreciated that being dismissive of sleep needs and stress management equated to being dismissive of my holistic well-being, something I was determined to never do again.

Although I knew I hadn't perfected embodying this type of essentialism by any stretch of the imagination, I was grateful that I was aspirationally embracing it as a goal. I smiled, looking around, feeling I was in the perfect context for working towards my goals - one of the biggest advantages of travel was opening one's eyes and mind. Exposure to other cultures was the ideal opportunity to gain a much-needed different perspective of what mattered in life and the Spanish way was exemplary without a doubt.

I glanced at Rafael, who was thoughtfully looking at me, as I had zoned out in contemplation amidst the wonderful chaos of the tardeo. I smiled happily at him before grabbing my journal to conclude my introspection. Although I knew the memories of my tardeo would be long lasting and that it was definitely not my last, I jotted down a few brief thoughts while the experience was still so vivid:

> "The Spanish tardeo is a cultural ritual that encapsulates the spirit of relaxation and social connection. It's a celebration of life's simple pleasures, a tribute to the art of enjoying good company, and a testament to the Spanish philosophy that life is meant to be lived to the fullest. So, the next time you find yourself in Spain, allow the rhythms of the tardeo to sweep you off your feet. Join the locals as they relish the joys of the late afternoon, indulge in delectable tapas, and bask in the warmth of the Spanish sun and camaraderie."

Rafael smiled at me deeply as I put my journal away. He put his hand on my slightly exposed thigh, asking if I were having a good time. "Oh, my, yes, the best," I replied, placing my hand on top of his, and returning his smile with equal intensity. I felt like I was on cloud 9 and dreamily envisioned many more social gatherings like this one to come, until that is that Rafael's friends burst my happy bubble…

******

Chapter 11

Deja Vu

Just as I thought the evening - at least for me and, hopefully, Rafael - was winding down, things suddenly got awkward. "So, Raf tells us you're a corporate lawyer," Adriano commented as he poured me more wine. "Impressive," Garcia chimed in with a complimentary whistle. I paused before responding, thinking the timing of the topic was interesting given my self-contemplation moments before.

"Well, thanks - I guess - but it was never my passion. I was kind of expected to go down that career path and then kind of got stuck in it for a long time. Too long," I looked down, trying to explain my history to myself as much as I was to them. Despite my well-intentioned self-admonition to not drown in regrets, my succinct articulation stung as the stark words highlighted the ludicrous nature of how I had lived my life - that I had spent most of it in pursuit of something I didn't want.

It was embarrassing that I "kind of" followed a path and "kind of" stayed on it because it's what validated me in others' eyes - even though it was never what I wanted. I made it pathetically sound like I had no choice in the matter - the painful truth was that I hadn't felt like I did because my low self esteem and people-pleasing pattern from desperately seeking validation. Way to harsh a woman's buzz, dudes, I thought as I started an unwelcome descent from cloud 9.

I thought it was obvious that I had no interest in discussing the matter. I grabbed my glass, taking a sip, and scanning the crowd, ready to change the subject or leave. "But you made a lot of money," Adriano persisted. "Sounds like a big waste of time and money quitting," Garcia added. I looked at Rafael for support, finding the duos' commentary more intrusive and inappropriate than even their earlier flirtatiousness. He looked away briefly before refilling my glass, remaining silent. I realized he probably thought the wine would calm me, but I was well aware that it would simply add fuel to my smouldering incendiary thoughts. I was disappointed in his silence, but I had no interest in making a scene - out of respect for him and for Juan.

"Well, I didn't find it personally rewarding. I wanted to help people - like the three of you do - not corporations. So I pursued my passions in holistic wellness." I looked at Rafael, proud that I had simply tactfully changed the conversation, but he still averted my gaze. "So what did you do with all the money you made - invest it?" Adriano rudely pursued. I took another sip of wine, negotiating with myself whether I unleashed or remained calm. I figuratively bit my tongue. I was still interested in Rafael and I didn't think it was fair to hold him responsible for his friends' obnoxious behavior.

It took all my determination to maintain my composure. Not only were the topics none of Adriano's and Garcia's business, but they were triggering my insecurities about my self-worth and my decision to leave my professional career for a pursuit that was not only uncertain but also required self-confidence in myself - a realm in which I already had sufficient doubts. I uncharacteristically paused, allowing the awkward silence to linger - while Adriano and Garcia just stared at me - as I willed myself to not let their rude questioning bait me or Rafael's silence to unravel me.

"Actually," I finally spoke, trying to change the subject again, "I was surprised there are gyms here. Fitness centers don't seem to be nearly as prevalent here as they are in the US," I silently patted myself on the back for keeping my cool, ignoring the impolite question instead of reacting hostilely.

"They aren't - most people engage in organic physical activity or simply exercise outside," Garcia noted. "So the gyms here aren't very nice. That's why the three of us want to open up an exclusive gym - it would be a huge success. We just don't have the money for it. It would make a great investment though."

I uncharacteristically continued holding my tongue, withholding that I thought it was a dumb idea and obnoxious that he had the audacity to imply I should fund their dream. Garcia basically admitted there was low demand and that's apparently why no one bothered investing in gyms, yet for some reason he had the gall to expect me - a total stranger - to make a risky investment over an afternoon of tapas.

This time, I reached for the wine bottle to refill my glass as Rafael continued to avert my gaze and remain silent. I felt deja vu like a dagger - the bitter memory of my ex-husband telling me he wanted his own restaurant one of our first nights together, stabbing me anew. Rafael's silence and Garcia's reference to the "trio's" plans was no longer affording me the hopeful assumption that Rafael's friends were being offensive while he was innocently ignorant…

******

Chapter 12

Sprouting- Tranquillo

Olivia always lovingly applauded my baby steps on my healing journey - initially calling me "sprout" and being my greatest cheerleader as I "grew" from a seed. I was never more proud of myself as I calmly and graciously made my exit from the Vineria - admittedly, after downing my last glass of wine, that is. "Well, what do you think?" Garcia probed. "Well, I think it's time for me to leave," I announced as I stood up to emphasize my point. "Tranquillo, tranquillo. Sit down," Adriano commanded as he motioned me to sit.

I stood defiantly, not wavering from his gaze, astounded by his audacity to tell me to calm down and his directive to sit back down. I raised my glass to make a departing toast, notwithstanding that their glasses were empty. "May you all make your dreams come true yourselves," the contempt in my voice, leaving no doubt as to my feelings, as I dramatically chugged the rest of my glass and set it down emphatically in front of Adriano, with a "cheers" and a wink.

It was the first time I truly felt I was "growing" - shedding my past and moving onwards and upwards. The whole evening I had remained composed, thoughtfully responding instead of reacting impulsively from self-doubt and my history of hurt. I walked decisively inside to pay 25% of the bill. Juan looked at me - quizzically, sympathetically - intuitively understanding that I had just been disrespected and was trying to salvage my self-dignity. He refused to accept any money from me, as he wrote his cell number on a business card, insisting I was his guest and that he and his wife were always available to me should I need anything.

Juan was definitely one of my "earth angels" - a designation I ascribed to my dearest friends and the random kind pure souls who reflected the best of humanity - unquestionably providing a spiritual hug of sorts to souls in times of trouble and need. I knew there was no sense arguing with him - I would have offended him had I tried. I meekly thanked him and hugged him with a ferocity I hoped imparted my deep gratitude.

Rafael had followed me in and silently watched my interaction with Juan. He gently smiled but we both remained quiet. I didn't know what part if any he had played in the tacit unbecoming investment request, but we both knew it didn't really matter. He was tainted by association at best. We stood there briefly, awkwardly - Juan protectively hovering nearby in a sweet gesture of support. Rafael finally asked if he could escort me home. I proudly heard myself respond that I preferred to be alone and I was grateful that for once I actually meant it.

I looked at him, lingeringly, trying to absorb the lesson I had just learned, steadfastly maintaining my composure. It was as if I was letting enough time pass to soak up the evening's events and let them pass through me so I could truly leave them behind. I finally hugged Rafael - sincerely but not romantically - thanking him for his hospitality. He stood looking awkward and kind of dumbfounded as I graciously made my exit, thoughtfully accompanied by Juan.

I nonchalantly waved to Adriano and Garcia as I walked past the table, reflecting how little they mattered. Juan escorted me to the garden in a fatherly manner as if to make sure my obvious desire to leave solo was respected. He gave me another much-appreciated hug, a to-go container, and a warm parting smile that I will never forget. Simple, random acts of kindness are priceless I thought as I glanced down, realizing the box was a piece of the pecan pie.

I slowly traversed the Murillo Gardens - alone and gratefully - shockingly - light-hearted. As I made my way "home," I thought of Olivia and how proud she would be of her little seedling sprouted. I smiled as I passed by the statue of the famous explorer, Christopher Columbus, as I realized I was exploring a new version of myself. It wasn't just Olivia who would be proud of me - I appreciatively acknowledged. I was pretty damn proud of myself.

******

I sat on the balcony when I got home, reflecting on the evening as I admired the twinkling lights of sweet Seville. I was all too aware that I was frequently taken advantage of. I refused to be bitter - I simply wanted to get better. I was fully cognizant of my accountability and was trying to figure out how I could stay true to my open, compassionate heart while not falling prey to others. I absolutely refused to be closed off or live in a guarded manner. I wanted to cultivate ways to try to discern people's intentions - I had spent a lifetime taking care of people who were fully capable of taking care of themselves, but chose to rely on me instead.

The evening's events reminded me of a sage admonition by the psychotherapist, Sigmund Freud - a man with whom I shared a birthday and a fascination with dreams. Freud's "prescription" so to speak with respect to the predicaments I seemed to forever be getting into was to not offer help to others unless - at a minimum - they at least ask. His suggestion made me profoundly aware that I was easy prey to manipulation. My romantic relationships may have frequently taken advantage of my generous and loving nature, but I was finally realizing I continually allowed myself to be manipulated. No one ever had to actually solicit my help - my exes had been masters at making their desires clear - knowing that paved the way for getting what they wanted. Nothing more was required since I forever prioritized them while endlessly, foolishly subjugating myself. I wasn't just terrible at saying "no" - no one ever even had to ask for my help.

Rafael's and his friends' gym aspirations had painfully brought Freud's advice to the forefront. The old me would have foolishly entertained the notion of helping Rafael - if not outright jumping right in - as the price of a relationship with him - despite having just met and despite thinking it was a risky venture. Touche, Freud, touche. Score one for healing.

I realized what troubled me most about the unpleasant turn of events was what type of energy or vibe I must have been projecting to have virtual strangers think it was acceptable to ask me for money. Regardless of how much progress I thought I was making, somewhere deep down I apparently still questioned my worth - outwardly signaling that I needed external validation based on what I could give someone else.

I needed to turn inwards - not outwards. My so-called relationships weren't happenstance. I had no interest in playing "victim" or abdicating responsibility for the way my life turned out. It wasn't my responsibility to teach people how to treat me as so many said. It was my responsibility though to not accept what I shouldn't tolerate.

I wasn't upset with Rafael. I looked down at my scarf and laughed. I didn't know what Rafael's story was - and that was a lesson for me unto itself. He was a stranger - I didn't know anything about him. My desire not to be alone was so overriding that I managed to find myself attracted almost instantaneously to anyone who came along. For someone who prided herself on not being superficial, it struck me that I found myself falling so quickly for men without really knowing much about them. I honestly didn't know if Rafael had ever been interested in me or if he had more or less played me. My gut told me that the funding "scheme" was more Adriano's and Garcia's doing and Rafael had succumbed to peer pressure. Rafael had never mentioned wanting his own gym.

With reflection, I realized Rafael hadn't mentioned much of anything. I knew nothing about his background or his family or his values. I didn't know his passions or his dreams. Even his "bucket list" seemed more or less like he was just telling me what he thought I wanted to hear. How could I fall for a guy I knew nothing about? He had been attentive and polite and seemed interested. That's all it took. It was dawning on me that I was always worried if I was enough - so if someone expressed interest, I felt validated, wanted, worthy. It didn't much matter whether I liked the guy or not - I set my bar so low - purport to like me, don't treat me badly, and you're "golden."

I shook my head, grateful that things had fallen apart quickly. I actually was glad that Rafael's friends had been so obnoxiously pushy while he had been determinedly silent. I knew myself well enough that if the trio's actions hadn't been so egregious Rafael would likely be with me now and I would be foolishly considering trying to help him get a gym. I was forever giving everyone the grandest "benefit of the doubt" because I always saw the good in people.

In any event, Rafael was no more to blame for wanting to possibly take advantage of me than I was to blame had I let him. People cannot take advantage of you without your acquiescence, Sofi, I reminded myself, vowing to take accountability. Instead of faulting Rafael, I needed to continue my introspection to truly understand what I was missing to where I would outsource my validation and externalize my worth. If deep down I didn't consider myself worthy for simply being me - instead of what I was able to do for another - no one else was likely to deem me worthy either.

I gently laughed as I twirled my scarf - the gift and the tapas and drinks didn't seem like a fair quid pro quo for a gym. I laughed harder, thinking manifestations can go horribly awry absent precision, as the realization dawned on me that I had wanted to get f—ked that night by Rafael and I more or less just had…

I went back inside to start packing - I wasn't sure where I was going, but I was sure I was going. I knew I would be back to Seville with my friends and I was ready for a change of scenery. I grinned as I came across the large economy size pack of condoms Olivia had given me as a parting gift. Looks like I'm going to be hauling most of them back at the rate I'm going here, I laughed, thinking of regifting them back to her.

I started feeling lonely as I looked at the empty bedroom - I had felt my desire for intimacy mounting since the moment I had met Rafael. I wasn't thinking about him though, I was thinking of Leo. I realized now that Rafael had pretty much just been a hot body - I was missing my oxytocin - the bonding hormone - that I thrived on. I sighed, cramming the box to the bottom of the suitcase. To my surprise, I heard a buzz - like a vibrating noise. I dug the box out to find a tiny vibrating satin pouch tucked amongst the condoms with the words "Love Honey" on it. Sounds like a name I would give someone or use as a code name, I lightly giggled as I opened it with great curiosity.

"Oh, Olivia," I murmured as I realized she had thoughtfully not only equipped me for safe sex but solo sex as well. The pouch contained a very small silver bullet-shaped stimulator. Olivia had even included the battery for heaven's sakes, I chuckled, having identified the source of the mysterious buzzing. "Love Honey," hmmm, I thought as I grinned, immediately getting over any disappointment that Rafael had not come home with me as expected.

I washed up quickly before contentedly crawling into my bed, accompanied by my new toy and thoughts of Leo. Physical pleasure without the risk of the type of emotional pain my exes had caused me seemed like an excellent idea. I was mentally exhausted from my introspection and revelations and I wanted to let my mind pleasantly wander. My imagination was without a doubt my biggest source of arousal. I toyed with Love Honey while letting my mind blissfully replay the night Leo and I had spent together in Marsala.

I shut my eyes while I reminisced about sitting together on the bed, simply gazing into each other's eyes. I felt the warmth of the memory teasingly spreading throughout my body as I started exploring myself, remembering Leo's soft caresses, his tantalizing breath as he sensually whispered in my ears, the passionate pleasure of feeling his skin on my exposed skin, and the heat of his firm body enmeshed with mine. My days of physical pent up desire from anticipation of Rafael, together with my amorous thoughts of Leo, and the expertly-designed Love Honey quickly gave way to a deeply satisfying release of emotions and physical satisfaction. I moaned Leo's name out loud, as I melted with pleasure, feeling a rush of joy and throbbing blood coursing through my body. An ethereal state blissfully took over my mind. "Tranquillo, indeed, a**hole," I thought of Adriano with a happy smirk. The day had certainly not ended as I had anticipated and that was more than fine with me, I concluded dreamily as I peacefully drifted off to sleep.

******

Chapter 13

Confessions

The towering massive cathedral - the "Catedral de Santa María de la Sede" - is one of Seville's most iconic landmarks and a masterpiece of Gothic and Renaissance architecture. Looming majestically over the historic center, it's like a colossal work of art in the heart of the city. As I approached the cathedral, I couldn't help but be overwhelmed by its sheer size. I had read earlier that morning that it is the largest Gothic cathedral in the world and the third-largest church overall. The structure is an impressive 126 meters long and 83 meters wide with a central nave that soars to a height of 42 meters. I had never seen anything quite like it and I was awestruck as I absorbed its grandeur standing in front of it and looking up for the first time.

The cathedral's exterior was a stunning example of Gothic architecture, with intricate facades adorned with countless sculptures and carvings. The central entrance, known as the "Door of the Prince," was particularly striking for its name and magnificent display of biblical scenes and saints.

The part I found the most fascinating was the Giralda Tower piercing the sky adjacent to the cathedral. I knew it had been built as a minaret for the mosque that stood on the site before the cathedral. I loved the co-existence of the different styles and the different religious influences; it reminded me of the Hagia Sophia in Istanbul. I love when history comes alive for me in the present from visual observations; I find it so much more intriguing and memorable than just reading dry historical facts. Observing seamless blending of various cultural influences in architecture and cuisine made me feel like I was able to grasp the true essence of the present and appreciate the imprint of the historical events. The tower itself, a blend of Moorish and Renaissance styles, was a true architectural gem. I climbed the Tower and was rewarded with panoramic views of Seville, providing a unique perspective.

I made my way into the Seville Cathedral after exiting the Tower. I was amazed by its stunning interior and intricate details. The sheer amount of artistic detail was astounding, from the beautiful stained glass windows that saturated the space in a colorful glow to the countless chapels, each with its own unique decoration.

I hadn't previously realized that one of the most famous features of the cathedral is that it houses the tomb of Christopher Columbus. I paused, appreciating that history was truly coming alive for me as I vaguely recalled learning about Columbus and other explorers in grade school. What I remembered more vividly was my fascination with learning about the Native American Indians in school. Columbus may have been a great explorer in the abstract, but it was shocking to me now that he had been portrayed in an almost saint-like manner when I was a child for discovering America. I didn't know what children were being taught in school now, but I hoped the tragic impact that Columbus' expeditions had had on the Indians was no longer being dismissed. A lot of traditions of the Native American Indians resonated with my holistic wellness passion. How sad it is, I mused, that we often lose so much with so-called societal innovations and "advancements."

With my somber reflections, I fittingly moved on to the cathedral's main altar, the "Retablo Mayor," - a masterpiece of Renaissance art. I took my time appreciating the immense gilded structure adorned with intricate religious scenes and statues, mentally comparing the different architectural styles reflected in the Cathedral.

I finished my visit to the Cathedral exploring the charming Courtyard of Orange Trees, a peaceful space filled with fragrant orange trees and fountains. I took a seat to enjoy the perfumed ambiance and reflect on my visit. Other than the mammoth Basilica of St. Francis in Assisi, Italy, I had never explored a cathedral more in depth. I had seen so many cathedrals and enjoyed briefly perusing the architecture, frescoes, paintings, etc., but this visit was a particularly memorable experience. Seville benefitted from such a mix of influences and I thoroughly enjoyed witnessing the visual reflection of this. I loved that the minaret had remained a part of the structure. As if on cue again, the melodious chant of the Muslim "call to prayer" started. I snickered, briefly thinking of Rafael and of Adriano's dictatorial, "tranquillo" - grateful they left my thoughts as quickly as they had entered. I felt a full-body chill as I exited the courtyard, appreciative of the peaceful embrace of different religions, regardless of one's beliefs or affiliations. My timing was fortuitous as I managed to capture a quintessentially representative video of the Cathedral, the Tower with the spiritual chant and iconic Sevillan horse and carriage buggies in the background.

I chose a perfectly-positioned nearby park area to sit down. I took off my sandals to feel the cool and grounding comfort of the earth while taking in the sweet surroundings and my thoughts. My visit to the Cathedral prompted a self-"confessions" of sorts. I knew I had barely known Rafael - he was a complete stranger. I had a tendency to attach so quickly - admittedly too quickly - ridiculously so before getting to know someone. Just because he had been attentive and thoughtful, I had thought he was the be all and end all. I thought so little of myself that I acted as if he were doing me a favor spending time with me.

I thought about "The Art of Happiness," and its wise passages about suffering and admonitions against attachment. My historical relationships had ended so abruptly, so tragically, it seemed - including, of course, losing my parents in the car accident. These were traumatic events of disconnection. I feared being alone to the depths of my soul. I was slowly realizing that my discomfort with solitude was inextricably wrapped up with my unhealed wounds from my prior detachments. I was blessed that my history had never caused me to close off my heart, to be guarded. My desperation to avoid the pain of the past though seemed to be positioning me to desperately attach for the sake of attachment. Rationally, I realized that was a recipe for disaster - desperation isn't a good foundation for a relationship. If I relied on another to fill a void, I would forever be fearful of that person leaving because that would leave me incomplete. I consciously knew I wasn't some half-assed human in need of another to complete me. I had to internalize that though before I could hope for any sort of healthy relationship.

I truly wasn't upset with Rafael - I didn't have a clue what his real intentions were and I had no interest in wasting energy on negativity. I was self-aware enough to know I was projecting my internalized belief that I needed to be needed in order to be worthy - that my conception of my value was my doing - not my simple being. I wanted someone to complement me - not complete me - and I wanted reciprocity in a relationship. I thought about Liam and his endless loving reassurances that I was never alone. I looked around at my peaceful surroundings as I contemplated Buddhist precepts about attachment and connection, concluding I was looking at things wrong.

I needed to expand my conception of intimacy and what it meant to be alone. I was always looking for love in all the wrong places. My endings with my exes had always made me feel discarded, defective. My eager heart was making me laser-focused on romantic interludes to make me feel wanted, not defective - worthy, loved. I wasn't some sort of misfit though that needed external validation of my worth or someone who needed to prove that she was loveable. Liam was right as he oft-repeated, hoping one day I would truly internalize it - I was never alone and I was loved.

Whenever things went awry, my oft-repeated nonchalant response was "live and learn." I grinned, fondly recalling how Liam was always imploring me to "learn" more and "live" less. My thoughts segued to my mom - she had always been resilient with an unwavering belief in herself and that everything would work out one way or the other, hence, no need to worry about it. I loved the saying "All's well that ends well. If it isn't 'well,' it hasn't ended." My mom's perception was more pessimistic while I was an eternal optimist though. She expected things to go badly, but was confident everything would work out, while I optimistically expected things to go well. She was more jaded while I had rose-colored vision. It brilliantly dawned on me out of nowhere that not only did I get my resilience from my mom, but my very name also encapsulated the "live and learn" precept. My mom had chosen my name, "Sofia," which was Greek for wisdom, while "Elan" was French for enthusiastic and assured vigor and liveliness.

I had no intention to "live less" - quite the opposite. I vowed, nonetheless, to focus more on the "learn" part -

and expand my conception of connection a la the Dalai Lama's wisdom. Connection, I mused. I had always struggled with the admonition not to become attached - assuming that meant a life of detachment - something that struck fear in my overflowing, energetic, affection-loving heart. I had been attaching though in an almost parasitic fashion - relying on my partner for my figurative lifeblood. Maybe my exes had used me - casting me aside when they no longer needed me. I couldn't be taken advantage of though without my acquiescence. I had been used because of my need to be used - stemming from my limited, misguided conception of what my worth was. I had been letting others define me.

I needed to focus on positive connections - not clingy, desperate attachments. I thought of his Holiness the Dalai Lama - the epitome to me of profound happiness and deep contentment. "Connection" came in many forms… I was certainly deeply connected with my friends, children, my passions, animals, and with nature, I appreciatively thought as I focused on the coolness of the earth beneath me and the warmth of the sun.

Compassion was also connection with humanity - with each and every soul and creature we encounter. My whole life's purpose now had become a compassionate endeavor of sorts - my mission was to help enhance other people's lives with my writing. A path - I was well aware - I would not be on but for my ex having left me. I thought of Rafael again and my extensive bucket list. I realized it was so lengthy because I had been pursuing my exes' desires, not mine. I wouldn't be able to explore the world or to travel with my friends were I still with my ex. He was jealous and had wanted to circumscribe my life. I had big dreams and ambitions that I would have never pursued had my life remained thusly circumscribed.

I smiled, realizing the irony that I wanted to be a writer - a "scribe" - and that my ex releasing me from that circumscription had been a prerequisite for me to not only become an author but to author my own life. I thought of the "we'll see" parable to not judge when things happen until seeing how they play out - often things that initially seem "bad" set off a chain of wondrous events and eventualities. The famous quote by the beautifully perceptive Helen Keller that when one door closes we often focus on it so hard that we fail to see the door that is open was a wonderful adjunct to the "we'll see" parable. It was also a nod to Buddhist teachings on impermanence - a concept that historically petrified me. I needed to stop focusing on my ex leaving me and embrace the limitless possibilities that wondrously lay before me - enabled by him leaving. I shut my eyes in gratitude, knowing I was progressing.

The "old me" would have funded Rafael's dreams as the price of admission to a relationship with him. I would have clung to him to distract myself from the pain of being alone instead of moving forward to effectuate my own dreams. My ex may have "circumscribed" my life, but until I truly let go of my past, I seemed destined to keep myself imprisoned in a "small" inauthentic, limited world of self-constraints.

I concluded my reflections, realizing that the sun would start setting within the hour and that I was hungry - one thing I could always count on to bring me into the present. I chuckled as I headed towards Plaza de América to enjoy the sun set with the illumination of the fountain. I picked up a "serranito" and a bottle of water from one of the many food kiosks as I made my way to the Plaza. It was known as the city's signature sandwich and I had never tried it before.

I watched Mother Nature's light spectacle unfold while appreciating the lights of the fountain as they illuminated. Nearby, a guitarist was playing sultry Spanish music. I felt as if I were being serenaded as I slowly enjoyed my sandwich - a new favorite, consisting of tender thin-sliced seared pork loin topped with serrano ham, tomato and grilled green pepper encased in a warm and crusty baguette.

What a perfect way to end my last day in Seville, I thought. Now what, I laughed? My feelings for Rafael had impetuously made me think of staying indefinitely in Seville. I had been eager for a lot of affection and a little bit of relative stability. A trio of beautiful men passed in front of me, each of them smiling at me, one winking, and all of them wishing me a beautiful night in Spanish. What is it with Spain and trios, I good-naturedly mused? I was making progress on my healing journey, but the youthful energetic sensual vibe that drew me to Seville didn't seem the ideal atmosphere for me to continue advancing. I wanted to embrace my novel focus on connection over attachment. I knew immersive nature would be the best place to do that and I knew exactly where I was going. I took one last long look at the Plaza, saying a prayer of silent gratitude for my experiences and revelations in Seville before heading home to finish packing and catch up with my friends.

******

Chapter 14

You Are Loved

Liam listened patiently as I briefly updated him about my visit and my plans. I was hesitant to share details about Rafael with him, but I was anxious to hear his thoughts on my recent reflections and revelations. I knew they were fledgling and could benefit from reinforcement.

"May I remind you, hun, of a quote by one of your favorite authors," Liam rhetorically queried, as he continued, "One is loved because one is loved. There is no reason needed for loving." I appreciated him citing words that resonated with me - at least in the abstract - and aspirationally as applied to me. I always lived life like I had to earn love while I forever bestowed it unconditionally on others. I enjoyed his intentional use of "hun," having lovingly, but not so subtly, explained his somewhat esoteric reference to Attila the Hun years before.

The quote was one of many famous quotes by the wise and poetic Paulo Coelho. Liam was a fan of Coelho's as well - we had read "The Alchemist" years prior as one of my "book club" selections for us. I really enjoyed simultaneously reading the same book and sharing our thoughts and we had always had a knack for engaging in hours-long marathon conversations.

Poor Liam I thought, in mild self-criticism for monopolizing "our" book choice. In theory, we had planned to take turns selecting the book to read, but I honestly couldn't think of one time when he had chosen. His selections would have been a little too scholarly for me - his primary goal of reading seemed to be learning. Although I loved reading for learning, the books I read for pleasure tended to be less academic with the primary goal of feeling. I had quickly - unintentionally - adopted a habit of preemptively making recommendations and he had always generously acquiesced.

Our relationship was a reflection of two best friends who truly wanted the best for each other, mirrored in unconditional mutual support and respect. Liam was the one man that had always truly listened to me. He knew me better than I knew myself. "You deserve love merely for your existence," Liam continued, trying to help me internalize Coelho's meaning, which Liam knew all too well, had been lost on me personally for all my life. He had always ended our conversations by saying "you are loved" - he was intimately aware of my low sense of self even before I realized. "Your worth isn't your doing for others, it's your being. Your very essence is love and light. You are the kindest, bravest, most worldly, humble, compassionate person I know."

For once, I let my dear friend continue without interrupting or self-deflecting. "You have the biggest heart, the most sincere smile, and a contagious positive energy for life in general and simple pleasures in particular. You know people gravitate towards you for a reason, and it's not only your damn irresistible natural fragrance," he joked, always telling me that my scent was his kryptonite.

"The problem" - he paused to drive his point home - "...is that you're the worst person I know about being selective about who you share your energy with. There are way too many takers out there with ulterior motives all too eager to take advantage of you and callously discard you at their whim. Of course guys fall for you - that doesn't oblige you to fall back. You need to raise the bar of who you let in, sweetheart. You deserve so much more than you get because your standards are woefully low." His words slightly stung despite his pure loving intentions and the kind way he had communicated them. I silently acknowledged that he was right as pent up bitter tears of regret and self-pity started unexpectedly streaming down my face.

Liam had a way of sparking necessary self-reflection in me, but oftentimes it took a really long time for me to fully absorb his advice. This wasn't one of them - probably because all of the time I had spent in solo contemplation just hours prior as well as already over the last months. My thoughts immediately went to GiGi - the precious little angel who had stolen my heart so spontaneously - in large part, I suddenly realized, because of personal traits akin to the ones that Liam had just identified in me.

It hit me like a thunderbolt thinking of GiGi like a mini me. I could never stand for this precious child enduring the type of narcissistic, materialistic-inspired, self-absorbed nonsense I had. If happiness is the purpose of my life, how could I stand for anything less for myself than I would for her beautiful soul? GiGi was like a reflection of my younger innocent self - before the negative limiting beliefs had developed. I had a bad habit of frequently thanking romantic partners when they told me they loved me - like they were doing me a favor and I owed them. I would apologize if someone rudely bumped into me - as if I were apologizing for my existence.

I wanted Liam to be proud of me and I was determined to take his words to heart. "I'll channel my inner Harvey Specter," I promised my dear friend, sharing the quote from the "Mad Men" character: "Ever loved someone so much, you would do anything for them? Yeah, well make that someone yourself and do whatever the Hell you want."

"Now that's going to be a long tattoo," I laughed. My burgeoning self-pity quickly transitioned to self-determination as I resolved to change the course of my life - thanks to Liam's pointed honesty and forthrightness. That's the thing about best friends - they always have your back when you fall; they catch you, but, equally importantly, they help ground you and propel you forward.

I knew Liam was right and that I had more work to do on myself - it's why I had reached out to him - he was always a great benchmark for me as to how I was doing objectively. We segued to lighter topics before I brought up our book club, inquiring if he had gotten George Sand's "Indiana" yet. He laughed, replying "No, no I haven't. I think it's my turn, don't you think?" I laughed back, not only acknowledging that he was he more than entitled to pick, but also admitting I hadn't had a chance to delve into "Indiana" yet any way.

"Ok, so what's it going to be?" I sighed in feigned exasperation, curious as to what his selection would be and hopeful it would be something not too academic or dense. "Meditations," Liam replied matter-of-factly, signaling his long-awaited pick was not up for debate. "Ooh," I practically cooed. "Perfect, I applaud your inaugural choice." Liam laughed at my humorous "inaugural" designation since we had been reading "together" for decades. I told him I was excited - I truly was looking forward to reading Marcus Aurelius' seminal work. Liam's choice really was perfect - I had wanted to learn more about stoicism for a while now and I was trying to embrace meditation in my life. It also was not lost on me that, although the book was more academic than I likely would have chosen, it synced with my philosophical nature. Liam knew I had been a philosophy major - we had talked extensively about philosophy over the years - and he knew I would be happy with his choice.

I promised to keep in good touch as we got off the phone and I called Olivia, making good on my promise to keep her apprised of my whereabouts. I summed up recent events - with a little more expansive detail about Rafael than I had shared with Liam - before discussing my contemplations and revelations. Not surprisingly, she immediately echoed my sentiments while generously applauding my progression.

"You want to complement someone, not complete them. You've always been filling voids in others. Your marriages have been hole-y more than holy," Olivia chuckled at her humorous delivery of advice. "You fill in other people's holes because you've always defined your worth as giving. It makes sense that you attract takers. Takers are always going to take so givers have to be vigilant to stop the cycle. You have such a good and generous heart and a giving soul. You struggle to realize that not everyone is like you. There will always be people willing to take advantage of you if you let them."

We segued to the pleasantries of Seville and my plans before concurring that we missed each other and needed to plan a joint trip to Seville soon. I got off the phone, comforted and buoyed by the warmth of my friends. I remembered one more promise - one I had made to myself - to expand my conception of intimacy. Even if I couldn't fulfill my heart's desire to explore a romantic relationship with Leo, that was no reason not to stay connected to the Valentinis even from afar. They were genuinely good people who had made me feel at home. I thought of GiGi, determined to find a way to stay in her life - in all of their lives.

My heart warmed, fondly thinking of her innocent, open, effusive nature. She was like a welcome torrential downpour of unapologetic, exuberant expressiveness. It dawned on me that I was borderline embarrassed and apologetic for the vulnerable, brave expressive traits I found so appealing in others - witness my insecurities about sharing my effervescent bucket list litany the first night Rafael and I had shared tapas. I had worried I was boring him or "taking up too much space." I wasn't used to being listened to in romantic situations - always shrinking to let my partner bask in the spotlight.

Whether Rafael had genuinely been interested or not didn't matter. Whether he had feigned interest for a financial or sexual ulterior motive - or perhaps both - shouldn't matter. I was finally "finding my voice" - something that naturally came to GiGi - to most children. If someone didn't care to listen to me, that wasn't a reason to suppress my voice - as I had habitually done most of my life in romantic relationships. It was a reason to move on. I needed to stop letting others dictate my perceptions, my behaviors.

I needed to be more like GiGi - more childlike. I loved her energy, her enthusiasm for life. Yes, when I "grow up," I laughed at myself, I want to be just like GiGi. I knew if I thought about it too much, I would talk myself out of it so I grabbed my phone to send my last message of the day. A simple "Thinking of all of you warmly and hoping everyone is doing well," should suffice, I thought as I typed my message to Isabella.

I paused before sending. Hmmm, maybe a tad too distant. I added "baci e abbraci" - the rhythmic expression for kisses and hugs in Italian. I only hesitated for a moment, contemplating if I should limit it to a singular "a kiss and a hug," before deciding to keep the plural. I hastily added "from Spain" though to the warm sign off before hitting send. It served two purposes in my head, making it subject to a more impersonal interpretation as well as not looking like I was trying to be mysterious as to my whereabouts.

I was starting to internalize my Buddhist contemplations, I gratefully thought. Buddhism wisely noted that overthinking - something I was always quick to point out in others - was also a source of unnecessary suffering. Here I was querying whether a simple expression of affection would be off putting in some way. "Mamma Mia," I said out loud, warmly thinking of GiGi and Gabriele, "Definitely enough thinking for the day for sure."

I finished packing, checking my messages before going to bed. I was hoping - more than I cared to admit - that I would hear back from Isabella although it was late and I had only recently messaged her. Fortunately, I got distracted, deeply touched and grateful to see that Liam had already sent me a copy of "Meditations." I decided to read a few pages before going to sleep. I was pleasantly surprised that the beginning of the book focused on gratitude. Seemed like the perfect way to what had been a lovely day, notwithstanding my unexpected change of plans and deep reveries. I drifted off to sleep thinking of Helen Keller's proverbial new "door of opportunity" as I fittingly focused on dreaming of the dreamy landscapes I knew awaited me the next day.

******

PART III

GORGEOUS GAUCIN - NATURE BECKONS - ALWAYS

Chapter 1: Tantric Masseuse

Chapter 2: Relieved & Refreshed

Chapter 3: No Such Thing as TMI - Again

Chapter 4: Recharged

Chapter 5: Sharing: The Art of Tapas

Chapter 6: Revelations in Ronda

Chapter 7: Tantalizing Tapas & Tantric Talk

Chapter 8: Yogic Sleep

Chapter 9: You're Never Alone

Chapter 10: Now What?

******

Chapter 1

Tantric Masseuse

I normally enjoyed train rides - a stress-free way to have a scenic journey. My trip from Seville to Gaucin, however, was anything but enjoyable, stress free, or scenic. I tried in vain to concentrate on the countryside vista. I just couldn't shake the feeling that something was "off" with me - way off. I had been trying to enlist "mind over matter," but I was failing woefully. I was getting worse, not better. I had had a fitful night of sleep - unable to stop thinking of Leo and "reading into" the fact that Isabella hadn't responded to my message. I was the one who apparently was "out of sight, out of mind," as far as the Valentinis were concerned - I had gotten that completely backwards. I was embarrassed that I had messaged - especially with the warm "kisses and hugs" sign off. Ugh, stupid woman, I thought, slapping my forehead as if my mental castigation needed physical emphasis. Leo didn't care, Rafael didn't care, my ex didn't care - no one wanted me, I concluded in a spiral of wallowing self-pity.

To make matters worse, I felt like I had some sort of virus I was desperately trying to conquer. I was feverish, faintish, weak, and exhausted. I tried to convince myself that I was just tired; I had been running myself ragged and barely slept the night before. I just need to catch up on some rest, I tried ineffectually to console myself, tears welling up in my eyes with the all-too-familiar pain of heartache beginning to take control in my chest. I started feeling nauseous and began sweating profusely. I didn't know if I were physically sick or just making myself sick - the origin didn't seem to matter much as there was nothing to do. I glanced around, criticizing myself for likely being dehydrated and not having bothered to bring water with me. How did I manage to get into these situations, I continued disparaging myself, bitterly and unproductively.

I tried breathing slowly, placing my hands over my heart - willing the calming heart coherence that had come to me so easily before to take over. "Gratitude, gratitude, gratitude," I silently - unconvincingly - recited, thinking of the excerpts I had read in "Meditations" the night before. My thoughts segued to Liam. I glanced down to acknowledge it was the middle of the night in the US. I wasn't proud that I needed a "safety net" of sorts, but there was no way I would let myself disturb him in the middle of the night. I thought of Olivia, knowing she wouldn't want me to hesitate to reach out. I didn't want to disturb her either and I sensed that I was more in need of the type of relatively direct, "harsher"- though equally loving - response I would get from Mike given my current emotional state.

I was the moron who had foolishly decided to up and leave the comfort and safety of the familiarity of my friends and surroundings - of my job. Ugh, I thought, don't go down that path, I implored myself. I truly couldn't bring myself to wake them in any event. Besides, regardless of how much they desired or tried to console me, they couldn't magically undo my literal reality - I was alone, all alone. "Alone" replaced "gratitude" on repeat in my head as I moved my futile hands from my heart to cup my throbbing, aching head in a visual show of despair to match the turmoil inside.

I was furious with myself for reaching out to the Valentinis - just when I thought I was making progress, I self-sabotaged, bringing my pain and strings of regret front and center. I thought of Rafael - less forgivingly than the day before - juxtapositioned with thoughts of my ex. I may have dodged a bullet with Rafael but I had squandered precious time with my ex. Had I met Leo sooner in life, things could have been so different, I ruminated - unable to muster the strength to channel Buddhism wisdom not to. Why didn't I just let it go, I rhetorically pondered.

I was unpleasantly shocked how I appeared to be deeply entangled in a tailspin of negativity - bordering on panic and existential crisis - in sharp contrast to the prior day's positivity and perspective. Ugh, I wryly thought - one step forwards and seemingly five steps back - par for the friggin' course. I knew healing wasn't linear, but I was feeling uncharacteristic despair and pessimism. I wanted to shift my mood by sheer will but it was nowhere to be found. I was mentally and physically shaky; the nausea was comprehensively intensifying - mentally and physically. I felt all alone - again - despite the real progress I thought I had been making - the reality of my circumstances washing over me in waves of queasiness.

You don't feel all alone, Sofi, I chastised myself, not even allowing myself to sit relatively comfortably in my self-pity. You are all alone - in a foreign country where you don't speak the language. You have no insurance, no income, no acquaintances, and no sense. My self-recrimination intensified along with the terribly unpleasant nausea, fueled by my feverish head and now full-on panic mode. What were you thinking, silly girl? You weren't - you weren't thinking at all. A dialogue of negativity and judgment was now ping-ponging in my throbbing head, my efforts at calming down utterly ineffectual. At least if I were going to die, I would be ending life somewhere pretty, I tried consoling myself as the gorgeous vistas passed by as the train approached my stop.

My decision to up and leave the life I knew seemed like a terrible idea all of a sudden. And not in that wondrous, mischievous, tantalizing way a la one of my favorite lines from the movie, "Under the Tuscan Sun," - "Terrible ideas - don't you just love them?" This felt like a terrible idea simply in a truly terrible way. I felt like I was completely unraveling from the day before. I scoffed derisively at myself as my inevitable struggle with my oversized luggage was approaching, my trademark energy and mental fortitude stubbornly refusing to be summoned. "You weren't exactly 'raveled' to start with, foolish, impetuous woman," I chided myself for the umpteenth time that day.

I mustered all the mental focus and physical strength I could as I weakly made my way to the vestibule to collect my luggage. Ugh, wtf, I thought in a Murphy's Law visual moment. The vestibule was filled with teenage school children who were too self-absorbed to see me wrestling with my luggage, struggling to procure my oversized bag that was - of course - on the bottom of the luggage space overflowing with heavy and cumbersome luggage. It was neither the first nor last time that I seriously contemplated just leaving my luggage. I thought of Rafael for a second, feverishly, fervently wishing he were there to help me navigate my predicament. I scoffed at myself again - this time for thinking I needed anyone but myself. My trademark resilience rose to the occasion - making a brief last minute appearance, as I yanked with all my might to finally get my luggage just in the nick of time - ungracefully, precipitously exiting the train with my odd assortment of luggage as the doors were enveloping it.

Thank God, I had arranged for a transfer from the station to my Airbnb in the center of town I thought. Score 1 for uncharacteristic planning, I thought, before looking up at my apartment on arrival. To my surprise - and chagrin simply due to my immediate circumstances - it was a four-story townhouse. Normally, my first impression would have been "delightfully charming," but the thought of four flights of stairs was completely alarming at the moment. I left my luggage immediately by the front door, practically crawling up the steep, narrow, twisting stairs to the second floor and crashed in a slump on the bed. I knew I needed water but I didn't care about that or anything. It had taken all my strength to get into bed and I wasn't moving.

I spent the rest of the day in bed followed by a troubled night tossing, turning, and sweating feverishly. I knew by then that I wasn't just in emotional anguish - I truly was fighting a virus. For me not to care one iota about food was clearly indicative that I was physically ill. I awoke the next morning still ill and weak and dehydrated but I felt like my body could begin to get the upper hand if I tended to it. I walked slowly into town, buying a large bottle of water at a small local store.

I slowly started sipping it to rehydrate while looking for a pharmacy - for what I didn't know - not even in English - and most certainly not in Spanish. I needed a magic elixir to miraculously cure whatever indescribable ailment was consuming my body and mind. I had no clue what was wrong with me or what I needed but I knew I needed something. The surrounding landscape appeared to be stunning but I was too laser focused on my mission to pay any attention to it. I intuitively knew I was pretty bad as my body was desperately trying to combat something.

For the first time in my life, I still wasn't hungry, despite not having eaten for over a day. I was relieved that I had gotten my wits about me sufficiently to focus exclusively on my physical condition. I wasn't wasting any precious energy on my emotional state. I realized I hadn't even charged or checked my phone as I stumbled into a store that looked promising, "La Pura Vida," - a natural health type store I optimistically hoped. ... or, perhaps - I briefly hesitated as I saw the green leaf logo on the door - some sort of cannabis shop. I'll try anything at this point, I resigned as I timidly entered.

Fortunately, my optimism was rewarded - as it so often is - and I was pleased to feel my sense of gratitude returning. I breathed a sigh of relief as I started scanning the shelves for herbal inspiration as to what could help cure me of whatever mysterious illness needed cured. The elderly, sweet-looking proprietor saw my disheveled and frazzled appearance as I was attempting to translate a brochure in Spanish, eventually realizing it was for massage services before I put it back down. She followed my glance and immediately summed up the situation.

"You are ill, no?" she questioned, the tone in her voice leaving no doubt as to the answer, as she placed her hand comfortingly on my shoulder, picking up the little pamphlet. I merely nodded yes. I had a lump in my throat and tears began welling in my eyes - her evident compassion was appreciated but somehow brought my "aloneness" front and center again. I was sick, I didn't know what to do, I needed help, I desperately wished I weren't alone in a foreign country, and I wanted my mom. The kind proprietor's solicitousness was as close a solution for all of that than anything else at the moment.

"This - massage. Help," she quietly, haltingly spoke in English, jabbing at the massage advertisement as if that summed up all that needed to be communicated. I didn't understand the nuances of the Spanish language on the flier and was far from expectant that a massage was going to cure me. I nodded my head in affirmation, too weak to disagree and too desperate not to trust proffered help. The maternal woman took down my number and address and arranged an appointment for me in a few hours. I thanked her in Spanish before more or less crawling back home to crash in bed again - after plugging my phone in and setting an alarm to make sure I didn't miss my appointment.

I was in deep sleep when my phone vibrated. I awoke disoriented, taking a minute to realize where I was. I gingerly made my way down the stairs, summoning all my strength to walk the short distance to my massage. I was relieved that I was feeling a little better, thanks to the rest and hydration. As I opened the door, I was startled to be greeted by a young man in his mid-20s. He seemed almost mystical, like a wizard in my still mildly feverish haze. I strongly felt that I had met him before but couldn't place him. He was tall with a solid build and his arms and legs were clearly extremely muscular. He had curly hair tied up in a bun and soft brown lipid eyes. He was carrying a number of bags that he set down to offer a handshake. I pulled away trying to explain in Spanish that I was ill and didn't want to get him sick. I didn't think I had anything contagious but figured why risk it.

"Yes, Sofia. I know, I'm here to care for you. Javier," he confidently introduced himself in a soulful voice, as if the mere introduction was synonymous with an explanation for his presence - as well as guaranteed healing - as he took my hand and reassuringly squeezed it. "Oh," I stammered, trying to make sense of the confusing circumstances, but immediately starting to feel better with his soothing voice and calming presence.

"Are we going to La Pura Vida?" I inquired as I stepped out of the apartment and started to close the door behind me. "No. We will do the massage here," he informed me in a gentle tone. "Oh," I stammered, my initial comfort quickly transitioning to suspicion. "Oh, ohh," I repeated and drawled, not managing anything other than monosyllabic words. I tried assessing the situation and the advisability of letting him in. I glanced at the bags having no clue what they were for but knowing there certainly wasn't a folded up massage table in there. "You have a bed, no?" his calm demeanor remained intact as he answered my unspoken query. "Well," I started, unsure how to proceed but too desperate and weak to think straight or protest. "Yes," I replied meekly as Javier basically turned me about face and guided us and the bags forward, gently but commandingly.

I planted my feet solidly at the entrance, trying to decide - with what little presence of mind and energy I had left - whether it was safe to rely on the store's proprietor. Javier's presence felt oddly immediately comfortable; I intuitively trusted him and the kind woman from La Pura Vida and went with the flow. Javier started taking out the contents of his bags and putting them on the countertop of the small kitchen. There was an assortment of vegetables and to my even greater surprise a lobster that fortunately had already seemed to have met its demise; I would never be able to cook one or even observe it. Wait, why am I thinking of cooking methods? Why does he even have a lobster? Did the flier say something about a massage and clambake? Am I hallucinating?

My feverish head started throbbing as I tried making sense out of the odd circumstances. I felt like I was in a Dr. Seuss book, a bit overwhelmed but confident the ending would be good. Is he going to massage me with the claws?

What's happening here? I was trying to make sense of the situation in my fiery head as Javier kept unpacking. Finally, I noted with relief some items that made sense - massage oil, creams and hand towels - and then incense. I looked at Javier quizzically, silently, head tilted like a puppy, trying to understand the odd assortment. My concerned initial thoughts transitioned into hope that somehow this mysterious man and his hodgepodge of items would miraculously heal me.

"First, massage. Second, I make soup," the sensual sorcerer summed up as if that answered all my questions. "I, I, didn't order any of this," I falteringly stammered, wondering if this were some sort of comprehensive Spanish take on Uber. I felt lightheaded, as if I really were mildly hallucinating - before I transitioned to giddy - Iberian Uber sounded like a catchy name to me. What a great business idea - tapas-style Uber Eats meets Uber home spa. Hmmmm, "soup and sex" - what an interesting combo. I started wildly imagining various du jour "specials of the day" for the novel business. I started giggling at the nonsensical rambling thoughts streaming through my head.

"No worries," Javier asserted with a mild look of concern on his face, having clearly observed that I was a bit delusional though we had just met. Or had we? "I feel like we've met," my fever loosened my normal introverted inhibitions and made me conversational. "Oh, yeah, mucho gusto, nice to meet you," I giggled, "…if we haven't already." Javier simply responded by carefully guiding me up the stairs from behind with one hand, clutching a couple of the bags in the other.

"Eschuchame, listen to me," I was belatedly trying to respond to Javier's "no worries" assessment. I could not stop my giddy giggling and suddenly felt confident with my elementary Spanish. "Easy for you to say dude," I started, locked and loaded, poised to go into the litany of reasons why I should be worried. I kept my mouth shut as I started silently inventorying what I should worry about - like having impetuously left my career and the United States for the complete unknown of foreign lands, and the fact that I was leading a strange man to my bed. I laughed, appreciating that this last decision was probably the wisest of the three. I obligingly started making my way up the stairs to the bed, having forgotten my elaboration of things to panic about, as Javier confidently, comfortingly, continued directing me from behind.

When we got to the bedroom, I glanced around realizing Javier had brought a whole lot of things but notably no sheet or anything to cover me up with - I didn't want to stain the bedding with oils. I giggled again, realizing at least that there was no lobster in sight. "Prepare," he directed, pointing towards my clothes as he went into the bathroom to wash his hands and soak the towels he brought in hot water. "Prepare for exactly what?" I softly chuckled rhetorically as I obliged, grabbing a towel, undressing - except for my panties and bra- and laying down on my stomach. I tried covering as much of myself as I could with one of the tiny towels Javier had brought. "Brava, Sofi," I sarcastically applauded myself as if the tiny towel and my adamantly-remaining lingerie were going to be of any protective use if protection were necessitated. I released another round of feverish giggles into the pillow - I wasn't the least but scared - just a lot confused.

When Javier returned, he lit the incense - it smelled like an alluring and relaxing combination of amber and lavender - before placing one of the towels that smelled of sandalwood near my head - fortuitously a fragrance that I always found deeply soothing. He removed the towel and unhooked my bra unceremoniously before placing one of the warm towels on my shoulders, gently pulling my panties down to place another over my buttocks. My body suddenly tensed, instinctively trying to resist the relaxed state of mind I had started to feel to my surprise.

Javier turned on some meditative trance chant-like music on his phone before asking me if I had ever experienced a tantric massage before. "What?" I groaned, my shoulders bolting up, knocking the towel off and exposing my breasts. He repeated the question as if my "what?" had simply indicated I hadn't heard him. "I, I," I began stammering again, "I didn't order that either." My response left no doubt that not only had I never experienced a tantric massage, but I wasn't expecting to now either. "Relax," Javier commanded, as he gently pushed my shoulders back on the bed, replacing the warm and comforting towel on my shoulders. "Easy for you to say, dude," I silently thought again as I obligingly sunk deeper into the bed. "No worries," I repeated, my favorite "we'll see" parable, commanding me to relax and try to make the best of the situation. Whatever the situation was - I broke out into another irrepressible fit of giggles - as I thought of what my facial expression must have looked like when Javier had pulled out the lobster. Hmmm, not "Iberian Uber Eats Meets Uber Spa" - simply alliterative, "Topless Tapas," I renamed the hypothetical business erupting in another childlike bout of laughter. I tried to stifle myself in the pillow as I tried contemplating what a tantric massage was and whether or not I did indeed desire one after all.

I was vaguely aware that "tantric" had a place in Indian yogic practice - or something ancient - I was clearly not at my most lucid. I had only exclusively associated it with sex though. I remembered getting a little tantric sex position "guidebook" as one of my bridal shower gifts eons ago for my first marriage. I groaned, racking my brain to try to remember whatever else I could about tantric practices beyond the cirque du soleil type acrobatic positions I vividly remembered.

Javier's presence was having a soothing impact on me despite my racing, nonsensical thoughts. The incense and the towels were helping me relax almost against my will; a blissful ethereal type lightness had replaced the prior throbbing, faint-like feelings in my head. I burrowed my face into the pillow deeper in grateful realization this time that Javier had placed one of the scented tiny towels over it, my giggling fit had subsided but had fortunately served to dissipate a lot of my mental and physical tension.

 I didn't know what to expect, but I felt extremely relieved and grateful. I didn't want to be alone and ill. This mystical man's energy was having a positive impact on me and I decided to embrace whatever was happening - except for sex. Well, at least I think… Hmmm, I started negotiating the pros and cons with myself in my head, as my body pleasantly started melting under Javier's touch. It would be a release of another kind… I started to giggle again and bit my lip to stop.

I tried to let go and heed Javier's command to relax as he took the towel off my shoulders and started massaging me with the massage oil he had warmed between his hands; it smelled like ylang ylang, another deeply comforting oil I frequently used. I felt my fever dissipating, my thoughts slowing, my body starting to release, and I started drifting in and out of an almost hypnotic trance between consciousness and subconsciousness. Our breath patterns magically started rhythmically syncing as Javier continued to massage me. I felt like I was hallucinating but I didn't care. I didn't know what was happening or what would happen, but I was all in at this point as I felt Javier's magical hands start to release the grip of whatever virus I had been combatting.

Javier slowly, tenderly moved down my back. As he removed the towel and started massaging my buttocks, he began chanting and I started silently echoing the chant in my head. I had never meditated with anyone before and whatever was happening felt like a powerful meditation. I was used to having my buttocks and breasts massaged in other countries so the placement of his hands neither surprised nor troubled me. Javier confirmed the pressure was fine as he massaged my buttocks, hips, and hamstrings in a flowing, circular, assertive manner. I murmured yes as I involuntarily sighed in multiple releases. I knew we hold a lot of emotions in our hip area and I felt myself sinking deeper into the bed and into a trancelike state as Javier massaged me with increasing pressure.

He had stopped chanting and started sharing details with me about the origins of tantric massage in his soft, soothing, soulful voice. Javier had quickly understood that I was embracing the massage despite my initial halfhearted protestations and trepidation and seemed eager for me to understand tantric practices. His voice was so peaceful, so melodious. I couldn't pay attention to what he was actually saying - it was like the "wah, wah, wah" sounds used to depict the teacher speaking in the animated cartoon, Charlie Brown.

I was interested but incapable of giving his explanation the attention it deserved. I was exclusively focused on the rhythm and tone of his deeply resonating voice which kept me in a relaxed fluctuating state between consciousness and "awakened" subconsciousness. I felt my mind, body, and spirit in fluid, comforting alignment like nothing I had ever experienced. I didn't understand what was happening, but, for once, I didn't really care and I certainly didn't want it to stop. I was blissfully centered in my body and out of my head - as if my mind had finally relinquished control, making way for the wisdom of the body to work its magic under the abracadabra touch of this talented tantric wizard. To my amazement and relief, I felt more at peace than I ever had.

Javier gently guided me to turn over, placing a warm, scented towel over my eyes. He started massaging my neck and I felt years of deep-seated tensions gloriously begin to melt away. I was in such a dreamlike state - I was only mildly cognizant when he informed me - seemingly randomly - that he had been celibate for several years. I had no idea if he was hinting for an award or a reward…

I inwardly groaned mildly - ugh, here it comes, my mental faculties disappointingly re-engaged. This was the most elaborate and bizarre lead up to a pick up I had ever heard. He gently whispered that he would be honored to break his celibacy with me if I so desired. "What was written in Spanish on that flier that I couldn't translate at La Pura Vida?" I thought to myself. "What the heck kind of package had I ordered? I can't wait to tell Olivia about this." A stream of consciousness thoughts started barraging my startled head as I meekly fought to stay on this side of consciousness in my dreamlike state. My mind was startled but my body stayed paralyzed. "Hmmm," I simply responded in a non-committal manner as Javier moved down to my breasts.

"Celibacy, of the intentional variety…," Javier thoughtfully started to explain his proposition in a serious manner. I lost it. Totally lost it. I broke out in uncontrollable laughter again, giggling like an unruly young child. Whether it was my slightly feverish nature, not knowing what to expect or how to respond, or my suspicion that his decision to suddenly abandon his years-long celibacy was some unique pick up line - I found his introduction unbelievably comical. "Celibacy, of the intentional variety" vs. someone who just couldn't "get any" struck me as extraordinarily funny at the moment.

Ironically, my introduction to tantric practices - that are characterized by thoughtful control - was defined by uncontrollable laughter. I'm all for celebration, but certainly hadn't anticipated signing up for celebrating the cessation of someone's celibacy when I had booked my massage. Fortunately, Javier "read the room," taking my reaction as a sign that now was neither the time to try to educate me about tantric practices nor the place to discuss his celibacy.

My mind started drifting away again as my body continued its relative state of immobility under Javier's masterful manipulation. He was definitely sensual but he wasn't my type per se. I had had no expectation of sex in my current state, not to mention he was a stranger and my masseuse. I had no clue whether it was due to my breaking fever, my comfort from not being alone, his soothing voice, his supernatural hands, or his solicitous nature, but I was starting to feel an undeniable longing - despite my initial assessment. I still had no intention of having sex - it wasn't sex that I longed for but an intimate connection. I had every intention though of otherwise fully enjoying the unique experience - it was a union of beautiful energy unlike any I had ever experienced or even could have ever imagined.

Javier seemed to have taken my lack of a clear "yes" to his offer as a no. It was obvious to us both that I was profoundly content though and no longer the slightest bit resistant to his touch as he worked his way down my abdomen to my upper thighs. Javier had pulled my panties up before I had turned over and I was relieved they had remained that way.

My mind and body were simultaneously melting under Javier's touch. I could feel all of the places where I normally store tension - my neck, my jaws, my shoulders - unclenching - the only thing that remained clenched was my pelvic region. As Javier rubbed my inner thighs, I started to brace in an effort to tamp down my mounting intensity. He politely moved down to my calves in a tacit acknowledgment. His physical pressure was unblocking knots of anxiety and his lack of pressure to have sex was making my mind deeply relax.

My calves were so tight, I kept jerking at his touch - he was on the precipice of literally being kicked out of bed accidentally. Javier liberally applied more massage oil before working all my tension out with long fluid, rhythmic strokes as he began chanting again. He excused himself to wash his hands after he had spent a blissfully long time on my lower body. I sunk further into the bed in a blissful voluntary-like quagmire as I sighed expansively, involuntarily again. I felt completely destressed - mind, body, and spirit - like never before. I wanted more though - of what I was unsure - of as I started letting myself slip back into a trancelike nirvana state.

Javier's return was nearly imperceptible to me in my dreamlike state. He started massaging my head and neck, something I find simultaneously extraordinarily pampering and erogenous. The tingles gloriously ran down my spine as I could feel myself release from head to toe.

Javier bent down to whisper in my ear, inquiring if I felt good. My whole body shivered from his warm breath as I nodded my head and purred my satisfaction. To my surprise and delight, my massage was not over, as Javier warmed more massage oil between his hands before starting on my feet. Good lord, what is this going to cost, I thought for a brief second before burrowing more into the bed, intuitively knowing I was about to enjoy the best reflexology - my absolute favorite. Cost wasn't the priority at this point. Peace is priceless, I assured myself.

Between my dreamy state and Javier's masterful touch, I started drifting hard towards a subconscious state. Javier started chanting again. I started writhing, slowly at first, trying to suppress the growing tension in my pelvic region. The effect of his massage on my feet was like a splendid slow tease that was driving me into a sexual frenzy no matter how hard I tensed to try to stop it.

I wasn't even fully cognizant of what Javier was actually doing with my feet. I was entranced by the connection his hands seemed to have to my pelvis in a paranormal way as I felt the undeniable build up to a mounting explosive orgasm. I opened my eyes to glance down and confirm he was indeed still only touching my feet. I paradoxically simultaneously felt intensely numb and alive; it was as if I were paralyzed with prolonged ecstasy; I felt like I was about to spontaneously combust. I shut my eyes as Javier quietly - sensually - commandingly implored me to let go.

I needed no further encouragement as I felt a cataclysmic release unlike anything I had ever enjoyed before. I was all electrical tingles; I felt a deep shiver while a fiery warmth spread throughout my body. I opened my eyes to look at him as if to confirm this mind-blowing, body-blowing experience was truly happening. He stared directly deeply into my eyes as he continued to work miracles on my feet. I was already clenching and convulsing as I experienced another gush of orgasmic waves rippling through my body purely from the direct intensity of his gaze. I gasped in a full-body release as I slowly regained control of my involuntarily gyrating body. It was the most cathartic experience I had ever had. Javier seemed completely unfazed by what happened. He quietly slipped away to wash his hands as I lay panting, the blood still coursing through my body in rhythmic waves, my light-headedness now from my "sexual" release. I was simultaneously exhausted and exhilarated.

******

Chapter 2

Relieved & Refreshed

Javier told me to rest while he made soup. Who is this amazing sensual sorcerer chef I briefly mused before immediately falling profoundly asleep, as he exited the room. I awoke about an hour later. I felt worlds better but still weak. I realized I hadn't eaten for over a day as an enticing fragrant smell of soup wafted from below. My tummy growled in appreciative anticipation as Javier timely opened the door to check on me. "Great. You're awake, I didn't want to disturb you. I'll meet you on the rooftop with dinner if you're up for it. You could use some fresh air," he endearingly, thoughtfully, nonchalantly said as if the afternoon's hocus pocus events were typical of your normal massage, followed by al fresco homemade lobster bisque.

I immediately jumped out of bed, feeling completely revived and suddenly ravenous. I washed up quickly in the bathroom, happily noting that my cheeks had a healthy glow now and my face didn't look so drawn and pale. I was excited to see the rest of the townhouse and the rooftop view and especially to eat now that my characteristically hearty appetite had reappeared. On my way up to the top, I noted the third floor was a cozy sitting room type area with lots of oversized pillows, an inviting looking chaise lounge, and a rustic wood-burning oven. I loved the style of the home, it was narrow and the rooms were relatively small but spread out over the multiple levels, each with its own unique charms.

I gulped refreshing breaths of air as I joined Javier on the gracious rooftop. He pulled out a chair for me to sit at the little terrace bistro table; there were two large bowls of soup, a loaf of brown crusty bread, a pitcher of water with orange slices, and a teapot. He had thought of everything. I thanked Javier as I sipped my tea. "Mmmmm, mint," I murmured in appreciation, a favorite of mine and a therapeutic one as well. I smiled at him, returning his "Buon provecho" in kind before we started enjoying our soup.

It was unlike any soup I had ever had before; it was extremely tasty, but it was also composed of things I knew would help me fully recover - garlic, leeks, ginger, turmeric, mushrooms, parsley, rosemary, and the unusual addition of succulent lobster pieces. "Definitely an elevated delicious soup," I complimented Javier's culinary skills and thoughtfulness as I slowly savored the inviting, warming concoction. "Coconut milk?" I queried trying to identify what was delightfully imparting a light, silky creaminess. Javier nodded before inquiring, "Did you know that lobster is not only high in protein but also has omega 3 fatty acids and is rich in vitamins and minerals, including selenium?" Hmmm, no I did not. I smiled, shaking my head in response, grateful for the immune-boosting soup. My new spiritual "guide" was even enriching me about topics I was quite familiar with.

"I have a curious soul," he explained, warmly smiling in return. I paused, a little choked up, thinking about the kindness this young, mystical man had bestowed on me in such a short time. The lovely proprietor at "La Pura Vida" had obviously told him I was ill and he had come prepared - even thoughtfully selecting ingredients he knew would help me recover. I wasn't used to such tender care from most people, let alone a complete foreign stranger.

I looked at Javier quizzically before admiring the view - he seemed too good to be true. I paused as I thought - just like I had felt about Leo. These were the best types of "co-regulation." Whereas, the saying is "misery loves company," I always quipped "happiness loves company." We should choose our company wisely - I hadn't exactly "chosen" Javier per se but I was ecstatic that we were happily vibing off of each other's positivity.

Our neurons were mirroring each other's energy - just as Leo's and mine had. I quickly focused on the vista, not wanting to harsh my happy buzz with thoughts of Leo. It was really the first time I was surveying the village. It was absolutely stunning, made more so by the fortuitously-timed impending rosy dusk approach of sunset.

My gaze returned to Javier. I was shocked at how comfortable I felt with this unworldly stranger - if one can call someone who had just made them orgasm multiple times - a stranger, I mused to myself. It was as if we were blanketed together in a field of elevated energy. "Good people simply help other good people," Javier quietly said, answering the inquisitive look in my eyes, as if having intuited my contemplation. It was so serendipitous meeting this gentle soul; he was definitely one of the people I refer to as "earth angels." It never ceases to amaze me how extraordinarily generous, kind, and positively impactful strangers can be, especially compared to how a lot of my romantic partners treated me. It confirmed my faith in humanity.

Javier's immediate presumption that I was a good soul was refreshing too. It reminded me of Buddhism and compassion. I longed to live in a world where we deemed strangers deserving of kindness and compassion simply based on our common humanity instead of viewing strangers with suspicion if not judgment. The world would be a better place if our default perspective and approach were akin to Javier's. I was grateful that Javier had taken charge and had made - and stayed - for dinner, despite my initial shock at the lobster. He hadn't just helped me recover from my unexpected illness - it was as if he had breathed fresh air into my soul. I felt connected with him in exactly the way I needed without even realizing I needed it. I had on proverbial blinders so focused on attaching to romantic partners. My sickness had caused me to be blindsided by Javier in the best way possible. Score 1 for intuition…

As we finished our soup and watched the glorious pastel sunset painting the sky with a brushstroke range of dusky rose and orange, we got to know more about each other. I summarized some of my background at a high level without getting too bogged down in details. Javier had been born in Madrid and tragically had lost his parents at a relatively young age. My throat knotted in empathy although I hadn't shared the loss of my parents with him yet. I held his hand warmly between mine as I listened intently about his childhood.

He had been raised by his older sister and, begrudgingly it seemed, by his aunt. Although his sister had done the best she could with the cruel hand she had been dealt, the aunt hadn't appreciated Javier's more soulful side. Instead of embracing and nurturing that part of him, she had always made him feel inadequate - that he should be chasing after things to make money instead of encouraging him to chase after his dreams. Thanks to his supportive sister and his determined spirit, he hadn't lost his spiritual zest. Although he loved his birth city and his sister, he had gravitated towards smaller villages as soon as he had become an adult. He was not only a masseuse but a yoga teacher and meditative guide. He more or less lived a nomadic lifestyle, traveling around Spain providing services in different villages.

Hmmm, a la carte services like tantric sex, I mused - an uncharacteristic tinge of jealousy brewing as I wondered how many other women had been offered the opportunity to break Javier's celibacy. I knew I shouldn't be jealous especially since I wasn't romantically interested in Javier but I momentarily wondered if I had been wrong about his genuine and authentic soul. I was immediately comforted when Javier, having felt my change in demeanor, made it clear that he too had felt a connection with me unlike any other and that he had been surprised himself about his proposition to end his celibacy. It seemed we were both searching for that elusive connection. I was certain - even without asking - that we were both glad we hadn't had sex - it was one of the reasons I felt so incredibly comfortable with him.

Javier realized I was no longer in my feverish, giggling state and was eager to learn more about tantric practices. I told him the slower pace of tantric sex and focus on connection and intimacy spoke to my sensibilities. I could easily understand how it could result in a much more satisfying experience and closer bond than instant gratification-type sex. I had never viewed sex in a more beautiful, loving way - strange that a stranger had made me perceive sex so differently than I had historically. The closest I had come to this perspective was with Leo. Although I had always had an active sex life, it had almost been akin to a sort of performance for me historically - the desire to satisfy my partner eclipsing my sexual experience. I recalled how unbelievably connected I had felt with Leo in Marsala - simply being together in silence, gazing into each other's eyes - no words, no sex. The eyes are a vision into one's soul... I remembered with a startle that I hadn't checked my phone.

Javier pulled me out of my reverie, inquiring if he could stay the night. I looked at him a little suspiciously, not sure what that would entail, and wondering if "too good to be true" was indeed too good to be true again. He quickly assured me that he just wanted to make sure I was really ok and that he would sleep on the third floor. I intuitively trusted him and immediately acquiesced. I was so touched by his help and comforted by his presence; I was actually relieved he offered to stay. I was sure we would remain lifelong friends. That being settled, he instructed that I would be taking a hot bath to help lull me to sleep while he cleaned up the kitchen. Still amazed by how at ease I felt with him and how he seemed prescient about what I needed, I obeyed his thoughtful directive unquestionably.

******

Chapter 3

No Such Thing as TMI - Again...

I ran my bath water hot and steamy like I love it - just like my men I giggled happily in a lighthearted - not feverish - manner this time. I added some of the bath salts and bubbles that apparently had been in Javier's bags. Wow, he truly had thought of everything I thought again as I gingerly got into the heated water, the fragrance of eucalyptus and lavender making the perfect combination. I knew as I gratefully sunk deeper into the luxuriant bubbles that the relaxing bath and a night of restorative sleep would ensure that I was back to normal the next day. Long-soaking baths always rejuvenated me mentally and physically; they were one of the simple pleasures I indulged in whenever I had the opportunity.

I realized I should check in with Olivia - plus I was anxious to share my memorable day with her. "I had the most unique orgasm of my life," I texted Olivia, not sure how to explain the experience I had and planning to withhold that I had been ill. Two seconds later, the phone rang, and I knew it had to be Olivia. "Don't leave me hanging, sister - spill," Olivia immediately directed in response to my "hello." "I don't quite know how to describe it," I began. Olivia patiently waited as I tried cobbling together an apt description. "It was like a combination meditation, breathing practice, craniosacral therapy, acupressure, and lymphatic drainage all culminating in an out of world full-body volcanic orgasm," I whispered my long-winded attempted explanation.

"Why are you whispering?" she endearingly whispered back. "Because he's still here." "Are you dating him or kidnapping him?" Olivia laughed, thinking I had just met the man of my dreams. "Oh, no," I chuckled, realizing I had forgotten the most interesting detail - "We didn't have sex." "Whoa, whoa back up the truck, Sof - and sign me up while you're at it. You had an incredible orgasm with a man without even having to have sex? What's this abracadabra magic? Sounds like the best kind of "friends with benefits to me." I'm ah going to need the 411 on this new age-y sex thing you got going on over there girlfriend," her tone demanded all the details. I grinned at her choice of phrase "having to have" sex as I explained it wasn't new age at all but a long-standing tradition. The moment I mentioned "tantric" Olivia divulged that she too began envisioning all sorts of contorted, twisted, cirque du soleil-type sexual positions. "My goodness, what's in the water over there?" she rhetorically queried, referencing my menage-a-trois dream in Mallorca. "Sounds like Spain is dripping with seduction and I should hop on over there."

"That's the thing - it was at least as mental as it was physical - even though I felt consciously "out of my head." It was like some supernatural holistic energy took over my body. It was more about intimacy and being present. Control is a part of it as well; he excelled at that. I failed epically," I shivered, remembering the simultaneously very tangible and spiritual impacts Javier had elicited. "It's like he was a sensual spirit animal," I laughed, knowing how ridiculous it sounded but it was how I felt. "Grrr…," Olivia gutturally growled animalistically in return. "Sounds amazing. He's part of your soul family, Sofia," Olivia said thoughtfully. She was way more spiritual than I - despite my aspirations - and I knew she was serious.

All I knew was that Javier and I had a special connection and I had a deja vu feeling from the moment we met. I laughed, knowing that Olivia probably hadn't expected that one of my so-called "soul family" she was always talking about was going to be a tantric masseuse. "I hope we can clone him," Olivia dreamily interrupted my own reverie…

I finished my luxurious bath, eager to crawl back into bed and put my illness firmly behind me. I sighed, remembering my message to Isabella, and wishing I hadn't - not the frame of mind I needed for the peaceful, restorative sleep I desired. I looked at my phone again before turning it off. I finally saw the lone message notification in my archived folder. I forgot I had "archived" Isabella to try to suppress thinking of the Valentinis. I opened the message with trepidation. "Everything is fine, Sofi. Everyone misses you terribly and can't wait to be with you again. Enjoy Spain, but don't forget about Italia and us! Baci e abbraci, cara." I chuckled at myself, thinking of the unnecessary suffering caused by my misperceptions and overthinking. I was the one trying to relegate the Valentinis to "out of sight, out of mind" status.

It seemed that the timing and intensity of my illness had been a reminder of sorts of the wisdom I was trying to internalize - I didn't know if I had actually had a virus or if I had made myself ill from my mental anguish and not taking better care of my body. I smiled - in relief from Isabella's message - and in bizarre gratitude for my illness. It had gotten my attention to take better care of myself mentally and physically and had introduced me to Javier and tantric practices. Hmmm, "we'll see" indeed… I quickly drifted off to deep sleep with an eclectic mix of gratitude and exhaustion and thoughts of Buddhism, tantric practices, and Leo.

Chapter 4

Recharged

I awoke early the next morning, feeling completely rejuvenated and energized. I was anxious to go for a hike and explore more of the village. I was hoping Javier would be able to join me. I was looking forward to learning more about my new friend. I was truly enjoying his company and I wanted to do something to thank him above and beyond paying him for the massage and groceries. He had not only cured my mysterious illness, but he had also helped me avert a spiraling panic attack; he had soothed me - body, mind, and soul - something that had been elusive my entire restless life.

I bounced down the stairs - quietly but with great enthusiasm - to make us a pot of tea. I was surprised as I got to the rooftop to find that Javier was already on the terrace doing yoga. He had been so careful so as not to disturb me, I hadn't realized he was up. He immediately interrupted his session as I stepped onto the terrace, jumping up to greet me with kisses on my cheeks before grabbing the pot and pulling out my chair. He asked me how I was feeling with a solicitous look on his face, beaming in relief and satisfaction when I told him how incredible I felt. He said he had slept perfectly and had already meditated. I told him I had recently started playing around with meditation and that I regularly did yoga poses but not yoga per se. He said he would be happy to share both with me. I was excited about the notion of taking both practices more seriously and encouraged him to continue with his yoga while I observed and learned.

Javier confirmed that he didn't have any appointments scheduled that day and would be happy to join me for a hike and show me the area. I was thrilled especially since I was out of my element - I love hiking but knew nothing about the area or trails. I was thrilled to be spending the day together, my usually introverted self truly felt like we had known each other for a long time.

The Andalusian countryside in southern Spain had always captured my romantic fascination and Gaucín - upon further exploration - became my all-time favorite place in the region. Nestled amidst the undulating hills and dramatic verdant valleys, Gaucín was a surreal picturesque gem that captured the essence of Spanish rural beauty for me. Like the other better known "pueblo blancos" - or white villages of the area - like Ronda - Gaucín had enviable stunning vistas, white-washed houses, rich cultural heritage, and warm community spirit. Relatively unknown Gaucín was the crème de la crème for me - it was a world of tranquility and authenticity - which made it particularly alluring to me.

I was delighted that Gaucín was a veritable feast for my eyes while exuding a palpable sense of peace. My impulsive impetuousness and trust in my intuition had not failed me again. I had taken a mental note of the beguiling village years ago when I was searching for places to visit after my first divorce. The photos had made the place look too good to be true - something out of a Disney fairytale. I was beyond grateful to find that the pictures had not even begun to do it justice. Sometimes our leaps of faith fail, sometimes they delight - that's part of the gamble. It had looked like a dream and it was even dreamier in reality - a rarity indeed. This is the reward I had claimed so many times for going "off the beaten" path. I truly felt if tranquility could come to life in a 3D-manner, I was experiencing it as I reveled in my first immersive vistas. I hadn't felt this unbelievably spectacular for a while - it was as if my body had not only been cleared of whatever virus I had but also of all negativity. Mother Nature never failed to charm me body, mind, and spirit - for me, it was the best antidote to any ailment, no matter the nature.

The village's strategic location atop a steep hill blessed it with panoramic views of the surrounding Serranía de Ronda mountains and the Mediterranean Sea in the distance. The picturesque landscape, dotted with olive groves, oak forests, and meandering rivers, understandably beckoned nature lovers, hikers, and artists. Although it certainly offered extraordinary photo opportunities, I knew I could best capture it with my mind's eye. One-dimensional photos fail to capture the multi-dimensional sensory feeling of exquisite natural beauties like this mirage-like mystical gem. Most of my favorite places were similarly seemingly insulated from the rest of the world and perched almost precariously atop a steep precipice affording the dreamiest of panoramic landscapes. Their relative isolation and precipitous setting made them all that more appealing to me - as if only the intrepid deserved to bask in their sheer grandeur.

Gaucín's architecture was also independently striking - it captivated me with its traditional white-washed buildings sharply contrasting with its endlessly green backdrop. Gleaming white structures, adorned with flower-filled balconies, winding cobblestone streets, and narrow alleys leading to incomparable vistas, created a postcard-perfect setting - where simplicity and charm reigned supreme.

Javier and I slowly strolled through the steep curvy lanes of the village before embarking on our hike. We soaked up Gaucín's rich cultural heritage, showcased by several art galleries, studios, and workshops, highlighting the unique talents of local and international artists. I window shopped, taking in a range of diverse artistic expressions, from traditional Spanish ceramics to contemporary paintings and sculptures. I appreciated that Javier matched my pace, languidly taking in the atmospheric village he already intimately knew so well. I loved his unhurried, carefree nature and contentment with simple things, akin to my own persona, and in sharp contrast to my exes.

We finished our village tour at the Castillo del Águila - or Eagle's Castle - which gracefully stood as a testament to Gaucín's historical past. The ancient Moorish fortress, perched on a hilltop, offered panoramic vistas of the surrounding landscape, serving as a reminder of the village's strategic importance during medieval times. I watched as eagles flew by - the lofty heights and omnipresence of these majestic birds had aptly served as the inspiration for the castle's name. I contentedly sighed, thanking Javier for his mini tour. The village somehow managed to exceed even the high expectations I had for her; it was the perfect place for cultural exploration, rejuvenation, and relaxation, I thought as we turned our attention to our hike in the surrounding hills.

We picked a fairly strenuous hike - I was so relieved my illness had passed as suddenly as it came and I was eager for physical activity. I felt as if I were cloaked in peace and the stunning scenery was the perfect backdrop to what turned out to be a wonderfully invigorating hike - mentally and physically. Nothing grounded me and got me more centered in the present more than hiking - it was like meditation in motion for me. I couldn't help but be immersed in gratitude while blissfully being immersed in the splendors of unspoiled nature.

I watched in amusement and admiration as Javier deftly navigated the inclines and declines effortlessly. It came as no surprise to me that Javier was a chivalrous and attentive guide, intuitively knowing precisely when I would welcome a helping hand as we made our way up and down particularly steep and rocky paths. It was almost comical to me how sure-footed Javier was despite only wearing sandals whereas I was "baby stepping" a lot of the more gravely parts of the terrain. I knew I would have been crouching, practically sidling down some of the particularly steep rocky paths, but for Javier's supporting hand. I fondly recalled a hike I had taken with Rachel where I had more or less been in that squatting position for a significant portion of our descent. She, of course, had to take a photo of me which, admittedly was quite amusing, because the hill appeared harmless in the photo. Baby steps, indeed, I laughed at myself in hindsight.

Baby steps, hmmm, I lovingly thought of Olivia next. I tried looking at Javier unobtrusively, peripherally. I nonchalantly, affectionately grabbed his hand, dreamily thinking of introducing Olivia to him. Javier was definitely her type and the idea of a prospective union between these two beautiful souls made me positively giddy as we finished our hike and reunited with the village center.

Chapter 5

Sharing: The Art of Tapas

Although I love cooking, I definitely wanted to explore a taste of authentic Andalusian cuisine at one of the handful of little unassuming eateries we passed by. Andalusian cuisine is a fusion of Mediterranean, Spanish, and Moorish flavors and I was anxious to sample the regional specialties. Locally-sourced ingredients, like olive oil, almonds, seafood, and fresh produce, featured prominently in the items listed on the chalkboards menus, which I suspected changed daily to highlight the freshest of ingredients. I looked forward to indulging again in tapas - the quintessential Spanish dining experience. Sampling a diverse array of items always pleased my foodie heart. There weren't any grocery stores of any real size to speak of either so shopping wouldn't quite be the experience I was used to in Spain.

I was practically giddy when Javier asked if I wanted to have tapas together - his invite answering my silent desire. I didn't want to monopolize his time and had been hesitant to ask him. I should have realized that this free spirit didn't make plans too far in advance. I beamed in reply, interlocking my arms with his as if we were lifelong friends. I was feeling like a new person thanks to this kind soul seemingly exorcising whatever physical ailment had taken hold of me. I realized I was running myself a bit ragged both from moving around a lot as well as my contemplations. My body was simply telling me to pause and focus on self-care.

Not only was I pleased to have Javier's company, but he had also instantly solved my tapas "discomfort" - my hesitancy about having tapas alone - as well as my slight trepidation about trying to navigate the experience with my rudimentary Spanish. These weren't the type of establishments likely to have either English-speaking proprietors or written menus - even in Spanish. Javier patted my arm affectionately, evidently pleased at my enthusiastic acceptance of his gracious invitation. "Whenever you're ready, mi amor," I didn't even flinch at his "my love" comment. I knew it was in a familial way and I felt the same. "Siempre, always," I gushed in happiness and anticipatory culinary ecstasy. Javier laughed appreciatively as he escorted me to indulge my omnipresent zest for food and life.

The place Javier led us to was a tiny but cute place; it was all dark wood and dim inside but Javier immediately led me to one of the outdoor tables on the terraced area. The cafe resourcefully and decoratively was using wine barrels as high bistro type tables. He helped me alight on one of the bar stools, selecting a seat for me that afforded an enviable vista of the breathtaking mountainside. The proprietor, an older gentleman with twinkling eyes, slowly came out to greet us; it was clearly his laid back demeanor and normal gait and no reflection on his service. I immediately sensed we were going to have a lovely evening. He greeted Javier enthusiastically with familiarity with a kiss on each cheek before turning to me. He took both of my hands in his in a warm welcome, introducing himself and telling me it was a pleasure to meet me. I took to Enrique, an endearing, sweet grandfatherly figure instantly.

"Mucho gusto, Enrique," I sincerely told him it was a pleasure to meet him before introducing myself, "Me llamo, Sofia." He turned to Javier to say "muy linda." I blushed and laughed, remembering an incident years ago when I was traveling to Argentina for work frequently. There had been a painting of a beautiful area in the South of Argentina and my host had always said "muy lindo," which translates to "very beautiful." It had become quite the joke when for months I would always say some day I planned to visit "muy lindo," mistakenly thinking it was the name of the place - which was actually Bariloche, Argentina, a place I visited years later that was indeed "muy lindo."

I was so happy to have Javier's escort; I knew I would have been too shy to come alone and would have missed out on what promised to be a memorable dining experience. I thought of GiGi, Dr. Seuss, and "Green Eggs and Ham," promising to challenge myself to be less shy and more bold about approaching new situations.

Javier and our host discussed the menu in Spanish which did indeed change daily depending on the availability of the freshest ingredients possible. I knew that there was a significant seafood presence in the region thanks to Andalusia's extensive coastline along the Mediterranean Sea and Atlantic Ocean. Javier politely paused their conversation to ask if there were anything in particular I wanted. I nodded no, indicating I was fine with whatever he selected.

As our host left, Javier advised me that my response was appreciated as we were getting whatever our host had fresh for the day anyway. We laughed together and I was grateful again to be in Javier's presence. An experience that would have been a tad uncomfortable for me in solitude would undoubtedly be a delight with my new friend. I wouldn't have known what to expect absent Javier's capable company. I was grateful being accompanied by him - being with a local always transformed and elevated the experience in a foreign country.

Enrique slowly shuffled back with a pitcher of sangria before returning to the kitchen to prepare our tapas. This was evidently a one-man show and would be a slow dining experience to savor. "Muy linda," I winked at Javier, complimenting the sangria - a deep red beauty generously filled with chunks of apples and grapes. Javier filled our glasses and we toasted as we watched the sun set over the magnificent mountains. It was truly a spectacular sight that I didn't even bother to photo. I knew I could never adequately capture its true beauty and preferred to simply soak in the moment.

Enrique had set the pace for the evening I noted as the charming man slowly shuffled back and forth bringing us a stream of various seafood items, hospitably wishing us "¡Buen provecho!" with a smile with the delivery of each tapa. Javier described each of the selections after giving me the Spanish name, which I greatly appreciated. I was unfamiliar with most of them and excited to try new things. I only cooked a limited amount of seafood myself and I particularly enjoyed having seafood when I dined out. I was quite pleased with the variety we were enjoying.

We shared "Pescaíto Frito," a platter of anchovies and sardines, coated in flour and quickly flash-fried until crispy. Although a lot of Americans often shy away from these small fish, I'm not one of them. I thought of Dr. Seuss, appreciative of how he helped children expand their horizons and be curious. Anchovies and sardines are not only healthy when prepared properly, they are also deliciously addictive. Javier told me Enrique only used olive oil and shallow fried the tiny fish - they were fresh and light and delicious - like sea "French fries."

Next, Enrique brought us a dish I had never had before, "Mejillones Rellenos," briny mussels stuffed with a flavorful, herby breadcrumb stuffing, served with a spicy tomato sauce that contrasted beautifully with the mild sweetness of the mussels. A different version of sardines that were equally delectable, "Espeto de Sardinas," was next in line; they were skewered and grilled, a novel preparation for me. They practically melted in my mouth; they were bright and citrusy from a scattering of parsley and lemon with coarsely cracked sea salt adding a nice textural contrast.

Our next tapa was a golden gazpacho made from ripe yellow tomatoes, peppers, cucumbers, onions, and garlic - it was a refreshing and light contrast to the fried fish. I complimented Enrique profusely as he brought us our next tapa - "coliflor salteada con aceitunas y datiles," - an interesting combination of cauliflower with olives and dates - another novel dish that I might have overlooked on my own but thoroughly enjoyed with Javier. I caught a glimpse of Enrique adoringly blushing at my well-deserved praise before he turned to Javier to see if we desired anything more. I simply nodded to indicate my satiation as we began savoring our final creative tapa. It was a delectable dish that perfectly combined textures and that addictive combination of mildly salty and sweet, which I already planned to recreate at home.

Never in my wildest imagination would I have dreamt of combining olives and dates - even though they were some of my favorite foods. It was one of the best things about being exposed to different cultures - I viewed meals out as living cookbooks, always thinking of ways to incorporate different things I tried in my own kitchen repertoire. It's one of the reasons I loved trying new things and it was a memorable way to always keep a part of my travels near and dear to my heart. Ooh, figs and olives too, my food-obsessed heart conjured up. Javier smiled at me, knowing I was lost in my thoughts but that I was having a splendid evening. "I love the creativity and individuality of cooking. What a sweetheart, Enrique is. Thank you so much for sharing this place with me, Javier." I knew if I had been alone, introverted me would have been sitting at home too shy and self-conscious to venture out on my own. I vowed to myself to work on my confidence, lest I miss out on experiences like the simple but incredible one Javier and I had just shared.

I deeply appreciated how Spanish cuisine was a tantalizing blend of flavors, encompassing traditional cuisine and innovative modern gastronomy. I was impressed by Enrique's combination of classics with creative preparations that simultaneously soothed my soul while piquing my interest. As the saying goes, "variety is the spice of life," and this was particularly true for me when it came to cuisine. At the heart of Spain's culinary scene was diversity - a wonderful multilayered richness thanks to the fusion of so many cultures over the years. Eating a diversity of small things was not only the most appealing way for me to eat but the healthiest as well. The tapas tradition perfected the health mantra of "eating the rainbow" for me - it was a feast for all the senses - and I loved the fact that all our food was fresh, seasonal, and homemade.

We were the only patrons at the time and Javier invited Enrique to join us when he popped back out to check on us. I knew Spaniards typically ate much later and that Javier had graciously accommodated me without even mentioning it. Enrique continued his one man show, clearing the table before returning with three glasses of sherry and a colorful plate of cubed melons, dried fruit, and nuts. Enrique pulled up a chair and he and Javier started quietly conversing. I slowly sipped my sherry while I admired the view and recited my blessings. In addition to my ravenous appetite, all my senses were satiated. I was quite content sitting in the presence of these two charming and hospitable souls as I watched the sun slowly continuing its descent, painting the sky a brilliant array of pink in stark contrast to the deep green mountains. What a perfect ending to a perfect meal - nay perfect day - with perfect companions, I thought, feeling worlds better from the prior day of my arrival. Life is good, life is simple, I thought, as I smiled in sincere appreciation at my lovely counterparts who had mirror beaming smiles on their faces and in their eyes.

*****

As we leisurely strolled back home, my heart as full as my tummy, I realized Gaucín's immediate allure for me, beyond its jaw-dropping natural beauty. Its ability to preserve the essence of authentic Spanish village life synced with my values. As the world moves forward a little too frenetically and recklessly for my taste, places like Gaucín that prioritize preservation of cultural heritage and the beauty of simplicity speak to my soul. There's no "schedule" in Gaucín, time slows down, encouraging the savoring of each moment and the present. It's a tranquil haven that dictates a peaceful interaction - gloriously, the only "distraction" was Mother Nature herself.

It struck me that my restlessness wasn't based on some need to randomly run from place to place. Although I had an exploratory nature, I desperately sought stability and some continuity in my life. My restlessness was from a sort of rebellion to feeling confined, to living inauthentically. I was perfectly content simply being, not doing, following my heart and dispensing with the limitations of succumbing to societal expectations. Nature's warm embrace soothed my soul. I felt like I could stay in Gaucín forever - well, I quickly realized, with a love of my life at least…

I made a collage of photos of the sunset, our tapas, and a sweet photo of Javier and Enrique together as a memento and to send to Olivia and Rachel. The evening had truly been the perfect ending to a perfect day and I wanted to assure my treasured friends that all was fine - indeed, I hadn't felt this "at home" for a long time. I was absolutely in unfamiliar territory and I was quite pleased at how comfortable I felt. Historically, I never ask for - or even accept - help. Javier hadn't asked if I needed help - he had just given me what I needed in so many ways. This kind soul was quickly becoming a wonderful friend and a sort of spiritual teacher all at once.

As if on cue, Javier asked me if I wanted to join him on the third floor to meditate before going to sleep and I eagerly agreed. As we got settled on the pillows on the floor, he told me that to "meditate" meant to become familiar with. I had never thought of meditation from that perspective - it was insightful and helped me to embrace it. Previously, I had practiced transcendental meditation a little - simply focusing on silently repeating a single word - or compassionate loving kindness meditation. I was interested in exploring different meditative practices. I sat quietly with my eyes shut, allowing my thoughts and feelings to arise naturally, non-judgmentally, while becoming aware of them. I intuitively placed my hands over my heart and started gently, rhythmically rocking back and forth. Javier's presence helped me stay "present" and prolong my meditation. I was surprised to see that almost a half an hour had passed when I opened my eyes to see Javier silently observing me. I felt light-hearted and blissfully light-headed - almost ethereal.

We were sharing a novel type of intimacy for me. Javier was so sensual but it was more about positive energy and embracing the present moment and all the senses - it wasn't about physicality or amorous urges. I hadn't felt compelled to have sex with him in some sort of twisted sense of obligation that unfortunately had colored some of my historical decisions and he was happy staying with me without having sex. He asked if I wanted to sleep together to just hug and I was instantly receptive. We had a deep connection and I needed my oxytocin bonding fix. I practically melted into his comforting, protective embrace instantaneously, reminiscent of falling asleep with GiGi. I smiled thinking of GiGi, my heart warmed as I peacefully drifted off to sleep…

******

Chapter 6

Revelations in Ronda

I awoke the next morning, feeling energetic and optimistic. I hadn't slept so deeply and restoratively for a long time and vowed to prioritize sleep going forward. Javier had to go back to "reality" - although I suspected his life didn't exactly resemble most people's sense of reality. We enjoyed a light breakfast and tea on the rooftop before going our separate ways. He had refused to accept money from me so I had put more than enough to cover the massage and groceries in his backpack. He had no idea how valuable what he had done for me was and I was particularly touched that he had refused money. We shared a tight hug and kisses on both cheeks before we parted ways, agreeing to spend the evening together.

Feeling wonderful and exploratory, I decided to take the train to visit the nearby renowned town of Ronda. Knowing I wouldn't have the educational benefit of Javier's companionship, I took a quick look at Ronda's history online during the train ride. Ronda, one of Spain's oldest towns, dated back to pre-Roman eras. Its history is an intricate tapestry "woven together" with threads of Phoenician, Roman, Moorish, and Spanish influences. I had wanted to visit for years and felt a tingle of excitement as the train approached the stop. I was feeling particularly grateful about life in general having quickly passed my illness and meeting Javier and was looking forward to a leisurely day acquainting myself with Ronda.

Ronda was cradled in the heart of Andalusia and she was as pretty and charming as I had expected. The fact that the village was perched precariously on the edge of a plunging gorge added to the dramatic appeal on first sight. I chose a bench at the edge of town overlooking the breathtaking vista to sit and soak up the ambiance before exploring.

I snapped my first of many pictures, eager to try to capture the essence of Ronda to share with Olivia - it definitely was her type of place and I desperately wished she were with me. I spontaneously chuckled out loud as I thought about our conversations and envisioned how much we would enjoy Spain's magnetic sensuality. I had quickly searched about tantric practices before leaving on my day trip - there were so many aspects of it that intrigued me. I was amazed by my experience and wanted to learn more about it as it had synced with me so well. I realized that Javier hadn't been feeding me a line just to have sex; he was seeking a personal connection between two kindred spirits with a lot of positive energy.

I thought about my time in Turkey in Isparta and how harmonious and ethereal developing heart coherence made me feel. I realized that Javier most definitely exuded coherence and that was likely what had made me feel that we had met before - our souls immediately synced and felt connected by the positive energies our hearts were emitting. I felt the kind of connection I yearned for in romantic partners with Javier notwithstanding that we weren't having sexual relations. I was happy that I could feel such a positive state of being - body, mind, and spirit - without being romantically involved. Meeting him was a serendipitous reminder to be open to such meaningful connections with people beyond a romantic context.

My brief exposure to tantric practices reminded me of the beauty of coherence and how it can profoundly benefit us not only individually, but in relationships as well as in communities - indeed globally. Tantric practices were, of course, more intimate, but positive energy and synchronized body, mind, and spirit were at the core of both from my perspective. Tantric sex seemed like sexual coherence to me and something that could be enjoyed individually as well as with a partner. I realized that was what was intriguing me about tantric practices and making me eager to learn more - and to experiment - given the appropriate opportunity.

Tantra originated in India and in Sanskrit means "woven together"; a lot of weaving together around here in Spain, I amusingly realized. The "weaving together" concept likely explained the intricate, interconnected sexual positions I vaguely recalled from the tiny guidebook I had been given years prior. The tantric practice of controlling physical sexual energy and sensations with the mind spoke to me in a number of ways. It reflected the strength of harnessing our incredibly powerful minds, and for someone who loves a slow tease and long foreplay, it also seemed to pretty much guarantee a deeply satisfying sexual experience.

I liked to think of the "woven together" concept individually too, reflecting the intimate, interconnected nature of our minds, bodies, and spirits - a la heart coherence. I had never met anyone more spiritual than Javi, as I was now endearingly thinking of him. Javi's spirituality - and kindred curious positive persona - made me eagerly anticipate learning a lot more from this young, wise "old soul" throughout life.

I was surprised at how I was randomly exposed to something that resonated with me so strongly. I would have never delved into tantric practices but for Javier, because I previously had no appreciation for what tantric actually was. I had ignorantly thought it was just about glorifying various twisted sexual positions - like a sexual-variation of the game Twister for adults. My interpretation of it now actually kind of put the "love" in lovemaking. Historically, I had viewed sex more as a physical performance. Although I "associated" it with love, that emotional aspect and connection was actually rarely at the heart of my sexual experiences - I wanted it to be going forward and that desire was making me a tad fixated on tantric practices.

I liked the extended bonding associated with tantric sex and emphasis on touching and eye contact. For a self-proclaimed hugaholic addicted to the bonding hormone, oxytocin, tantric sex sounded blissful to me - deep intimacy was my primary goal. I had always been so focused though on the physical act of satisfying my partner and had sacrificed what I really desired - historically it was about performance over pleasure.

My thoughts suddenly segued to Leo; I realized that our sexual encounter had been the most tantric-like experience I had had without even realizing it. It also had been the most satisfying sex of my life and I better appreciated why now. I sighed, imploring myself to focus on the present - there was no sense pining away for Leo. I couldn't give him what he wanted so any hypothetical relationship would inevitably end in heartache, a path I was wisely trying to avoid now. C'est la vie…

I realized my thoughts had been conflicted after Leo. I didn't want to be alone, but I didn't know if I wanted to date different men or be in an exclusive relationship. There was no question in my mind that a monogamous relationship was what I ultimately wanted. I wasn't sure though if I were seriously interested for the time being in seeing more than one man or if I were afraid of getting hurt given the painful demise of my marriage and my sadness over Leo.

I thought about my 2-for-1 "happy hour" dream in Mallorca, trying to determine whether it held any insights into what I really wanted. At least subconsciously, I was apparently embracing my freedom and my sexuality, uncharacteristically prioritizing what I wanted. I didn't interpret the unusual threesome nature of my fantasy as an actual desire to experience a menage-a-trois, but rather as embracing my sensuality outside of a romantic, monogamous relationship. Historically, my fantasies revolved around the man I was with at the time. The odd nature had made me reflect to try to understand what my dream was trying to tell me.

It struck me that I had really never been alone much once I started dating at a young age - I had jumped from one long-term relationship to the next. I took the dream as a cautionary one - to not jump into a relationship merely from attraction or from a desperation of not wanting to be alone - something I had a pattern of doing - which never ended well. I was a monogamous, faithful woman - I had conjured up a context in my dream that precluded an actual relationship with anyone. I hadn't equated sexual desire with anything more than what it was.

I also knew I was self-conscious about being with younger men and I took my "taboo" dream as at least subconscious acceptance and as a prod to not judge myself. As Olivia was quick to remind me, Sergio and Diego were full-grown men, and indeed, they were. I was tired of certain societal factions not batting an eye with respect to older men and younger women while judging older women with younger men. Men in comparable age-gap relationships didn't have a derogatory term comparable to "cougar." I thought of the French author Amantine Dupin and her relationships with younger men and the themes of her stories, applauding her conviction to follow her heart. I always admired the French President, Emmanuel Macron and his wife Brigitte, 24 years his senior. I particularly liked how they were still drawn to each other notwithstanding they had to wait to be together until the younger Macron was older, Brigitte having been Emmanuel's teacher.

Talk about scandalous circumstances and being in the public eye, I mused, reflecting that Americans seemed particularly judgmental of older women-younger men relationships. There was definitely a double standard. From my experiences, - "age is just a number" and "love is love" - seemed to be the more prevalent perspectives in the Mediterranean countries I frequented. It didn't seem coincidental to me that women in many other countries generally appeared more effortless, more natural, more comfortable in their skin - it seemed to be largely a reflection of society.

I couldn't discern what the difference in judgment between age-gap relationships with older men or women was other than one premised on superficial appearances, outdated gender-specific measures of attraction, and ageism. In the US, it seemed that the prevailing societal image of female "attractiveness" was predominantly one of a youthful appearance, while for men it was predominantly one of professional success and wealth. Of course, a "youthful" appearance decreases naturally with age, while one's success and wealth generally tend to increase with age.

These societal conceptions and diverging trends seem to create a societal perspective of a relationship between an older male and a younger woman an "appealing" one -

while an older woman with a younger man is considered "cougar-like" - having to "prey" on her unsuspecting younger counterpart since what would she possibly have to offer as her "beauty" is deemed to fade with age. I hadn't appreciated that my dream had put me on a contemplative roll. I had been self-conscious about being with younger men for absolutely no reason other than American stereotypes which I wanted no part of. I hadn't even realized I was doing it until I tried analyzing my dream.

No wonder I was drawn to the Macrons, Ms. Dupin's writing, and other cultures I was enjoying where women seemed to be appreciated differently from my observations and in my experiences. A mature woman who knew what she wanted, who had lived life, and was confident in her own skin appeared to be revered as she should be. My dream, I concluded, wasn't just a matter of embracing my sensuality - it was also a nudge not to judge myself by societal age standards - something I hadn't even been fully cognizant of. I was determined to stop judging myself about being with younger men by happenstance. Olivia was right - these were men and my interactions weren't a community project. My romantic interludes and relationships were my business and no one else's. I smiled - always happy to decipher my dreams. I knew that a threesome wasn't my fantasy - as odd as it seemed, the contextual oddity for me was really just a prompt to break free of societal confines and expectations - something I had thought I was doing but apparently not as much as I had thought.

For heaven's sakes, I laughed at myself, recalling how reticent I had initially been to share the details of my dream even with Olivia and how I had felt self-loathing simply for having the dream. Funny, I thought - thinking of Javier and looking forward to seeing him again - how my unexpected exposure to tantric sex had taken me down this path of self-exploration. Now, I felt foolish having previously let discriminatory, societal judgments make me judge myself. I felt lighter having cast off the ignorant cloak of judgment and looked forward to reading the works of "George Sand."

I looked down to see to my surprise how much time I had spent in contemplation. I smiled as I focused on my surroundings - while some thought I was trying to "run" away from my "problems," I felt as if I had "run" to where I needed to in order to truly get grounded and - although not a fan of cliches - "find" myself. Indeed, before I had supposedly "fled" with a one-way ticket to Sicily, I hadn't realized how "lost" I had been.

I was proud of myself, I realized as I soaked in the natural beauty and tranquility. I had listened to my heart, I had trusted my intuition. My open heart had never let me down. While some thought my resignation and departure had been foolhardy - while others, in contrast, thought it was courageous, it had quite simply been what was best for me. It was the first time in a long time that I had simply followed my heart and trusted in myself. To do otherwise - ever - I pointedly reminded myself - would be the foolhardy thing. I started gleefully laughing again, thinking of my otherworldly massage and my new relationship with Javier - oh how terribly many wondrous things we stand to miss out on if we simply don't follow our hearts. Following societal norms and expectations and being confined by others' opinions seemed unbelievably, comically ludicrous with the clarity that had come to me. I loved my "why not?" spirit and all the literal and metaphorical places it had taken me.

I couldn't quit thinking about Dr. Seuss - this time "Oh the Places You'll Go" came to mind. His wisdom really was timeless and universal. I thought wistfully of my mom, putting my hands over my heart - she had instilled a love of books in me from a young age. She was the most avid reader I had ever known and I was sorry I wouldn't be able to share my writing with her. She would always be a part of it though as she had instilled the passion in me. I kept my hands over my heart, appreciative of the values she had instilled in me since childhood - little did I appreciate the worldly lessons I was learning from Dr. Seuss sitting in my bedroom while my mom sent me off to sleep with magical, meaningful stories. Being transported to other times and other places through books was what drew them to me and what I hoped to share with others with my writing. Books were like a magical flying carpet to me. I said a prayer of gratitude as I felt my mom with me - she had exposed me to different morals and philosophies and I would forever be connected with her through what we had shared and what I would always carry in my heart.

******

My heart warmed with thoughts of my mom, I got up to check out Ronda in greater detail. I challenged my brain to remember more about Ronda's history as I began leisurely walking around the center. The brief highlights - like a "Cliff's notes" version - was as far as I cared about particular historical details. I liked learning a little about the places I visited to gain insights into the present culture of a place. I focused more on the visual appeal of architecture and natural beauty and the day-to-day pace of life and simple pleasures. Ronda was a key stronghold for the Moors during their rule over the Iberian Peninsula - I admired remnants of their legacy reflected in the town's architecture and layout. Although I wasn't a stickler for details, I did like knowing the style of architecture when I found types I liked. I was a big fan of Moorish architecture and Ronda did not disappoint.

I approached the most iconic symbol of Ronda - the Puente Nuevo - or New Bridge - reflecting how countless centuries of history had unfolded beneath my feet. It was easy to appreciate why Ronda's dramatic landscapes had captivated the hearts of artists, writers, and romantics for centuries, including Ernest Hemingway. The views overlooking the plunging gorge and the El Tajo River were nothing short of breathtaking. I envisioned how spectacular it would be to witness sunrise or sunset when the warm Andalusian sun cast a golden glow over the landscape.

The bridge was built in the 18th century - it spanned the incredibly deep gorge below, connecting the old and new parts of the town. I thought of Javi again gratefully - I almost felt as if his impact on me was serving as a sort of metaphorical bridge between my past and my future. I took several photos before continuing my tour on the other side of the bridge.

The old town, "La Ciudad," was a labyrinth of narrow, winding streets, white-washed buildings, and charming squares. There were Arab Baths and a Moorish palace, "Casa del Rey Moro." Ronda reminded me of a number of sites from Seville and Granada - home to the exquisite Alhambra Palace - that I intended to visit again one day - it had been built to resemble heaven on earth and was indeed paradisiacal. I admired highlights of the town's Spanish heritage, including the stunning Plaza de España and the Church of Santa María la Mayor. I loved the vibrantly-colored and intricately detailed Spanish tiles, reminiscent of my visit to Seville - where they seemed to be everywhere. I paused in the plaza to soak in the beauty and was rewarded with a flamenco performance. The beautiful natural flow and artistry of the graceful dancer made me think of tantric sex again - the fluidity and synchronicity were mesmerizing.

I strolled along the Alameda del Tajo, a stunning park stretching along the edge of the gorge. It was a serene setting for a leisurely walk. I listened to the sounds of birds chirping and the gentle breeze rustling through the trees. What a romantic village, I thought as I wistfully watched couples strolling hand in hand or sitting intertwined on park benches. "Weaving together" is indeed the theme - maybe particularly notable to me given my solitude - I mused as I continued my aimless wandering.

The Serranía de Ronda, the mountainous region surrounding Ronda was clearly a haven for outdoor enthusiasts just as it was in Gaucin. I had read that there were hiking trails meandering through lush forests, leading to hidden waterfalls and panoramic viewpoints. The Sierra de las Nieves Natural Park was also close by, offering even more exploratory opportunities. I passed by many boutique wineries, apparently attributable to Ronda's proximity to the Malaga wine region. What a lovely place to savor local varietals while enjoying the scenic vineyard landscapes, I thought as I passed by the charming wine shops.

What a spectacular romantic region to explore with a loved one, I silently mused, starting to feel pangs of self-pity. I immediately chastised myself and thought of Liam's advice to embrace my solitude. I was having a lovely day - why on earth was I letting random couples sightings harsh my happy buzz? What a spectacularly idiotic way to ruin my fabulous visit. I laughed out loud at myself as I realized it would also be an incredible region to enjoy with Olivia and Rachel to share our passions - like hiking, food, and wine. Indeed, my trips with my girlfriends had been the best trips of my life because of our common interests.

My trips with Things 1 & 2 didn't compare. Thing 1 always had me follow him around, we did what he wanted, and he was always making me feel bad about spending money on my well-deserved vacations - the money I made working so hard. I never did anything extravagant whatsoever but he always managed to take the pleasure out of trips. He insisted on making little sandwiches at the breakfast buffet to avoid lunch and insisted on takeout food for dinner. Thing 2, on the other hand, was more than willing to be extravagant with my money - only the best for him. He also wasn't into exploring and could spend countless hours inside on the Internet. He'd make me feel guilty for venturing out alone because of his jealousy and concern that something would happen to me. Either of them would have diluted - not added - to my experience here. It wasn't them I was pining away for though - it was Leo.

I paused, taking in my spectacular surroundings and focused on what an incredible day I was having doing exactly as I pleased. My budding pangs of self-pity quickly dissipated when I admitted how unbelievably ridiculous I was being. Gratitude and perspective truly are life-altering. I was more than happy exploring alone when I wasn't gratuitously making myself sad, fixated on couples. I was profoundly appreciating my blessings when I stopped wallowing in self-pity as if something were wrong with me - as if my single status screamed to the world I was damaged goods. I didn't normally care much about what other people might think and I knew that no one even noticed - let alone cared - that I was alone. I was the only one judging myself. I needed to stop relying on external validation of my worth and embrace myself like never before. I was excited about coming back some day - it certainly didn't have to be with a romantic partner - it would be spectacular with Olivia, or Rachel, or Javi, or my brothers or nephews, or even Isabella and the twins... My novel conception of "intimacy" that I was determined to embrace was a much-welcomed one that I knew would comfort me whenever pangs of loneliness started hijacking my head.

******

I continued my stroll, all smiles now with my new perspective. An adorable little cafe with an outdoor terrace fringed with planters filled with a rainbow of geraniums and gerber daisies soon caught my eye, making me realize I was hungry. I was thrilled to see "Calamares a la Plancha" on the handwritten list of specials of the day. Calamari is a favorite of mine and I'm particularly pleased when I can get a grilled version of it. I knew it would pair perfectly with another of the day's specialties, and another favorite of mine, "Pimientos de Padrón," flash fried green peppers. "Ooh," I thought as an intriguing special that I hadn't tried before caught my eye - gazpacho de remolacha - an interesting variation of the classic chilled soup I was eager to try.

I ordered excitedly without hesitation without even looking at the rest of the menu. My garçon smiled at my enthusiasm and decisiveness as he asked if I would perhaps care for a glass of wine. I only hesitated slightly before saying , "Porque no? why not?" with a grin, impulsively ordering an Albariño, one of my favorite Spanish white wines - the crispness of which would undoubtedly pair beautifully with my meal. I was practically giddy with contemplation for my lunch of favorites together with a new version of gazpacho.

I smiled deeply, feeling more profoundly relaxed by myself than I had in a long time. I admired the stunning surreal vision in front of me, a wave of gratitude palpably washing over me. The vista was incomparable. I shut my eyes as I basked in the solar warmth of the sun and silently recounted my gratitude litany with my hands automatically gravitating to my heart. I felt so peaceful and so energized.

I opened my eyes to see my sweet garçon bringing me my Albariño accompanied by a salad that I tried to politely wave off, wondering if he had misunderstood me. He had impeccable professional but endearing service, his one arm behind his back as he placed the salad in front of me over my protestation, advising me with a broad smile that it was complimentary. I smiled my gratitude in turn as he left me to enjoy the unexpected endibias con queso de cabra y naranjas, a pretty endive salad with goat cheese and oranges topped with pistachios that was as visually stunning as it was refreshingly delicious. I took a photo of my table with the vista in the background, futilely trying to capture the perfect lunch and setting. Such simple ingredients combining to make a pleasant and refreshing starter, I thought as I languidly enjoyed my salad and my Albariño.

I sent Olivia the photo with a simple, "Heavenly - could only be dreamier with you. Wish you were here. xoxo." I liked to keep her in the loop - at least visually anyway. I loved how we shared everything and that Olivia wanted to be kept apprised of every detail. I often felt like I was selfishly inundating her with information and never wanted to look like I was showing off with my experiences. She was one of those oh-so-rare true friends though who genuinely felt my pleasures as well as my pains. I could never adequately express my appreciation to her; I always felt her presence and support. It made me feel less alone - whether I was enjoying something I wanted to share or whether I was struggling with something. She was one of my many blessings for which I regularly expressed gratitude.

As my waiter returned with my order, I took another look at my vista before saying a silent prayer for my meal and focusing on my lunch. I snapped a photo for Rachel, wishing that my two best friends were enjoying the lovely day with me. The grilled calamari was cooked to perfection - it was tender, slightly smoky from the grill and slightly sweet from the sea delicacy's natural sweetness. Its brininess contrasted beautifully with the brightness from the chopped parsley and hints of citrusy lemon. It was presented on a delicate bed of arugula drizzled with the ubiquitous pungent green olive oil, adding visual appeal and a peppery back note. I was struck again by the simplicity of the dish, allowing the natural flavors of the star ingredient to shine.

The gazpacho - a unique combination with beets and tomatoes topped with crumbled goat cheese and slivered slmonds was nothing short of gorgeous. As it delighted my palate, I knew this was another novel dish that I would recreate at home. My peppers were the perfect accompaniment, they were left whole, stem and all, flash fried and sprinkled with coarse sea salt. My meal was served with slices of crusty slightly charred bread with an addictive side of lemony aioli for dipping.

My garçon came to check to see if everything were alright. He warmly smiled when I simply replied with a smile in my eyes and a slight nod of my head; I had no words. He kindly offered to take a photo of me and I uncharacteristically acquiesced, it would make a nice memory of my oh-so-memorable lunch. When I looked back at photos, it was often a great reminder of how happy I always was even when solo. I was trying to appreciate the benefits of experiencing things by myself - it provided a different dynamic that I often took for granted. Solitude enabled a type of profound savoring that can easily get lost in the company of another. I was soaking up my culinary experience in my incredible surroundings. I was completely focused on the present and my blessings and I felt extremely peaceful.

Despite my extremely relaxed vibe, I was like a ball of anticipatory tingling excitement. My characteristically high energy levels were often the result of the intense somewhat paradoxical feelings I simultaneously had. I was at my most energized when I was my most relaxed. Fittingly, my solitude made me realize that it was my solitude that was making me so happy at the moment.

It dawned on me - albeit slowly - that my happiness wasn't premised on being with someone - as I had always assumed. It was the simple result of sheerly living authentically and feeling worthy for simply being. The periodic times my happiness had felt elusive or slightly diluted were when I was catering to basically self-absorbed - if not narcissistic - people or when I questioned my worth and floundered accordingly. I had been self-conscious about my aloneness - like my solitude were some sort of "Scarlet letter" - a stamp of unworthiness for all to see.

When I was either alone - and living authentically - or with emotionally healthy, respectful people - like my best friends - my happiness knew no bounds. My epiphany made me realize that my happiness wasn't dependent on my relationship status, it was simply dependent on being authentic and true to myself and not depending on external validation of my worth. Wowza, I thought, as the life-transforming realization hit me like a lightning bolt, admittedly an extraordinarily slow one. Tears of joy welled up in my eyes and I couldn't wait to share my momentous lunch with Olivia and Liam - and Javier, I realized - surprised at how quickly and deeply we had bonded.

As I took in my awe-inspiring vista one last time, I took my last sip of Albariño in a self-celebratory toast in grateful acknowledgment for my present and grateful anticipation of the beautiful future I was confident undoubtedly lay ahead of me.

******

Chapter 7

Tantalizing Tapas & Tantric Talk

As much as I had loved my visit to Ronda, I was anxious to get home to share the details of my contemplations with Javier. I couldn't wait to get his insights. I messaged him and was touched to hear that he missed me too and was looking forward to our evening together. We agreed to meet at one of the local stores to pick up provisions for a tapas meal to enjoy at home on the rooftop. I couldn't remember the last time I was so excited. I felt like I was on a precipice between my past and my future and it seemed like a particularly splendid cause for celebration.

Javier and I synced beautifully in the kitchen. I sighed, reminiscing about Leo and wondering what he was up to. Oh, if only things were different. C'est la vie, I told myself to stop my unproductive thinking. Back to food, always, I chuckled out loud. The kitchen was my happy place and cooking was almost a meditative outlet for me. I was joyous sharing the kitchen with Javier who couldn't help but notice my particularly playful mood. We had picked up a few prepared things to reduce our time in the kitchen.

We had "Boquerones en Vinagre," fresh anchovies marinated in vinegar, garlic and parsley. A novel dish for me that I would never have tried but for Javier's suggestion and the emboldening effect of "Green Eggs and Ham." I smiled wistfully, acknowledging how frequently my thoughts returned to Valentini B&B, and, more frankly, the Valentini family. I missed GiGi and made a mental note to check in with Isabella. I had been purposefully avoiding communicating with Leo but I certainly didn't want GiGi to think I had forgotten about her when in reality she was so frequently in my mind.

We also had "Escalivada," which was a new Spanish word for me but was basically roasted and marinated vegetables, a mainstay of my diet - I was looking forward to trying the Spanish version. Javier was working on preparing "Gambas al Ajillo," one of my favorite Spanish tapas and all-time favorite dishes in general. I had featured the addictive tapa of garlicky shrimp sautéed in olive oil with garlic and chili peppers on the menu for the restaurant with my ex. Focus, I reminded myself to not go down a path of regret.

While Javier tended to the shrimp, I was preparing a platter of some more of my beloved Spanish staples and all over favorite dishes. We were enjoying a repeat of the number of items I had enjoyed in Seville and earlier in Mallorca: Manchego cheese, a sheep's milk cheese; and thin-slices of Jamón Serrano, dry-cured Spanish ham, and the highly-prized Jamón Ibérico de Bellota, revered for intense flavor due to the diet of the pigs who are left free to roam and eat "bellota," or acorns. The acorn-rich diet imparts a unique nutty and sweet flavor to the ham. Last, but not least, I was making "Pan con Tomate," toasted bread rubbed with garlic, grated juicy ripe tomatoes, drizzled with olive oil, and - in my case - always fresh coarsely cracked salt and pepper and a sprinkling of oregano. I was practically jumping inside in culinary anticipation. As we headed upstairs with our feast, I knew I would have to refrain from my endless "mmmmm mmmmm mmmmm's" culinary seals of approval with each bite if I were to keep up my end of the conversation with Javier. Despite my saturating lunch, I was ravenous again - for our meal, for our conversation, and for life in general.

We chatted while we happily grazed, it was a perfect meal and I couldn't be happier with the setting and my companion. Although I frequently enjoyed the rest of the tapas, the intense, savory, slightly salty, complex flavor of the Ibérico ham was a rare treat that I only had in Spain. It melts in your mouth, while the nutty and slightly sweet notes from the acorns and the lengthy aging process contribute to the ham's depth of flavor.

Our conversation ended up segueing to tantric sex. I admitted to Javier that my preconceived notions of it had been wildly off; I had generally thought about it as bending into strenuous poses and uncomfortable positions. I had always assumed it was a male-centric practice that tried to use spiritual justification for basically encouraging sex every and any which way purely for men's gratification.

From my novel exposure, I was quite intrigued. I was looking forward to learning more and experimenting with tantric sex in the future. Tantric practices were grounded on principles completely contrary to what I had erroneously assumed. I chuckled thinking of the wise advice of Dr. Seuss again - don't judge it until you try it. I couldn't stop laughing as my Dr. Seuss tangent led me in a direction of picturing characters like the real Thing 1 and Thing 2 from the Dr. Seuss books comically depicting the different tantric positions. After I explained to Javier what I was finding so funny, he patiently went on to school me in the real practice as he personally approached it, noting there were many variations.

Contrary to my former belief that tantric sex was a sort of strategic sexual means to a quick end, Javier explained that tantric sex is quite the opposite in every way. It's meant to be slow and satisfying, with sessions typically lasting quite long. Many people delay orgasming to enjoy the closeness and intimacy as long as possible.

I listened intently as Javier explained the practice in greater detail. I couldn't believe how comfortable I felt discussing the topic with him. "Tantric sex is rooted in the ancient Indian spiritual and philosophical tradition known as Tantra. It is a holistic approach to sexuality that aims to integrate the physical, emotional, and spiritual aspects of human beings." I nodded, encouraging Javier to go on, noting that the underlying body, mind, and soul union shared between two people deeply resonated with me. "Tantra encompasses a wide range of teachings and practices, including meditation, mantra chanting, and rituals," he continued, "although it is most well-known for its unique approach to sexuality. Tantric sex emphasizes the importance of deep connection and presence between partners. Tantra views the human body as a sacred vessel for spiritual growth and self-realization." He paused, reflecting, "Tantric sex certainly doesn't shy away from the physical aspects of sex, but it celebrates the body as a means to transcend ordinary consciousness. It emphasizes the flow of energy throughout the body - known as "prana" or "kundalini."

"Sounds quite involved," I interjected, listening intently, trying to absorb all the nuances of tantric sex now that I appreciated it was a practice that profoundly synced with my sensibilities. "Breathing exercises - pranayama - are integral to tantric sex," Javi explained. "I never thought of conscious breathing in connection with sex," I began. "Well, actually, that's not true," I remembered breathing in sync with Javi almost unintentionally - it had come so naturally - and intuitively trying to sync my breathing with Leo in an effort to be as close as possible. "Tantra believes that synchronized breathing enhances a couple's connection and exchange of energy." "How truly intimate and beautiful," I replied dreamily.

"Yes, it really is, isn't it?" Javi seemed pleased that I was understanding and appreciating Tantra - as opposed to my feverish fits of giggling when I had thought Javi was making up pick up lines. "Conscious breathing not only promotes relaxation, but also facilitates the movement of energy. The goal is to harmonize and intensify the energy to lead to heightened states of consciousness and pleasure."

My goodness, I thought, completely enthralled with the energy perspective and the bliss-like state that could be reached from such a profoundly intimate union of mind, body, and spirit between two loving souls. "Boy was I wrong about what Tantric sex is," I laughed at myself before, making sure I understood, "Sooooo, in contrast to a lot of conventional sexual interactions - especially casual ones - that are laser-focused on reaching orgasm - often rapidly - tantric sex prioritizes delayed gratification and prolonged connection. Sounds extraordinary," I murmured. "It's about enjoying the journey rather than fixating on the destination," I concluded, looking at Javi for confirmation. "Precisely," he clasped his hand together, beaming that I was a convert.

He went on to explain the basic practical aspects as I let my mind wrap around Tantra. "The first thing is to practice eye contact together, facing each other, fully clothed. Practice the breathing techniques and synchronize the breath. Once you've gotten into a rhythm, you can begin to incorporate tantric techniques. After you undress, you can begin touching, feeling, and moving with your partner however feels best for you. The key is to maintain eye contact and to continue to focus on your breathing. The only thing that matters is the present moment and enjoying every sensation."

I couldn't help but think of my beautiful sexual experience with Leo - it had been as close to tantric sex as I had ever encountered. I knew it had been so special and so beautifully different than any sexual interaction I had ever experienced before. Whereas I had ignorantly thought of tantric sex as a contorted sort of free-for-all, focused on the sheer pleasure of various positions, it was a sacred and intentional space for lovemaking to my pleasant surprise. When I had been with Leo, it had been as if the ultimate orgasms - though glorious - were afterthoughts - the time would have been just as special even without climaxing - it had just been a natural outlet for the overwhelming emotions I had felt. I knew I would never be interested in tantric sex in a casual relationship, but to my surprise, I wastarting to wrap my mind around the appeal of the optional celibacy aspect. "Wow, what an extraordinary example of not judging something before understanding it," I reflected to Javi who had remained silent, patiently observing my inner contemplations. "I couldn't have been more misinformed," I readily admitted, having associated tantric exclusively and superficially with the physical aspects of sex and pure bodily pleasure. For someone who prided herself on using all her senses, I hadn't taken advantage of the profound sexual experience that one could enjoy with a tantric perspective and approach.

Thanks to Javier, I had an entirely new appreciation for tantric practices and I was eager to try it with my expanded knowledge. Tantric sex seemed like the natural adjunct to my new perspectives and philosophies about life in general. I couldn't help but wonder if Leo were familiar with Tantra, before thanking Javi for enlightening me. Turned out that something I actually thought was quite shallow and lascivious was actually very profound and aligned with my desires. Don't judge a book by its cover, I reminded myself, wishing I could explore the ancient tradition with Leo. I asked Javier where the celibate aspect fit in to understand his personal motivations better.

"That's the real interesting twist," Javi began. I tried stifling my childish laughter as I thought again about an adult version of the childhood game, "Tantric Twister." Javi generously smiled at me before continuing, "Yes, many mistakenly associate tantric just with sex and contorted bodies, but Tantra is not solely focused on sexual activity, and celibacy is just one aspect of the broader practices." I was listening attentively, eager to learn more about this sensual man's decision to be celibate. I was intrigued and had such respect for his physical restraint and power over his mind. "Some view celibacy as a preparatory phase in which they abstain from sexual activity for a period of time to build up their physical and energetic reserves. This can help them better channel and control sexual energy during tantric practices." Sounded like a long slow tease, I thought to myself, with an ultimate volcanic-like explosion. It reminded me of the bizarre "delayed orgasm" potential side effect of benzodiazapenes I had experienced years prior having briefly tried them after my first divorce before switching to natural anti-anxiety remedies. Admittedly, the ultimate orgasm had been extraordinarily mind and body-blowing. Fortunately, the fact that a pill could have such an effect promptly made me get off prescription anxioltyics.

I could see the appeal of mastering one's mind and body via tantric-induced celibacy. But for years??? I pondered, looking at my friend inquisitively. Javi read the question in my eyes before explaining that some practitioners of Tantra - like himself - believe that temporary celibacy allows them to redirect their sexual energy toward spiritual growth and self-awareness. By abstaining from sexual activity, they aim to harness and transmute their sexual energy for higher states of consciousness. "Hmmm… Sounds like sexual fasting. Mad respect," I concluded - making it clear that my more instant-gratification-type persona likely made me incapable of such prolonged abstention. "Precisely - it's about delayed gratification and holistically experiencing each other." "Now that part and the focus on intimacy I love. I would also enjoy the delayed gratification within a sexual encounter. I just don't think I'm ready for lengthy celibacy. Maybe I could work on "tantric-light" and earn a tantric-in-training star."

******

Chapter 8

Yogic Sleep

Javi and I slept together again that night - my time with him was the most intimate, non-sexual connection I had ever had with a man. Seemed ironic that this young man had exposed me to the world of tantric sex while our relationship was a completely pure one. Meeting him was extraordinarily serendipitous - my time with him was helping cement my desired expansion of intimate bonds. I longed for physical affection like no one I knew - struggling without it whenever I was alone. Although historically, I had gravitated towards sexual encounters for cuddling, bonding, and oxytocin, I was expanding my perspective and was grateful for Javi's presence and the relative novelty of fulfilling my need for connection outside of sexual engagement. My time with Javi was eye-opening and mind-expanding. We were mirroring each other's energy, serving to intensify my overall positivity and optimism.

I awoke early the next morning feeling restored from another deep night of restful sleep. Javi's presence gave me the feeling of connection and bonding I deeply longed for without any of the tension or fears associated with my traditional relationships. I was learning so much from him, so quickly. He had transformed my life and although I knew we would be forever in each other's lives, I was sad contemplating our separation.

My mood shifted from the tranquility I had felt the past few days as I began anticipating my departure. "What am I going to do without you?" I started pouting and feeling panicky. I buried my head in his chest, trying not to cry.

"Sofia," Javier turned my face upward to his and looked intently in my eyes, pausing for effect. "You are going to do you - maybe for the first time in your life - and it's going to be splendid. You are going to shine like the luminous star you are. You radiate positivity and energy. I want you to channel that for you," he emphasized for effect. "I cannot wait to hear all about it. I'll be wherever you need me whenever you want. You are never alone. We are forever connected. You are loved," Javier cited Liam's oft-repeated reassurance.

"Sofi," Javier kindly held my hand as he continued trying to comfort me, his words having brought tears to my eyes. I adored how he intuitively knew how to make me feel better instantly - taking me by the hands as a physical demonstration of his verbal assurance - as I was beginning to feel woefully untethered. "Have you ever tried yoga nidra?" Javier queried. Hmmm, I thought, anxious to learn more about this magical-sounding practice as I imagined powerful covert yoga ninjas soaring through the air or parkour enthusiasts masterfully bounding from object to object with agility and lightning speed. Parkour mesmerized me - not just the physical prowess but the fact that it was about a disciplined mindset as well - one that seemed to view the world as a playground of possibilities and employ a determined mindset to overcome seeming obstacles. I was drawn to holistic disciplines that merged physical feats and mental mastery. My enthusiastic inquisitive smile and the eagerness in my eyes prompted Javier to continue.

"It's an ancient tradition that can help you attain inner peace and deep tranquility," he began explaining to me. Just as I had been way off base with my misinterpretation of the essence of tantric sex, my vision of stealth ninjas and parkour-type acrobatics was equally off. "Ohhhh, interesting. I was actually picturing something like parkour." Javier chuckled, "That's another story entirely. Yoga nidra is a profound form of guided meditation and relaxation that has been practiced for thousands of years. In sharp contrast to the energetic ninja activity you had imagined, yogic nidra is often called 'yogic sleep.' The name is from two Sanskrit words: 'yoga,' which means union and 'nidra,' which means sleep. Together, they encapsulate the essence of the practice – a path to union with one's inner self through a state of profound relaxation that resembles sleep."

I was floored in the best way possible. I couldn't believe I hadn't known that "yoga" meant "union" and was even more incredulous at how much I had learned from Javier in such a short time. I was so grateful that I hadn't turned him away when he had showed up at my door just a few days before. Trusting my heart and embracing the "we'll see" parable was paying off with incredible rewards.

Whereas Tantric practices would enrich my intimate interactions with romantic partners, it sounded like yoga nidra held the potential to be a tremendously beneficial tool to help me deal with my restless nature and my discomfort of being alone. I loved Javier's simple explanations that highlighted the aspects of importance to me without any extraneous details that I likely wouldn't remember any way. I was totally intrigued and excited to give yoga nidra a try. Tantric practices seemed ideal to connect more deeply with another, while yoga nidra sounded like an almost magical way of connecting more deeply with oneself.

Although I regularly did yoga poses, I didn't actually practice yoga per se and I was intrigued by this version. I was astounded at how incredibly unaware I had previously been about so many of these ancient practices, like Tantra, meditation, and yoga. My fortuitous experience with Javi was helping me understand the practices I was trying to wrap my head around to embrace.

Focusing on active relaxation instead of the more active physical postures or stretches I associated with yoga sounded promising. I was relieved when Javier led me up to the third floor instead of the bedroom. I would be more likely to relax, not concerned Javier would have had me in a perpetual preorgasmic state as I had experienced with his massage. Javier had me lie down on a mat and instructed me to close my eyes, while he guided me through a systematic process of relaxation and inner exploration.

The primary goal of yoga nidra, Javier explained, is to reach a state of conscious relaxation where you remain fully aware while your body and mind enter a state of profound rest. It is a state where the subconscious mind becomes more receptive, allowing for deep self-discovery and healing. "Whoa," I simply uttered, astonished that this type of yoga that I had never heard of before sounded just like what I needed. I was deeply touched by how intuitive and caring Javier was. As I listened to his soothing melodic voice, I felt almost trancelike again - alternating between full conscious awareness and subconscious sleepiness - as I had when he had massaged me.

Javier started by encouraging me to set a personal intention, a short, positive statement or affirmation. "Let it go," I stated simply, a summation of my desire to leave my history firmly in the past to truly embrace the limitless potential of the future. Next, he guided me to scan my body to bring awareness to different areas of tension and then to release them - similar to programmed muscle relaxation. I consciously got as relaxed as possible - making a point to focus on releasing where I normally store my tension, reflected in hunched shoulders and clenched jaws and fists, without even being aware of it. Next, he had me focus on my breath to deepen relaxation and encourage my mind to let go.

Javier guided me through a series of visualizations to encourage mental and emotional exploration. To my surprise, tears started to flow - tears of joyous release from bottled up emotions and embedded physiological manifestations of those emotions. Eventually Javier had me reflect again on my intention to reinforce it. Finally, he guided me back to sensory awareness, having me focus on sensations and sounds to gently awaken me back to full consciousness.

I was an immediate convert. I felt incredible - lighter, almost ethereal. It was almost a mystical experience. It was extraordinary how this practice that was novel to me had basically harmoniously blended the different healing tenets I had been working on separately - self-awareness, release of muscle tension, breathing practices, affirmations, etc. I had never tried unifying body, mind, and spirit with yoga - I simply had focused on the physical aspects for strength and flexibility. This was definitely a powerful yogic practice that intuitively spoke to me. I loved how accessible it was - seemed like a practice that pretty much everyone could adopt and benefit from. I was excited Javier exposed me to this wondrous new ritual - it was like a sanctuary of tranquility that I could access at will.

I grinned - the parable about withholding judgment when something seemingly "bad" happens to take a "we'll see" approach to see how things ultimately transpire - coming front and center to mind for the umpteenth time since having met this extraordinarily special human being. I would have never met Javier had I not felt so desperately ill when I first arrived in the village. My arrival may have been marked by sickness but my departure was marked by profound gratitude.

Javier had become "soul family" immediately. Not only did I have the blessing of a strong bond with this incredible human but also the amazing gifts he had shared with me in such a brief time. He had graciously taught me so much. I had new practices and rituals that would help me holistically heal, enhance my relationship with myself and others, and help my restless nature feel at peace. Tears of joy welled up in my eyes for having connected with this special soul.

I appreciated how intuitive Javier was; he had quickly grasped my essence and my issues and was teaching me ways to overcome my challenges, while elevating my spiritual essence and enhancing my overall life. It's amazing how transformative a little selfless compassion and positive energy can be. I hugged Javier effusively in gratitude. I complimented him on his stealth transformation of me from the pouting, panicking woman that was about to unravel that I was before he introduced me to yoga nidra to the calm, grateful one I was now. You are my "yoga ninja," I lovingly teased, kissing him on the forehead.

******

Chapter 9

You're Never Alone

I couldn't believe how simultaneously lighthearted I felt from having experienced such an incredible connection with Javier and how heavy hearted I felt separating. "Forever" had historically been an empty cruel promise to me and I was struggling, quelling my abandonment issues as Javier and I said our "goodbye."

"There's nothing "good" about a "bye"," I pouted - almost childlike to the much younger, wiser Javier. "Sofia," he gently said softly as he wrapped his strong, comforting arms around me in an enveloping, loving embrace. "You know this is not goodbye," he tilted my head towards him to look me seriously in the eyes. "You are never alone," he repeated the oft-quoted assurance that my truest friends frequently made, intimately familiar with my biggest vulnerabilities. "I know," I started sobbing and I did know as well as anyone could. "I never cry," I said as I wiped my tears, realizing how many times I had professed that over the prior months. "You should," Javier gently admonished as he put his hand under my chin - not allowing me to avert his pointed gaze as my head started downward in habituation.

"You are limitless, dear heart," he continued. "You feel - vulnerably, sensitively, multidimensionally - in an often one-dimensional, superficial world filled with callousness, fear, and self-absorption. It's what makes you beautifully you. That way of living is going to inevitably come with some ups and downs, but you're more than strong enough to traverse through them. At the end of the day, it's the price of truly living. Isn't that what you want?" I hugged him closer in deep understanding and gratitude.

He pulled a satin pouch out of his pocket. I giggled childishly as it reminded me of the one Olivia had hidden in the box of condoms. He told me to turn around and close my eyes, which I did with unconditional trust. I felt him putting a necklace on me before asking me to feel the charm. I thought of Helen Keller as I slowly felt the coolness of the stone and the warmth in my heart from the unexpected gift. "A heart?" I guessed the shape as I turned to him, tears starting to stream down my face from this gentle soul's perception and thoughtfulness. It wasn't just any heart though - I saw as I opened my eyes that it was a rose quartz heart. The significance was not lost on me. Rose quartz is known as a healing crystal and the stone of unconditional love.

I simply couldn't imagine a more perfect or impactful gift as I hugged Javier tightly again, hoping to silently express my gratitude, as words escaped me. "You are always welcome with me - wherever I may be - whenever you want. I'll take care of you," he paused thoughtfully. "We'll take care of each other. You will always find "home" with me. We are family."

We wrapped our arms around each other with a ferocity borne of sincerity and a deep desire to impart a protective field of positivity and strength to each other until we inevitably reunited. I had never felt more connected with anyone despite having virtually just meant. We were both open hearts and expressive beings. I truly believed the respective magnetic energies of our feelings had inextricably bonded us instantaneously - it gave me the comfort I longed for that our relationship would be a forever one. Now I had a constant tangible reminder that I was loved and never alone, literally caressing my heart.

Javier's gift and words deeply resonated with me. I realized that "home" wasn't the place we grew up as children. Indeed it wasn't a place per se for curious, spirited souls like us. "Home" was within us and with the real authentic connections we made. It wasn't a static location. My thoughts went back to my discomfort with the fundamental Buddhist concept of impermanence. I realized with deepening gratitude that I was getting more comfortable with the concept in general, as well as the prospect of feeling "alone," or "abandoned," or "homeless." Whether my encounter with Javier had truly been by chance or not, I gratefully acknowledged that the positive effect of it would last forever…

******

Chapter 10

Now What?

I am much more motivated and disciplined and practices are more effective when I understand the science behind them so I researched yoga nidra while I was on the train en route to the airport. I intuitively felt that the practice would be beneficial to me - helping me deal better with my feelings of aloneness. I was anxious to anchor my belief in it even more. I found numerous studies demonstrating the effectiveness of yoga nidra in reducing stress and anxiety and improving sleep quality. I was quite familiar with the nervous system from my research for my writing and had been exploring and incorporating ways to calm my sympathetic nervous system "fight or flight" mode and engage my parasympathetic nervous system "rest and digest" mode. I was so grateful for discovering a new way to activate the relatively calmer, more peaceful parasympathetic nervous system, thanks to Javier.

I understood how yoga nidra could result in greater tranquility by counteracting the body's stress response and reducing cortisol levels, enabling profound relaxation. It was easy to translate that impact to improved sleep. As a lifelong insomniac, I was thrilled to learn that yoga nidra could have a trifecta of positive impacts on my sleep challenges - it could help me fall asleep faster, experience deeper sleep, and wake up feeling refreshed! I was also fascinated to learn that yoga nidra could help promote emotional healing and enhance focus and creativity - this previously unknown practice that Javier had shared with me was perfectly suited for my needs.

These benefits made perfect sense to me given my understanding of the subconscious. Yoga nidra provided an avenue to confront and process traumas and emotional blockages. By calming the conscious mind and allowing the subconscious to surface, it could also encourage greater insights and creativity. I was amazed at the incredible array of beneficial insights that Javier had given me. The practices that he had introduced me to - that I had shockingly been so ignorant of - seemed perfect to help me combat the various challenges I had been struggling with. I had shown up in Gaucín at one of the lowest points of my life - but for my extreme mental and physical anguish at the time - I would have never met Javier or benefitted from my truly transformative time with him.

Indeed, I reflected, since my arrival in Mallorca, my solo trip to Spain had impacted me deeply. I had experienced and learned so much - about myself and life in general. I was leaving, a changed person - something that wouldn't have been possible if I hadn't come alone. I had saved the best for last without even planning. I appreciated how Gaucín's tight-knit community added to the appeal of its breathtaking natural beauty. It had a timeless allure that made it feel like home and a unique authenticity and exquisite nature that managed to effortlessly calm my normally restless soul. Few vistas had ever captivated me like the breathtaking panoramic views of the majestic verdant Serranía de Ronda mountains and the Mediterranean Sea in the distance. A sanctuary of serenity for the contemplative, an endless opportunity for exploration for nature and fitness enthusiasts alike, and a source of muse-like inspiration for creative artists.

Although I had enjoyed my visit to Mallorca and Seville - despite some unexpected twists and turns - I had been most touched by my time spent in Gaucín. I was grateful to end my Spanish visit in the village that had become synonymous with a haven for my body, mind, and spirit. In

Gaucín, my head finally found the peaceful escape I had longed for; in Javier, I had found the peaceful presence and connection my soul desperately desired.

Although my overall time in Spain had admittedly been characterized by a bit of floundering - a metaphorical one step forwards, two steps back - I felt I was progressing in the right direction. I was starting to construct a sort of comforting grounding - rooted in my unwavering belief in myself and the omnipresence of my extraordinary friends. In Gaucín, my belief in myself had cemented a bit more while my intimate circle of trust had expanded with the inclusion of Javier. I knew Gaucín was an enchanting experience that would linger long in my memory and heart and I knew Javier would forever be my treasured friend - a source of spiritual inspiration and comfort - a mere thought away.

It wasn't lost on me that my restless soul was feeling relatively grounded and my body and mind were feeling invigorated - due in no small part that I hadn't engaged in any romantic interludes in Gaucín. I chuckled at myself, remembering that my only plan for my time in Spain when I had arrived was to revel in simple pleasures. An intended loose itinerary of sorts to distract myself from my past and my heartaches. I had never expected my trip to be a sort of contemplative, spiritual journey. Gaucín was a loving example of the simplicity of the beauty of nature and the rejuvenating power of self-care.

Although I was leaving for a change of scenery, I would continue focusing inwards while reveling in the sheer magic of the simple pleasures in life. I couldn't think of a better place than France to continue my novel theme of intimate solitude and serenity - and searching - finding clarity about what I wanted now that I had a better appreciation of what I didn't want. I laughed as I thought of Rafael and our supposed bucket list plan of exploring the Champagne region together. C'est la vie - you win some, you lose some.

I was in good spirits as I reflected on my Spanish experiences, gratefully clutching my rose heart. This trip had been unconventional and unusual and I wouldn't change a thing. I had learned a lot of lessons - a couple about life and a lot about myself. I had found intimacy of an unexpected nature in Javier and I was cultivating my self-love. Life is good, I thought gratefully as I enjoyed the scenery en route to the airport. I smiled deeply, knowing it was about to get amazing, saturating myself in the quintessential French joie de vivre, the simple joy of life…

*****

To Be Continued...

Please join me in France for

French Rendezvous,
Searching
Part V
of the
Happily Ever Now Collection

Sofia xo

What Readers are Saying*

"French Rendezvous"

"A captivating novel that touches your mind, body, and soul."

"An inspirational story of life lessons and love lessons, based on true events."

"Not your typical love story - an engaging, thought-provoking and evocative delight with something for everyone as Elan poignantly weaves an inspirational tale of personal transformation while immersively transporting us to her beloved idyllic Mediterranean gems with an insider's perspective. I thoroughly enjoyed Elan's perspective on creative geniuses - like da Vinci and Picasso - and the present-day impact they had on Sofia. I feel like I am intimately familiar with the characters. I know which love interest I'm rooting for and can't wait to see how Sofia's journey turns out. Highly recommended!"

"I felt magically transported and inspired by French Rendezvous. I found Elan's storytelling gripping - I felt as if I were experiencing the dreamy locales she describes in such alluring detail while my heart strings were pulled as Elan intimately depicts Sofia's challenges and triumphs. I was particularly drawn to Sofia's vulnerability and strength - determinedly moving onwards and upwards - despite setbacks. This isn't your normal romance novel - I was touched how the story embraces intimacy in all its forms - including the enviable friendships Elan describes throughout the series. I cannot wait to see how things turn out for Sofia. With Elan's cinematic detail, I can envision Sofia's journey unfolding on the big screen and I hope one day it's made into a movie!"

www.ingramcontent.com/pod-product-compliance
Ingram Content Group UK Ltd.
Pitfield, Milton Keynes, MK11 3LW, UK
UKHW022238230426
12048UKWH00018BA/1336